LOVE'S LAST STAND

LOVE'S LAST STAND

S. B. MOORES

FIVE STAR
A part of Gale, a Cengage Company

Farmington Hills, Mich • San Francisco • New York • Waterville, Maine
Meriden, Conn • Mason, Ohio • Chicago

LIBRARY OF CONGRESS CATALOGING-IN-PUBLICATION DATA

Names: Moores, S. B. author.
Title: Love's last stand / S. B. Moores.
Description: First edition. | Waterville : Five Star, 2018.
Identifiers: LCCN 2018000907 (print) | LCCN 2018006025 (ebook) | ISBN 9781432838614 (ebook) | ISBN 9781432838607 (ebook) | ISBN 9781432838591 (hardcover)
Subjects: LCSH: Pioneers—Tennessee—Fiction. | Frontier and pioneer life—Tennessee—Fiction. | Love stories gsafd | GSAFD: Historical fiction
Classification: LCC PS3613.O5695 (ebook) | LCC PS3613.O5695 L68 2018 (print) | DDC 813/.6—dc23
LC record available at https://lccn.loc.gov/2018000907

First Edition. First Printing: July 2018
Find us on Facebook–https://www.facebook.com/FiveStarCengage
Visit our website–http://www.gale.cengage.com/fivestar/
Contact Five Star™ Publishing at FiveStar@cengage.com

Printed in Mexico
1 2 3 4 5 6 7 22 21 20 19 18

ACKNOWLEDGMENTS

The popular image of a novelist is that of a solitary individual who sits in a lonely room, banging away on the keyboard and sipping endless cups of coffee. Occasionally, the author will gaze out a window for inspiration, usually at a snowy mountain range or at a set of dramatic waves crashing on the seashore. For me, only the endless cups of coffee applied.

The histories of Kansas that my Aunt Mary authored were my earliest inspiration. More recently, my motivation has come from the many friends and writers who unfailingly inspired me along the road from idea to story. Thank you to the past and present members of my amazing critique group. I owe you so much. Thank you to my wonderful wife. And special thanks to Tiffany Schofield, who had faith enough in my writing to make me a Five Star author. You all inspire me to do my best.

—S. B. Moores, 2018

PROLOGUE

I am an old woman now, but I was young once upon a time, and in love.

My love took me far away from the safety of my Tennessee home, but I survived the journey. Others did not. I saw it all and I can tell you about it. A gentle breeze warmed us as it blew softly between the sharpened points of the stockade wall. The redwing blackbirds sang, glad that winter had left the Béxar Valley early. Pink and white flower buds speckled the gnarled branches of fifty-year-old apple trees in the courtyard, and there should have been a fine crop, come fall.

But it wasn't to be. The trumpets blew and the battle was joined. So many men on both sides died, simple as that. History would not accept any survivors. Neither Texas pride nor the honor of Mexico would permit it.

In a manner of speaking I died, too, on that day. At least what I was and who I was died. It's not all a sad story. I returned to my Tennessee home, reborn into a life with such a love that might never have been possible if there hadn't been so much death on that fine spring morning.

Life, death, and love. These are my stories.

CHAPTER ONE

Ridgetop County, Tennessee, Late September 1825

"It's the most beautiful thing I've ever seen." Justin Sterling's fascination overcame the shadow of jealousy he'd felt when Tobias Johnson had first pulled the new knife from his belt. He was glad his best friend had received such a fine gift, even though he knew he might never be so lucky, himself.

"My pa brought it all the way back from Nashville two weeks ago," Tobias said, "just for my tenth birthday." He lifted the blade over his head as if brandishing it at the unseen Indians the two boys knew were somewhere in the forests around their farms.

"What'd your pa give you for your birthday?" Tobias asked.

"My daddy?" The idea that his father should give him something as special as a knife just because he'd been born had never occurred to Justin. "Nothin' much," he said. He kicked at the school ground dirt with his toe, unsure whether he'd suffered some sort of injustice. "But my ma cooked me the biggest dumpling you'd ever ate. Baked it with apples!"

"Aw," Tobias said. "That ain't nothin'. We eat dumpling pies most every week. The sharecroppers' women bring 'em to my ma."

An uncomfortable feeling dawned in Justin's mind. He had heard his father called a "sharecropper" once, but he couldn't remember whether his mother had ever taken pies to the Johnsons. She could have, he figured. After all, they lived on

9

neighboring farms. But the idea that his family might be different from Toby's settled over Justin, and the unseen barrier he felt rising between himself and his best friend worried him. True, the Sterlings and Johnsons were both farming families, but Toby's father worked the rich, dark bottom land along the Tennessee River, while Justin's father had always farmed in the rocky hills to the north. Justin didn't know how much land either family owned or leased. It never seemed important to him before.

Tobias's knife glinted in the morning sunshine. Justin closed his eyes and turned his head away when reflection off the blade flashed over his face. When he opened his eyes again, his gaze was drawn to a girl playing tag with kids on the other side of the schoolyard. She was a little younger than he. Her long red hair bounced in fiery curls across her face and her blue cotton dress swayed back and forth as she dodged her schoolmates. Her laughter resonated in Justin's mind like the melody of a song drifting to his ears over the cold, clear air.

"See how they wound the handle with strips of leather?" Tobias asked. "It's so you can get a good grip when you stab."

Toby thrust the knife out in front of him, chest level, but Justin barely noticed. He had never seen the young girl before. Any newcomer would have been noteworthy in the small farming community, but this particular girl struck a chord somewhere deep in Justin's soul.

"Who is *that*?" Justin asked, pointing at the kids. He immediately regretted saying anything, once he realized what Toby would think.

Tobias quit admiring the knife long enough to give Justin a questioning look. His gaze followed Justin's outstretched arm to the other side of the schoolyard, where the children were playing.

"You mean the new girl?" he asked. It was obvious to Toby.

There hadn't been another new student at the Ridgetop school in two years. "Her name's Abigail, but folks just call her Abby. Her family's been working the Talbot farm since old man Talbot died of consumption." Tobias ran his thumb lightly across the blade of his knife, testing its sharpness for the hundredth time. "Her pa and my pa are start'n a cattle company," he added absentmindedly.

Justin listened with one ear, but kept his attention on the figure of the lithe young girl. She seemed to dance on the air, rather than madly dashing about to escape being caught.

"Maybe we should play tag," Justin said.

"What?" Tobias looked at the jumble of kids and then back at Justin. A wicked smile spread over his face. "I think Justin's in *love*," he said, dragging out the word "love" to give it as scornful a sound as possible.

Justin glared at his friend and growled, "I am *not*! Besides, *you* love Louise Gunderson."

Tobias's eyes sprang open, not in shock at the offensive comment, but in his surprise that Justin knew of his affection for the girl. He worked his jaw, groping for some kind of denial.

"That's a lie," he said. "We only held hands once, and she made me."

At the tender age of ten years, it was still unthinkable to the boys that girls, who didn't hunt, fish, or fight Indians, could have any importance in their lives. The accusation that they would pay girls any attention at all was an insult. Never mind those increasingly frequent occasions when their thoughts inexplicably turned to the wonder and mystery of the softer sex.

Tobias dropped his knife in the dirt and the two friends crouched, facing each other, obliged to spring into hand-to-hand combat to defend their honor. Thankfully, the school bell clanged before they could come to blows.

★ ★ ★ ★ ★

The teacher, Miss Murphy, put her finger on her chin and looked at her assembled students. "Tobias Johnson," she said. "Why don't you move to the back of the room this year and give someone else a chance to sit near the blackboard?" Her stern gaze turned on Justin as she physically divided the boys with her hands and Toby went to the back of the room.

"Justin Sterling," she said, her voice artificially sweet. "Why don't you sit next to our new student, Miss Abigail Whitfield."

Justin rolled his eyes as he and Toby parted for the school year. They both knew Miss Murphy wanted to avoid the disruptions she'd suffered at their hands the winter before. He dutifully took his seat next to Abby on the hardwood bench and immediately felt a wobbly electricity run through his head at the nearness of her. She smelled fresh, like tumbling creek water. He squirmed a little, then managed a quick sidelong glance at her. She was smiling directly at him! Now what was he going to do? Would he have to sit next to her and suffer like this for the entire year? His head swam at first, but then a strange calmness came over him. He turned toward her, looked into her eyes, and returned her smile.

"Hi," she said.

"Hi," Justin croaked. He looked down at his hands, hoping she wouldn't notice the pink rushing into his cheeks.

No doubt about it. Toby's knife was no longer the most beautiful thing Justin had ever seen.

CHAPTER TWO

Christmas Eve Day 1827

Christmas, Justin decided, was his favorite time of year. During no other season were the homes in the Ridgetop Valley decorated so gaily. Pinecones and mistletoe were gathered from the surrounding forests, and extra candles decorated everything. Christmas trees displayed in the windows of the houses of the well-to-do were covered in metallic tinsel that sparkled like long curly diamonds. Even the Sterlings had an abundance of venison, oranges and other fruits from the south, as well as chestnuts. Justin's farm chores were fewer, which gave him more time to read and think, and anything seemed possible.

Everyone's attention focused on the coming Christmas day. People set aside their earthly concerns and differences, at least for a little while. It was as though the inhabitants of the valley had forgotten each other during the rest of the year, but at Christmastime they drew together, seeking to renew a biblically inspired fellowship with their neighbors in the cold of midwinter.

While Christmas may have been his favorite time of year, Christmas Eve wasn't always Justin's favorite day, since it meant extra time spent in church. He looked at his mother across the congregation and tried not to fidget on the hard wooden pew. His mother liked being on the side of the church nearest the stove. But Justin and his father thought it too warm. They sat with the rest of the men, next to the windows, which were opened a crack to let in the crisp winter air.

Henry Whitfield stood behind the lectern at the front of the little church, dressed in a long black coat and exhorting the assembled worshipers with outstretched arms to remember why Christ was born a man—so he could die to cleanse all mortals of their sins. Justin thought hard to remember which sins he'd committed that might have caused Christ to die for him. He blushed and looked down at his shoes when he remembered some thoughts he'd had about Abigail Whitfield. "Lascivious" thoughts, Justin decided. That was a word Henry Whitfield used a lot when he presided over services in the absence of the regular, circuit-riding preacher. When he wasn't watching Abby, Justin stared at Henry Whitfield and wondered how he would react if he ever found out that his daughter was the object of Justin's sinful thoughts.

"Thank you for sparing me, Lord," Justin whispered. He hoped that by acknowledging Christ's forgiveness, he could erase his sins and prevent any possibility that they would be revealed.

Services ended. His mother kept one eye on him as she socialized with other grownups, so he tried not to rush down the stairs, eager to be free of the stuffy church. Out in the yard, he could see his breath, and he exhaled as hard as he could to see how big a cloud he could make. When the air cleared he saw Abby Whitfield standing on the bottom rung of the nearby corral, gazing at the milling horses. He glanced around. His parents were caught up in talk about the weather and plans for Christmas celebrations. Toby was nowhere to be found. Justin and his friend often sat together during the service, but when Henry acted as their preacher, Toby had church obligations that required him to sit elsewhere and stay behind after the service. Justin wasn't sure why Henry had chosen Toby, or why he, Justin, wasn't required to help, too. The adults probably thought it was a privilege to help the preacher, but Justin couldn't be

14

jealous of Toby. Sitting through a service at the back of the church was punishment enough.

Watching Abby out of the corner of his eye, he reached down for a small stone, and tossed it casually in the general direction of the corral. Then he walked that way, as though he were going to retrieve the stone and throw it again. When he drew near Abby, he changed directions and stepped up onto the corral rail next to her.

"Hi," he said. "What are you doing?"

"Hi." She glanced at him, smiled, then turned back to the horses. "I'm looking for my Christmas present."

"Did you lose it in the corral?" He wanted to help, but he thought it odd that she had received, much less lost, a present on the day before Christmas.

Abigail laughed. "No, you silly goose. My father says I'm old enough to ride a horse now, and I want him to give me one for Christmas."

Justin stared at the horses with new appreciation. He was two years older than Abby and already an experienced horseman, having ridden almost daily as part of his chores. But the idea that someone not quite his age—and a girl, besides—could be given a horse as a gift bestowed a value on the animals he hadn't appreciated.

Abby sighed and rested her chin on her crossed forearms. "They're all so beautiful," she said. "Don't you think?"

"Sure." He looked at Abby and back at the horses. They milled about quietly, blowing steam from their nostrils, anxious to get back to their own warm stables. Abby's statement sounded like one of those odd things girls said that they really didn't want an answer to. He felt vaguely jealous of the animals and the way Abby looked at them.

"Someday I'm going to raise my own horses," she said.

Justin thought about that. He knew Abby's father raised

horses, so it didn't seem out of the question that she could too, when she grew up. But all of the breeders in the valley were men, as far as he knew. He'd never heard of a girl who owned a farm or raised her own horses.

"Me too," he finally said.

She gave him a sidelong glance, and the unexpectedly sad look in her eyes took Justin by surprise. Didn't she believe him?

"Really, I want to." He looked off at the tree line beyond the corral and scuffed his foot on the rail. Did she think he'd said it just to please her?

"My father says horse breeding is hard work," she said. "Do you think I can do it?"

Justin studied her for a moment, trying to tell whether she meant to challenge him with her question. He had an idea that Abby was serious, so he decided not to say anything about her being a girl and how all the people he knew who raised horses were men.

"I don't see why not," he said. "But you might need some help."

"Would *you* help me, Justin?"

Justin thought about it. The truth was, he had always loved horses, but he didn't want to look to Abby like a copycat.

"Maybe I will," he said. "If you need me."

"Oh." Abby beamed. "It'll be wonderful. You wait and see. We'll have a big green pasture, and red barns, and lots of little colts to play with." In her excitement, Abby turned and stepped off the rail. Justin stepped down, too, and Abby gave him a hug.

"Abigail!" Henry Whitfield's voice boomed from across the yard.

Abby let go of Justin, who had been too surprised by the hug to return it.

"Abigail Whitfield, you come here this minute." Henry strode toward them.

Confusion crossed Abby's face, but it was quickly replaced by an expression of resistance.

"Father," she said, "I'm only watching the horses with Justin."

"I can see very well what you were doing," Henry said.

Justin stood by dumbly as Henry snatched Abby by the arm and pulled her a few feet away from him.

"And what were *you* trying to do?" Henry pointed an accusing finger at him.

Justin's sudden shift from pleasure to guilt left him confused and unable to speak. Thankfully, his own father appeared. "Is there a problem, Henry?" Walter Sterling asked, lighting his pipe.

"Not as long as young Justin here can keep his hands to himself. I found the two of them embracing like animals."

"Father, it was nothing like that," Abby said. "We were just watching the horses."

"You hush," Henry said. He was about to continue his indictment but Walter Sterling spoke first.

"The way I see it," Walter said, lingering over his words, as if to slow down the confrontation, "it's better we found them in a hug than in fisticuffs, like so many other children their age." He straightened Justin's jacket and brushed some imaginary dust from the lapels.

"I'd rather have our children learn from the apostle Paul." Henry pointed a finger at the heavens. "In Galatians, he said, 'Walk in the Spirit and ye shall not fulfill the lust of the flesh.' "

"I agree with you there, Henry," Walter said. "And I can't argue with good old King James, but these youngsters are hardly old enough to know what 'lust of the flesh' is. Don't you think?"

"Perhaps. But let's you and I see to it they don't learn about such things any time too soon, shall we?" He placed a firm hand on Abigail's shoulder and guided her away from the corral.

"And the pews are still warm from the service," Henry grumbled.

Justin watched as the Whitfields climbed into their covered carriage. Abby glanced at him behind her father's back and, as she did so, Justin waved. She did not wave back.

Abby's hug had sent a thrill chasing through Justin's body like a blazing meteor from heaven. But judging by her father's anger, Justin figured he'd committed one more lascivious sin. He wondered how much patience God had for such a frequent and hopeless a sinner as himself.

Two months later, Henry Whitfield took over as the community's full-time preacher, after the regular circuit rider caught the pox and died somewhere in Missouri.

Justin wasn't sure whether he was at fault, but two more years passed before Abby got a horse for Christmas.

CHAPTER THREE

July 1828

"Where should we go?" Justin whispered.

"Follow me." Abigail lifted her skirt over her ankles and ran toward the creek, suppressing the urge to giggle. She heard Justin's padding footfalls behind her as he followed her on the narrow dirt path.

She had discovered the low overhanging bank of the creek days earlier, and knew instantly that it would provide the perfect concealment from her friends in a game of hide-and-go-seek. And the idea of hiding with Justin stirred something deep inside her, something that hinted of danger and excitement. She started to zigzag as she ran, just in case Toby hadn't completely closed his eyes again. She didn't want to give away her special place too quickly, and she relished the idea that she would be alone with Justin, hidden from the world, if only for a few minutes.

She ran through an opening in the tall grass and trees lining the creek. With Justin close on her heels, Abigail jumped down onto a small patch of sand where the cold, burbling water had undercut the curving creek bank, then receded with the spring rains. It left a short stretch of dry sandy beach. By crouching near the bank, they would be hidden from view, even from someone standing immediately above them. She sat down with her back to the water and reached up for Justin's hand, pulling him down next to her.

"Toby will never find us here," she whispered.

"No one could find us here," Justin said. "Not without walking the length of the creek." He gave her a knowing look. Abigail felt her chest swell, and she hooked her arm around his elbow, as if to keep him close.

At that moment, a large gold and brown butterfly fluttered silently in front of their faces and landed on top of Abigail's head. She stifled a giggle, not wanting to frighten the creature. It sat there, slowly fanning its wings.

"I can *feel* it," she whispered. Justin pulled close to her and watched the insect.

"It looks like Mother Nature's dressing you up," he said. Then his gaze lowered until their eyes met. "Maybe she thinks you look a bit drab today."

She wrinkled her nose and gave him a look of mock irritation, but her heart skipped a beat when she felt Justin's sweet breath mingle with her own. A sudden flush of embarrassment rose to her cheeks when she thought he might be going to kiss her. She held her head statue still, a temporary resting place for the butterfly, even though modesty told her to pull away from Justin. She knew that coming to this hidden spot with him might lead to trouble, either the good kind or the bad. Which was which, she wasn't sure, but she'd wanted it, anyway. She'd been driven by an undefined longing for intimacy that only recently had begun to dawn in her chest. Now she felt caught between the sensual craving to feel Justin's lips on her own and a sudden fear of the consequences.

But the matter seemed out of her hands. She would not move and disturb the beautiful butterfly resting on her head, and she could only watch as Justin's soft eyes filled her vision. Her breath stilled, her lips parted slightly, and she closed her eyes in anticipation.

"Ow!" A young voice rang out in the field over their heads.

"That's Toby," Justin said. "It sounds like he's hurt."

Justin scrambled up the creek bank, and the butterfly flew away across the water. Abigail squeezed her eyes shut and let out a quick, low sigh. Had Justin really been about to kiss her, or had she simply imagined it? She might never know. Reluctantly, she opened her eyes and climbed up the creek bank. In the field they found Toby lying on his back, rolling to and fro, and holding his left leg. Through a ragged hole in Toby's pants, Abigail saw an ugly but not very serious scrape on Toby's shin. It bled slightly.

"What happened?" Justin asked.

"I fell over a stone," Toby groaned.

"It doesn't look very bad," Justin said.

"Oh, but it must hurt like the devil." Abigail bent down and lifted the flap of his pant leg carefully, to look more closely at his injury. Toby sucked in his breath, but let her do it.

"That is going to leave a nasty bruise." She ran her fingers through Toby's hair to comfort him.

Justin turned away and started walking in the direction Toby must have been running when he fell. He had gone only a few feet when he stopped and looked down at something hidden in the tall blades of grass. He knelt down and started pulling away grass from around a granite stone.

"Would you look at this?" He had uncovered a gray stone with three flat sides, each about a foot wide. It had a peaked top and stood, or rather leaned, about two feet tall.

"What is it?" Toby asked. He quickly got to his feet, injury apparently forgotten, when he saw the curious object he'd fallen over.

Abigail took a sharp breath. "It looks like a tombstone."

"Yes," Justin said. "It's even got someone's name carved into it."

"I hope I didn't step on someone's grave." Toby shivered.

21

"That would be bad luck."

Justin grinned. "A dead person might have reached up and tripped you when you ran by."

"Hush," Abigail said. "What is the name on the stone?"

Justin looked at the gray surface more closely, brushing away dirt, moss, and debris that must have been collecting for years.

"It says 'Johnson'!"

"Oh, stop teasing." Abigail stooped down and looked at the carving on the side of the stone facing her. When she saw the name it was her turn to shiver.

"This side says 'Whitfield,' " she whispered.

"Well this side says 'Sterling,' " Toby said with some satisfaction.

After a moment of silence, Abigail said, "It can't be a grave. They wouldn't put three people in one grave. It would be sacrilegious."

"No," Justin scratched his head. "If people we knew were buried here, surely we'd have heard about it."

"Then what is it?" Toby asked.

"It must be a marker," Abigail said.

"Maybe it marked the boundaries of our families' property at one time," Toby said.

Abigail glanced at Justin. She knew his father leased land from her father, and she wasn't sure the Sterlings actually owned any property in the valley, or how much.

Justin arched one eyebrow. "Perhaps it marks the location of buried treasure."

"Really?" Toby's eyes grew wide. "Like pirates? Why do you think that?"

"Why else would such an odd stone be out here near the creek? It's well inside Abby's family's land, so it can't mark any kind of property line. And it doesn't seem to have any other purpose."

Abigail considered this. She didn't really believe there was any buried treasure, but the possibility of it excited her. "Maybe our families buried some money together, to keep it safe from Indians. Back then Indians wouldn't be able to read the names on the stone, and they might think it was just a grave. If they were superstitious, they wouldn't go digging around to find a buried treasure."

"I've never heard about this," Toby said, as if he were giving the idea great weight. "Our parents would have told us about that, too, wouldn't they?" He looked worried, as though he still might have committed some indiscretion by tripping over the stone.

"Maybe they've forgotten about it," Justin said.

"Maybe it was buried by our grandfathers, and they all died before they could tell anyone," Abigail added.

"All of them died of the pox, didn't they?" Justin asked.

"Yes," Toby said, "and I think they all died at the same time, more or less."

"So that's it," Justin said, crooking a finger on his chin. "I wonder exactly where the treasure is buried."

"We should ask our parents before we go digging up Henry Whitfield's land," Toby said.

"You're right about that." Justin had been the subject of Henry's angry gaze more than once.

The three of them leaped to their feet and ran in the direction of the Whitfield home, since it was closest. They found Henry in the horse barn with his field hands, tending to a mare lying alone in its stall. From the looks on the men's faces and their muttered conversation, it was clear that something was wrong. Justin and Toby stopped a few yards shy of the stall and the knot of men, cautious of Henry Whitfield when he wasn't in a good mood. Abigail went ahead.

"What's the problem, Father?"

"It looks like she's eaten nightshade. She's dying."

Abigail gasped and put her hands to her mouth. "How could she do that?"

"I have no idea," Henry growled. "We should have no nightshade on Whitfield land. I've tried to be sure of that."

He looked up and saw Justin and Tobias, and Justin felt the man's stony gaze linger on him longer than he thought it should.

"Somehow the gates were open, letting the cattle out," Henry said. "It's happening more and more these days."

"I'm so sorry." With tears in her eyes, she knelt beside the dying horse and gently stroked its neck.

Justin and Toby gave each other a wary glance. They put their hands in their pockets and went their separate ways, each toward his own home.

CHAPTER FOUR

June 1830

Abigail closed her copy of *The Mysteries of Udolpho* and set the book in her lap. She gazed out the bay window of her second-floor bedroom, thinking about the story. The heroine, Emily St. Aubert, was only slightly older than she, but she had already lost her mother and father. How horrible. As if that weren't enough, Emily's guardian aunt married a scoundrel who stopped at nothing to keep the love of Emily's life away from her. Where did authors get such fanciful ideas?

Abigail's own parents were, so . . . so stable. Not dull, exactly, but so much the same from day to day. Then again, nothing exciting ever happened to anybody she knew in Ridgetop. That was a good thing, she supposed. Her life wasn't nearly as difficult or dramatic as Emily's. Still, sometimes Abigail wished for a dashing young hero like Valancourt, to sweep her up and take her away to an exotic castle where all of her dreams came true. How lovely that would be. She sighed but shook her head. She wasn't a storybook heroine, and life wasn't a novel. In reality, Abigail's future in Ridgetop seemed awfully limited. All that was truly expected of a woman was to get married and have children. That was fine, as far as it went. She would be lucky if she were ever allowed to raise horses, with or without a man like Valancourt to help her.

When her eyes focused, she found herself looking at a small gray smudge in the distance. She realized it was the slate roof of

25

the Sterling farmhouse, up the slope of the Ridgetop Valley, more than two miles away. She wondered what Justin Sterling was doing at that moment. Could he see her bedroom window from there? That idea made her blush, and she turned her head away from the view.

At school and elsewhere, most of the boys she knew would act the fool around the girls, tease them or try to impress them with their skill with a knife or a horse. Every so often, some poor boy got all moon-eyed over a particular girl. It was the source of great amusement among the girls, except for the girl who was the object of the boy's awkward affection. Usually nothing came of it. But the Ridgetop Valley was sparsely populated, and it dawned on Abigail that all of the boys and girls she knew might eventually pair off with each other in marriage. The idea that she already knew the boy she'd marry distressed her. At that moment, she'd rather some handsome stranger like Valancourt come to the valley and find her. Sadly, that wasn't likely. Still, there were a number of boys living around Ridgetop who might interest her. Could any of them capture her heart?

She thought again of Justin Sterling. Justin was no stranger, and she surely noticed the way he looked at her. It wasn't the same looks she got from the other young men. Their intentions were obvious from their childish grins. They would steal a kiss, or more, the first chance a girl gave them, and they wore this urgent desire on their sleeves for everyone to see. But Justin didn't grin at Abigail. He had a way of smiling that took her off guard. He made her feel that she was his equal. It was more than the look she might get from a friend. Much more. But Justin didn't make her feel she was the object of an adolescent courtship. She felt his quiet strength in his smile. He knew what he wanted, and it wasn't to play games. It was an unexpected maturity at such a young age, but Abigail only saw it when she was alone with him.

With his male friends, Justin was as much an unruly boy as any of the others. Oddly, it was his quiet demeanor that drew her to Justin, made her want to know him better. Where did he find that strength, his sureness? Did he ever think about her, as she was thinking of him now? And who would Justin Sterling marry? She looked out the window again at the small gray smudge in the distance.

"What do you want out of life, Justin Sterling? Will you live your whole life in Ridgetop, get married and have children?"

If only life were like a novel, one with a happy ending. She picked up her book and started reading again.

Justin had finished his chores for the day. Now he reclined on his favorite flat rock, next to a relatively quiet pool on the edge of the Little Elk Creek. He kept one eye on the line angling down from his fishing pole and the cork bobber as it drifted among a few floating leaves. A fish could strike at any moment. He already had four fat bluegill and a smallmouth bass on a stringer to bring home to his mother to cook up for dinner. If he caught a couple more fish, they would eat well and maybe salt a few for later. He liked the way his mother hugged him when he came home with his catch. It was just fishing, after all, but she made him feel like he'd done something important, like they might have had nothing at all for dinner if he hadn't gone fishing. He sensed that might have been true, once. Still, they always ate his catch.

His father said he had a knack for fishing, said he could talk a bass into biting the hook. He'd tried that a couple of times, but it never worked as well as a wriggling earthworm, so he wasn't sure his father understood the mechanics of fishing.

Every few minutes the sun peaked through the trees overhead, warming his arms and legs in the humid summer breeze. The sound of the water burbling down the creek next to the fishing pool soothed him, lulling him until his eyelids drooped. He propped his pole up between some rocks and lay on his back with his hands behind his head. Then he tilted his hat over his eyes to shield his face from the sun, the way he'd seen some Whitfield farmhands do when they napped behind the tobacco barn and they thought no one was looking.

He let his mind drift and he idly wondered if Abby Whitfield ever went fishing. She was a girl, so he doubted it. But if she did, she might be fishing on the very same creek, only farther downstream. He pulled his hat from his eyes, sat up, and glanced downstream. He could walk in that direction a ways. If he found her, he could say he was looking for a good fishing spot, not for her. Then he remembered that the Whitfields had a big fish pond all their own, right in front of their house, which they kept regularly stocked. He couldn't imagine fishing in a pond next to his house. How sporting could that be? You might as well catch the poor fish in a net and harvest them like you would corn or potatoes.

Still, if he could fish with Abby, it might be worth trying once or twice in an open pond. He lay back and put his hat over his eyes again. Thinking about Abby, his eyelids drooped and he felt he might take a nap. Then he heard a splash. Something had taken the bait. He leaped up and grabbed his pole. Sure enough, a fish big enough to be a smallmouth thrashed through the water, trying to lose the hook.

"Not today," he said. "You're coming home with me." He carefully played the fish as much as he could, pulling the line closer to the rock when the fish gave it slack, letting the line out when the fish struggled enough that the line might break free. Finally he managed to pull the fish out of the water. As he watched it wriggling on the end of his line, he saw two kids watching him from the bushes. They stood next to a tree, partially hidden by the undergrowth, about twenty feet away. They were Indians. Surprised, his blood surged. He almost dropped his pole in the creek and ran.

One of the Indian kids was a bare-chested boy about his own age and wearing buckskin pants. He had a small knife tucked under his belt. That alarmed Justin, but even though the boy's dark eyes stared at him, he didn't strike Justin as dangerous, as long as he kept his distance. The other Indian was a girl, younger and probably his sister. She wore an off-white cotton dress with a colorful sash. They were both skinny and Justin could see the boy's ribs. They both had big brown eyes and long hair, gathered together and trailing down their backs.

Justin quickly scanned the trees around the children, looking for any other Indians, adults or warriors, which might mean real trouble. But the brother and sister appeared to be alone. When he'd regained his composure, Justin laid the fishing pole and fish down on the rock and looked again at the Indians. He had no idea if they spoke English.

"Hi," he said. The girl jumped, covered her mouth with her hands, and ran away like she hadn't known Justin could see her until he'd spoken. The boy didn't react. His brow knit as he looked back and forth between Justin and the fish flopping around on the rock. He seemed concerned. Was he worried about the fish? Justin didn't know, but he felt uncomfortable having an Indian stare at him.

"What's wrong?" Justin asked. "Are you okay?"

The Indian boy put a shelled acorn in his mouth and started to chew.

"Hey," Justin said. "Don't eat those things. They're awful bitter." Didn't this kid know any better? Then it came to him. The boy was hungry. His sister probably was, too. He'd heard that life was hard for Indians, even in summer. Most of them didn't grow their own crops but relied on hunting and fishing. And

Justin knew from overhearing adults' conversations that wild game was getting scarce in the county.

"Are you hungry?" he asked.

The boy looked at the bass, which had stopped wriggling. Justin bent down on one knee and pulled the hook from the fish's mouth. Then he pulled his stringer of fish from the creek and added the new bass. The Indian boy's eyes grew wide at the sight of the collection of fish.

"Look," Justin said. He held up the stringer in the direction of the boy. "Why don't you take these? I can always catch more." He took a step forward and lay the stringer down on the rock. He pointed at the boy, then down at the fish.

"They're yours, all right? I'm going home now." He gave the boy a slight wave with his hand, stepped off the rock, and walked away in the opposite direction.

The next day he went back to the creek. As he approached the flat rock, he could tell the fish and his stringer were gone. A bear could have eaten them, or a raccoon, but when he stepped up onto the rock he found a bone-handled knife lying where his stringer had been. He picked it up. The six-inch blade was sharp, clean, and new. A hawk's feather was tied around the hilt by a strip of leather just below the blade. At first he thought the Indian boy must have forgotten the knife. Then he understood. It had been left there for him. Not as a gift so much, but in trade for the fish. The knife wasn't fancy, certainly nothing like the prize, custom-made knife Toby had received for his birthday once. Still, Justin thought this knife must be too valuable to trade for a handful of fish. But maybe that wasn't the point. When you're hungry and a total stranger helps you out, that's significant. Maybe more so than the meal itself.

He scanned the woods along the creek but couldn't see anyone. Even so, he held the knife up over his head, knowing someone could be watching.

"Thank you," he called. "Thank you very much."

CHAPTER FIVE

September 1831

Abigail set out from home on foot, walking down a path she knew well. It was a shortcut that would take her to the road that eventually led to the commercial center of Ridgetop, such as it was. It had never been more than a few shops, the modest roadside inn, some residences, and a few farm-related businesses. Even so, Ridgetop was big enough to host the annual county fair, and that was her destination. She was happy her parents allowed her to walk to the fair unchaperoned, even though her parents would arrive shortly thereafter, and she was to meet her friend, Sally Marston.

She had both arms wrapped around a napkin-covered, quart-sized clay pot, full of her mother's dark clover honey, which she was to enter in the fair's farm products contest. Her mother was rightfully proud of Whitfield farm's honey, which had taken the blue ribbon on a number of occasions, usually in years when Anne Sterling's honey wasn't judged the best. The two women were locked in a friendly rivalry that had gone on for years.

After turning onto the more traveled road, she started to cross a short covered bridge when she saw a young man bending down, near the far end, tying his shoe. She skipped a step and her lips drew back in a mischievous smile. Even though he was partially hidden in the shadows of the bridge cover, she recognized Justin Sterling's broad shoulders and strong jaw. He had set something next to him on the bench that ran the length of the bridge. It looked like the same pot Abigail was carrying, and she guessed that he, too, might be headed for the county fair.

Justin's back was turned, but Abigail didn't call out to him. She wanted to surprise him with her appearance, if he didn't notice her first. She stepped lightly over the thick wooden planks until she stood directly behind him. Giddy that her prank was working, she spoke at the moment Justin stood up.

"Having some trouble?" she asked.

"Yow!" In his surprise, Justin spun around. His forearm knocked the clay pot out of her arms. The string holding the cloth cover broke, sending it fluttering away. The pot smacked against the side of the bridge and landed upright on the bench, but a large crack had split the pot nearly in half, and Henrietta's prize-winning honey began to ooze out.

"Look what you've done!"

In a flash Justin grabbed the pot he had been carrying, pulled off the lid, and held the pot under Abigail's to catch her honey.

"Sorry," he said. "I won't be able to save all your honey, but I'll catch what I can."

She put her hands on her hips and watched in dismay. "What good will that do? That was my mother's contest entry. She will be furious."

"All the more so when she finds out I was the cause."

"It wasn't your fault." she moaned. "I shouldn't have snuck up on you." But she knew Justin was right. Even if she had caused the mishap, her parents would be suspicious of Justin if he was involved.

"My mother won't be happy, either," he said. "Now that I've mixed her honey with Henrietta's."

"You were going to the contest, too?"

He nodded. "I wonder what the two of them together will taste like."

"It doesn't matter. I'm doomed."

"Can't you go home for more?"

Abigail shook her head. "There's not enough time."

They both watched as her honey dripped into Justin's pot until it overflowed and ran down his hands. He set his pot on the bench and covered it with the lid. Then he looked at the honey covering his fingers. "I have an idea."

"Like what? We could run away to Kentucky. That's about the only thing that would save us."

"Don't tempt me."

The intimacy of the idea flashed through her mind, as it must have his. She was suddenly aware of his closeness, that his coffee-brown eyes were focused on hers. He held out his hand and she took it in hers before she remembered it was covered with honey.

"Ooo!" She tried to pull away, but he held on. He rubbed her hand in his until it was as covered by the sweet, sticky mass as his.

"What a mess." She laughed and rubbed her one clean hand around his, spreading the sticky mess further.

"I can't let you go to the fair like this," he said.

"Oh, no," she said. "That wouldn't do at all."

"Let me clean you up." He raised her hands to his mouth and licked her fingers.

His tongue darted between her fingers, tickling her.

"Oooh." She giggled.

"Delicious," he murmured.

"You're awful," she said. "But don't stop."

"Your mother makes a very fine honey."

She glanced in either direction and saw that they were still alone and hidden in the shade of the covered bridge. "Let me try that." She pulled his hand to her mouth and licked, keeping her gaze on his. They took turns that way, laughing when it wasn't their turn to lick, until most of the honey had been smoothed from their hands. When that was done, he pulled her to him. She thought he meant to give her a hug, but when she raised her head, he kissed her softly, briefly. She tasted the honey on his lips. When he pulled away she kept her head raised, her lips still parted and her eyes closed. Her heart raced and she felt her cheeks turning pink.

"You never kissed me before," she whispered.

"You were never covered with honey before."

She opened her eyes and scowled. "I'm not sure that's a good excuse."

He laughed, but her unexpected elation faded, and the problem of the honey recaptured her attention.

"What are we going to do about this tragedy?" She gestured at the pots, one messy from overflow, and one cracked and dripping its remaining contents slowly onto the floor of the bridge. "You can't very well enter *your* mother's honey in the contest, mixed as it is with *my* mother's."

"Contaminated by it, you mean."

She scowled. "This isn't funny. I don't know about Anne, but my mother is not going to be happy."

"Listen. Whatever you do, don't tell her what happened."

"Well, I wouldn't tell her everything." She popped a finger in her mouth.

"You know what I mean. If neither of our mothers win this year's contest, that's simply the way of things, isn't it? Surely they can accept that."

"That assumes they were beaten in a fair competition, but now they can't even enter."

"Oh, they'll have an entry," he said. "They will surely have an entry."

35

That year, to everyone's surprise, the blue ribbon for best honey was awarded to a previously unknown competitor, someone named Whiting. No one had ever heard of this Whiting person and, mysteriously, they never came forward to claim the prize.

Justin sat on a wooden bench outside Jacob Byrne's general store, waiting for his father to call him to help load their wagon. With his legs stretched out in front of him, he whittled on a short length of pine with the knife he'd found on the flat rock by the creek. A shadow fell over his hands. When he looked up he saw Abby and her mother, Henrietta, standing nearby in front of the store.

"As long as we're here," Henrietta said, "would you like to see what new fabrics Mr. Byrne has in stock?"

Abby gave Justin a quick glance. "You go ahead, Mother. I'll join you shortly. It's such a fine day, I think I'll sit outside and talk to Justin for a minute."

Henrietta looked at Justin as if seeing him for the first time. "Oh, hello, Justin Sterling."

"Good morning, Mrs. Whitfield." Justin touched the brim of his hat with the knife. Henrietta raised an eyebrow and averted her eyes from the blade. "Very well, Abigail. But don't be too long."

Justin heard Henrietta's reluctance at leaving the two of them together, but she disappeared into the store and Abby sat down beside him.

"What are you making?" She pointed at the piece of pine.

"I'm not sure," he said. "I won't know until I get a little further along. Maybe I'll carve myself a fine, long pipe." He grinned and looked at Abby sideways. "Wouldn't I look grand with a pipe?" He set his jaw and held the rough piece of wood up to his lips.

"Oh, yes. So manly," she said. "But don't ever smoke such a thing in my house."

"No smoking in your house? A fine thing for the daughter of a tobacco farmer to say. I've seen your father smoke a pipe many times."

"I wasn't speaking of my father's house." She casually looked over his shoulder, down the dusty street that ran in front of the store.

"Ah," he said, catching her meaning. "Thank you for the warning. I'll make sure to never take up the devil's weed in your house." He set the chunk of wood and his knife down on the bench, away from Abby. "It's very nice to see you, Abby Whitfield."

"It's very nice to see you, Justin Sterling." She smiled and his heart thudded for a moment. He wasn't sure why Abby had stopped to talk to him, but he was glad she did.

"You know, the older we get, the less I get to see of you," he said.

"I know." She smoothed her hand back and forth along the wooden bench surface. Each time her fingers came close to his thigh, he wanted to jump. "It's our family obligations, I think. My chores keep me very busy."

"Does Henry lay on the whip at home?" He was kidding, but he watched her meadow-green eyes, trying to guess her thoughts.

"Not as such." She gave him a look of mock disapproval. "But I wish we weren't growing up so fast. I'm not ready for the worries and obligations of the world, and I miss playing with you as we did when we were younger."

He nodded and looked down at his feet. As they'd acknowledged, casual meetings were becoming rare occurrences, and for Justin this one was an opportunity. He wanted more of a connection with Abby than small talk and, against his better judgment, he said, "Can I ask you a question, before your mother returns?"

"Of course." Abigail glanced over her shoulder at the shop.

"Why doesn't your father like me?" He was instantly afraid he might have offended her, but it was too late to withdraw the question.

It was Abigail's turn to look down at her feet. She folded her hands in her lap. "I'm not aware that he dislikes you. What makes you say that?"

"He's never told me as much. I suppose that's to his credit. But whenever I see him, and he sees me, he never seems very pleased."

"Perhaps you should talk to him more. Could you be reading too much into my father's behavior?" She smoothed a lock of long red hair behind her ear.

"I think not. But it occurs to me that, on most occasions when I see your father, I'm also seeing you. And when I see you, I'm not much inclined to talk to your father. That may have something to do with it."

"Perhaps he sees the evil intentions in your eyes whenever you look at me." Her eyes crinkled in a grin.

Justin nodded. "No doubt when your father looks at me, he just sees a fool. After all, I am nothing more than that, and I must sound like one when I'm talking to anyone in the presence of such beauty." He gave her a slight bow, meant partially in jest.

She laughed but she gave him a shy, coy look. "Talk like that will get you in trouble with my father every time."

"Abigail. Let's go." Henrietta had come out of the store and stood next to the bench. Abby stood up, placed a hand on Justin's arm, and gave him a gentle squeeze.

"I hope we can work on your speech difficulties again soon." She winked at him. "I always like it when you express yourself clearly."

As Abby and her mother walked away, Justin heard Henrietta say, "How nice of you, Abigail, offering to help the poor boy."

Justin stared at his arm. He could still feel the pressure there from Abby's fingers.

CHAPTER SIX

Mid-May 1833

Abigail Whitfield sat, leaning against the trunk of an oak tree, shaded from the hot noonday sun. She drummed her fingers on the top of a rattan basket and watched Justin Sterling, across the field in front of her. Justin fought with a team of oxen as they pulled an iron plow through the questionable soil that made up much of the Sterlings' land. She watched him wipe the sweat from his brow with the back of his hand. He adjusted the leather straps of the plow around his shoulders, then slapped them on the backs of the oxen. The plow moved forward a few more feet and then stuck fast. Where most men would have taken to swearing, Justin simply shook his head, loosened the harness, and knelt down to see what was obstructing the plow. He brushed away at the loosened soil and exposed a stone as large as Abigail's basket.

In her relatively cool hiding place, she caught her breath as Justin stripped off his shirt, revealing his broad back and tanned, well-muscled shoulders. No doubt his conditioning was the result of years of such chores. He tossed the shirt onto the back of one of the oxen, then went down on his knees to wrestle the stone out of the ground. Abigail watched in admiration as Justin, back muscles flexing, lifted the stone from the ground and heaved it out of the way of the plow. He threw the shirt aside, too, and started gathering up the harness leathers.

Now, she thought. Now's the time. She stood up, grabbed

the basket, and walked from the shade of the trees onto the field toward Justin.

Justin reined the oxen to a halt and watched the cool vision coming toward him in the sweltering mid-day heat. There was no mistaking Abigail Whitfield's flowing red mane and shapely young body. And to his delight she carried a lunch basket. Could it be for him? How thoughtful of her to remember him on such a hot morning. He tossed the harness aside and picked up his shirt, but he realized it was too late to pretend any modesty.

To his surprise, Abby walked to one side, as if she would pass by and continue on, but she stopped and turned toward him at the last second. She held the basket low in front of her with both hands, but did not offer it to him.

"Good morning to you, Justin Sterling," she said.

"Good morning to you, Abigail Whitfield." He felt embarrassed and at the same time exhilarated that she should see him in the noonday sun, dirty and half naked. Holding his soiled shirt in one hand, he bowed as gallantly as he could. But the intensity of her smile weakened him so that he had to look away, but just for a second. His own smile felt clumsy, as though he were drunk or a crazy man. Funny that she always had that effect on him.

"Are you lost?" he asked. "We're not often favored by the presence of a Whitfield on the modest Sterling farm."

"No," she said, as if she were considering the notion. "It seemed like a fine day for a walk, and this way seemed as good as any other."

Justin had a fleeting image of Abigail as a farmer's wife, his wife perhaps, delivering lunch. But she looked a bit out of place in the middle of the field. "Are you on a mission of mercy this morning?" he asked, gesturing at her basket.

"Yes, I guess I am," she said. "How clever of you to notice." She paused, as if in thought, then said, "Justin, I was wondering

41

if you were intending to race this year."

Since she had changed the subject, he realized she hadn't brought the basket for him, but he understood that she was asking about the county fair horse race. He was rightfully proud of his family's breeding operation, which won the annual contest on occasion, besting horses from far richer farms.

"I wouldn't miss it for the world," he said.

"I hear your friend Toby is going to enter this year, too," she said seriously. "And I understand the Johnsons have a mare who's never lost a race."

Justin had heard this before, and he was more than a little irritated at all of the talk swirling around Toby's unbeatable mount. Since the Johnsons had taken the horse to more profitable races in Tennessee and Kentucky, Justin had never competed with the storied animal.

"I thank you for the warning," he said. "I guess we'll see about Mr. Johnson's mighty steed in a couple of months or so, eh?"

"It will be an interesting competition," she said.

To his annoyance, he couldn't tell who she'd favored, him or Toby, but he couldn't keep his eyes off the basket. "Is that why you came all the way out here?" he said. "To talk about the race? Aren't you saving a poor field hand from dying of hunger?"

"Why yes. I am indeed."

"That's very sweet of you, Abigail Whitfield." He almost reached for the basket.

"Yes, I suppose so, but it's the least I could do for those poor men slaving away in my father's fields. They work so hard."

She had set him up for a joke. Justin's smile vanished and he rolled his eyes.

"And I should be getting on to them," she said. "It must be nearly noontime, and they're liable to rise up and beat the foremen senseless if I don't get this dinner to them quickly."

42

"Oh, I understand. All too well." He gave her a wry smile, conceding that she'd successfully kidded him.

"It's been nice to see you, Justin Sterling. Good day."

Justin's mind reeled. What kind of woman would go so far out of her way to pull such a prank? He wiped his grimy face and gawked at Abby as she started walking away.

She took two steps and stopped.

"Oh," she said, "I almost forgot." She set the basket down, opened it, and withdrew a covered glass jar. It dripped wet and cooling with condensation. "I've had this quart of lemonade setting in the creek for an hour or so." She walked back to him, took his hand, and placed it around the jar. Then she kissed him lightly on the cheek. "I hope you like it." She turned around, picked up her basket and walked away.

Justin stood there with the cold jar in his hand and shook his head in bewilderment as he watched her go. First she plays a cruel trick on him, then she kisses him. It was only a peck on the cheek, but he would like to have kissed her back if he wasn't covered with dust and sweat. Still, that hadn't stopped her. Maybe she'd planned the whole episode, knowing he was helpless to take advantage of her kiss. He marveled at her boldness. She was a mystery and a challenge at the same time, and everything about her drove him wild.

Then he looked at the jar in his hand as if seeing it for the first time. He ripped off the cover and drank the cool, sweet liquid in a series of long quick gulps, not caring that some of it spilled onto his face and chest. When it was empty he tossed the jar aside and took one last look at Abigail. He turned and snatched up the reins of the oxen team. Raising them high, he slapped the animal's backs and bellowed "Whaahoo!" at the top of his lungs.

Abigail smiled without turning around.

CHAPTER SEVEN

August 1833

Every young man a certain age in Ridgetop looked forward to competing in the annual county fair horse races. It was a chance to show the young, single ladies, not to mention the male competition, what kind of man you were. For Justin it was no different, although he wished to catch the eye of only one young lady, whom he was certain would be in the viewing stands, near the start and finish line. He hadn't forgotten Abby's love of horses, or her dream of raising them.

Racing at the county fair required a certain degree of riding skill, of course, but often much more than that. The signature competition of the fair was a free-for-all, point-to-point event that ran across fields and forest, over fences and around or through whatever obstacles might lie in the path of horse and rider. The distance of the race varied each year between two and four miles.

Because of the rough condition of the course, those who truly wanted to win needed a kind of determination and fearlessness not usually found in the casual rider. Indeed, the county officials who organized the race sometimes deliberately left a downed tree in the path of the riders, or routed the racecourse over a stream, which, depending on the amount of recent rain, might force riders to swim their horses.

Horse racing in Ridgetop County was more than a casual sport. It was a chance for the spectators to see what sort of stock the various farms in the region had to offer. Breeders would come from other parts of the state and from as far away as Kentucky to evaluate Ridgetop County stock. The area was known for above-average horses, and Justin understood this well. The Sterling farm wasn't as well-known as others in the county and, for Justin, winning the race was a means of getting the recognition he thought his family's stock deserved. It was the one way he could think of that might lift his family's fortunes and provide them with a more comfortable living.

Justin dearly wanted to win the race to impress Abigail Whitfield, too. More than that, he wanted Henry Whitfield to take notice, so that someday he might give Justin a chance at winning Abby's hand. It was just a dream but, when Justin considered it, he set his jaw and redoubled his race preparations.

It was not uncommon for neighbors to wager a friendly silver dollar or two on their horses as a matter of pride. But sometimes other, less reputable, characters attended the fair, hoping to make a more substantial investment in the outcome of the race. And so it was that Justin noticed two strangers as he cinched up his saddle. One man wore a brocade vest, visible beneath his top coat, and a high top hat. None of the local men, even those with means, would dress in so ostentatious a fashion. More likely the man came from Nashville or from as far away as Louisville.

Justin might have paid the man no more attention, but for the fact that he was talking to Tobias Johnson. The two of them stood at the edge of the barn with a third man, who also didn't appear to be a local. The second stranger dressed more like a teamster or a longshoreman, and he wasn't doing much talking. His tri-corner hat was worn at the edges and out of fashion. His simple woolen overalls had not recently been cleaned. His nose had been broken more than once, and one ear had cauliflowered like that of a man who'd spent time in the boxing ring, but hadn't bettered his opponents. Justin wouldn't have played cards with either man for more than matchsticks.

The three men were deep in discussion and, since they were at the far side of the barn, it looked as though they did not wish to be interrupted or even overheard. Justin went about his preparations, but Toby glanced in his direction once, apparently pointing him out to the other two men. Why he would do that, Justin had no idea.

Toby left the men after slapping the back of the man in the top hat. He walked past Justin toward his own horse.

"Making new friends?" Justin asked, nodding in the direction of the strangers.

Toby glanced that way. "More like business acquaintances. They have an interest in racehorses and, as you know, the Johnson farm breeds the best."

"I guess we'll learn more about that today." Justin checked his rigging one more time.

"That we will," Toby said. "And good luck out there. You'll need it."

"You'll need more luck than I if you don't step lively. They call the next race in ten minutes."

"Blast!" Toby whipped off his hat and ran to his horse's stall.

Justin chuckled. He took his reins and walked the bay stallion out of the barn and into the bright noonday sun. His path took him past the two men who'd been talking to Toby moments earlier. The man in the top hat paid Justin little or no mind. His attention seemed fixed on Justin's horse. The other man had no eye for horses. He saw only Justin, and his eyes narrowed when Justin met his gaze.

"Good day, gentlemen," Justin said without breaking stride.

"Oh. Good day to you, too," the man in the top hat said. He put two fingers on his hat's brim in greeting. The other man kept his arms crossed and looked at Justin as if he'd insulted his mother. But he said nothing.

At the starting line, Justin mounted his bay. Other horses sidled back and forth, as nervous as their riders. A crowd had gathered, filling the small viewing stand and spilling along the first part of the course. Most people were there to cheer on one rider or another and talked up their chances. At the nearby fairgrounds a small brass band played "Blue Eye'd Mary," and everyone was in high spirits. The competitors formed themselves in a crude row, side-by-side behind a rope stretched out on either side of the course, which acted as a starting line. But, at the appointed time, nothing happened. The starter, a man named Hawkins, looked from his watch to the county barn. Justin couldn't tell what the trouble was until Toby rode up and took a position next to him.

"Good, I've made it," Toby said.

"Not a moment to spare." Rank had its privileges, Justin thought. Hawkins had waited for Toby to get ready.

The starting gun sounded and the rope dropped. Spectators cheered and the horses sprinted away with thundering hooves in a cloud of dust. Justin leaned forward, urging on his bay, but it seemed as though the sudden crack of the starter's pistol had silenced every other sound and caused time to slow down nearly to a standstill. With his horse in mid-stride, he glanced over at the viewing stand. He hadn't been able to pick out Abby's face from the crowd earlier, but in that still, quiet moment he clearly saw her crimson hair, fair skin, and those green eyes, lustrous as a June bug's wings, watching him. With her hands raised, her lips parted as she cheered. All the other faces in the sea of onlookers remained a blur. He smiled and looked ahead at the racecourse. Time sped up and the race resumed its chaotic, breakneck pace.

Riders whipped their mounts like they were chased by a

tornado. In the confusion, men's arms flailed, some slapping at the competitor next to them, accidentally or not. Not to be outdone, Tobias, too, laid on the whip. This year's course was all of twenty furlongs, and Justin made no immediate attempt to take the lead. He intended to let the other riders confront the obstacles ahead of them first and tire their horses more quickly. Then, as the knot of contestants thinned out, they would be easier to pass.

Galloping steadily, Justin kept his gaze fixed on the flapping coattails of Tobias's tweed riding jacket. Its distinctive checkered pattern stood out from the brown and gray leather outfits of the other competitors. In the long run, Toby was the one rider Justin needed to beat.

And Toby rode with abandon. He whipped his horse with more desperation than Justin thought necessary. Still, his Thoroughbred took the beating in stride, and its long legs inevitably pulled Toby toward the front of the jostling, colliding pack of riders. A great, gnarled oak tree marked the first half mile of the racecourse, and by the time the riders had reached it they'd become an uneven line, led by a small pack of contestants who traded off the lead. Toby rode near the front, Justin four lengths behind.

At the oak, the racecourse took a sharp right-hand turn. Such was the enthusiasm, confusion, and aggression of the lead riders that a number of them collided at the turn. Riders on the outside of the pack were pushed farther out, away from the best line. Several horses lost their stride completely and careened away into a fallow field. Cursing, their riders whipped them all the harder to regain their momentum and catch up. Toby's horse was bumped by a rider on his right as he made the turn. His horse took a sideways leap, nearly throwing Toby off balance, but horse and rider quickly regained their composure and lost little time racing away from the turn.

Dodging sod thrown into the air by the horses' hooves, Justin easily passed two slower riders and rounded the oak tree without incident. He'd brought himself one length closer to the group of front-runners, none of whom seemed capable of claiming the lead for very long. Several horses blocked Toby's way on either side, preventing him from riding cleanly. Justin hoped to stay out of that melee until more horses tired and dropped back. The bay was cruising now, and so far Justin's strategy appeared to be working.

At a mile and a half the riders were forced to jump a low, split-rail fence onto Jacob Russell's property and then follow along the side of a creek. The first two riders cleared the fence together without trouble. The horse of the third rider balked, coming up short and failing to jump. The rider intended to backtrack and take another run at the fence, but he turned into Toby's path and surprised Toby's horse. The Thoroughbred was already in jumping stride when the head of the other rider's horse struck it on the shoulder.

The collision was minor, but enough to cause Toby's Thoroughbred to hesitate. It jumped short and struck the fence with both cannons. Toby came out of the saddle as horse and rider tumbled headfirst over the fence and collapsed on the far side. Seeing this, Justin stood in his stirrups and raised one hand overhead to warn the other riders. He reined the bay to a stop in front of the fence, opposite where Toby had fallen, and waved the other riders around. The other competitors had seen Toby fall or took Justin's warning and jumped the fence away from the accident. The rider who initially failed to jump the fence cleared it on the second try and kept going. Toby lay still, facedown on the ground. The Thoroughbred whinnied in pain, clearly unable to rise. When all the riders had passed, Justin dismounted and leaped over the fence.

Toby had no visible injuries, except that his right leg was

bent at an unnatural angle below the knee. His head was turned to one side. Justin placed his hand near Toby's mouth. His friend was breathing but unconscious. Gingerly, Justin took Toby by the shoulders and turned him over on his left side, careful to keep any weight off the injured right leg. Toby had blood around his nose and a split lip. Except for that and the fact that Toby's tweed jacket was covered with dust, his friend could have been napping.

"That was quite a tumble young Master Johnson took." A farmer named Jenkins appeared at Justin's shoulder. "How is he?"

"His leg is broken and his head may have concussed. I don't know."

"Aye, it's not a compound fracture, but a bad break anyway."

It would have to be set, but by the time a doctor arrived, Toby might be awake. Given the likely pain involved, Justin knew Toby would much prefer to be unconscious when the leg was manipulated. Justin had seen the procedure many times. He decided to do it then.

"Hold him by the shoulders," Justin said. "I'll set the leg."

Jenkins sat down and cradled Toby's head and shoulders in his lap. Once he had a strong grip, Justin slowly but firmly pulled Toby's right leg and turned it back into line.

A deep moan escaped Toby's lips.

"Better he should have a few bad dreams than feel that when he's awake," Jenkins said.

"Stay here. I'll find something for a splint."

Jenkins nodded. Justin ran to the creek a few yards away, where a stand of straight willows grew. He found two that looked the right size and snapped them off. Then he broke them again until he had two pieces almost two feet long. He laid the lengths of willow on either side of Toby's leg. They were long enough to immobilize the leg as much as could be expected, and long enough to keep Toby from bending his knee.

Justin was removing his shirt and tearing it into strips he would use to tie the splint when Toby's father, Thomas Johnson, arrived on horseback, along with Abby, Henry Whitfield, and several other men.

"Oh, it's Toby!" Abby leaped from her horse and knelt by his still body. "Is he all right?" She put the palm of her hand on his cheek, and Justin felt vaguely jealous of her attention.

"I think he's okay," he said. "But for a busted leg. We won't know more until he's awake."

"Yes. And thankfully I can see you're not injured." She allowed one short glance at his bare chest and looked back down at Toby. Justin's skin tightened around his nipples. He felt fairly naked, kneeling next to Abigail with his shirt off.

"What's happened?" Thomas demanded. "What have you done?"

Justin started to glare at Thomas but checked himself. The man assumed someone else was at fault, anyone but his fair-haired son. He ripped another strip of wool from his shirt and kept tying the willow strips to Toby's leg.

"Tobias's horse failed to clear the fence," Jenkins said, getting to his feet.

"Impossible," Thomas said. "It's the finest horse in the county."

"I saw it with my own eyes." Jenkins looked at Thomas like he expected to be challenged.

"And you?" Thomas said to Justin. "What part did you play in this?"

"I'm playing the part of a doctor," Justin said, not bothering to hide his irritation. "Someone should look to the horse."

The men turned as one to see the Thoroughbred, about twenty feet away. It had given up trying to stand and lay quietly on its side, exhausted and huffing deep breaths. Its leg, too, had clearly been broken.

"Good God," Thomas said. "Such a waste."

"Now, Thomas." Henry Whitfield objected. "The good Lord appears to have spared Tobias any more serious injury."

Thomas shook his head. "You're right, Henry. You're right. But this should never have happened." He glanced again at Justin like he, the poor farmer's son, must somehow have caused Toby's fall.

A buckboard arrived and the men lifted the still-unconscious Toby into the bed. As they gathered up their horses and prepared to leave, Thomas Johnson handed Justin a pistol, butt first.

"It's primed," he said. "Since you're the doctor here, Sterling, see if you can manage this operation with only one shot."

Justin understood. Even if Thomas couldn't blame Justin for Toby's accident, he could make him put the Thoroughbred down. Justin accepted the pistol without saying anything. The men left, along with Abby, who rode next to the buckboard. Naked to the waste, Justin stood in the hot sun, held the pistol at his side, and watched them go. Abigail didn't look back.

Jenkins placed a sympathetic hand on Justin's shoulder. "Sometimes I think we're only here to serve them." He winked. "I'll let the renderer know he has work."

CHAPTER EIGHT

Still unconscious, Tobias was placed on a goose-down mattress on a divan on the covered porch at the rear of the Johnson house, where there might be a cooling breeze and relief from the summer heat. The doctor had come and gone. He was unable to do anything more for Tobias at that moment, except to place a more permanent splint on his broken leg. Servants were available, but Abigail volunteered to sit with Toby until he woke up. It was assumed that his unconscious state was temporary, and that he would awaken shortly. He appeared comfortable enough, and there wasn't much Abigail could do, but someone needed to be there just in case. She limited her attention to occasionally dampening Toby's brow with a cool kerchief. Every few minutes, Toby's closed eyes would dart about. He'd mumble something Abigail couldn't understand, then lapse into a deeper, more comfortable slumber.

How young he looks, to have such troubled sleep, thought Abigail. She remembered the start of the horse race, and how Toby had lain on the whip, eager to take the lead and prove his mettle. Her friend was still full of youthful vigor and enthusiasm. She wondered what fate awaited him, or her, for that matter, as they grew older. As an only son, undoubtedly he would take over the family's farm. Who would he end up marrying? What kind of a husband would he make? Ridgetop was a relatively closed society, and whatever future Toby had might well include Abigail.

A woman could do worse than marry Tobias Johnson, but at that moment she wasn't sure. She still planned to raise horses of her own, even if part of a larger farm. She would insist that whatever man she married help her live that dream. Surely Toby wouldn't object, but she might need more than permission. What of other men? Justin Sterling came to mind. There was a man who knew what he wanted from the world, if not how to get it. If she needed a partner to fulfill her dreams, Justin had an inner strength that might make it possible. If her plans fit his.

There came a soft knocking on the screened door. Abigail looked up and saw two men standing at the top of the steps outside the porch. One wore a silk top hat and looked the part of a travel-worn gentleman. The other man stood slightly behind and looked more like an employee, but at what rough service? Between the two, he looked like the one who did the heavy lifting.

"Good afternoon, madam," the gentleman said. "The name's Bailey. Hutchison Bailey. This here's my associate, Mr. Smith. We've come to inquire of the boy's condition." He pointed a gloved hand at Toby.

"Hello," Abigail said. From their unannounced and somewhat irregular appearance at the rear of the house, she wasn't eager to introduce herself to these strangers.

Bailey continued. "We spoke to Master Tobias before the race this morning, and we're real sorry he took such a bad spill. We hope he's not seriously injured."

"His leg's broken, but he's resting well enough." Whoever these men were, apparently they were acquainted with Toby.

"A bit of bad fortune." Bailey removed his hat and held it to his chest. The other man said nothing, but he looked to and fro, as if he'd never seen a house as large or nice as the Johnsons', and he wanted to memorize everything he saw.

"We believe he'll be okay when his leg is mended." She wondered where the servants were, or if she should call for the Johnsons.

"Excellent," Bailey said. "Excellent. As a matter of fact, our discussions with Master Tobias this morning concerned a certain business arrangement we—that is, Mr. Smith and I— have with him. Has he by any chance mentioned us to you, or anything about our business?"

"I'm afraid he has not," she said. "And I don't believe Tobias will be in any condition to conduct business for a few days, possibly more. Can you inquire of him at a later date?" She couldn't imagine what kind of business Toby had with two such disreputable-looking characters as Misters Bailey and Smith. Obviously they were not from Ridgetop County, and Abigail was beginning to wish they would go on their way.

"That would be a problem for us," Bailey said, glancing at Mr. Smith. "Our business with Master Tobias was of a rather immediate nature, to be concluded at once, after the competition this morning."

"I'm afraid there's nothing I can do for you," she said.

"How unfortunate." Bailey put his hat back on his head. "Mr. Smith and I must insist that the matter be addressed—"

"Excuse me." Justin appeared, standing at the bottom of the steps. He'd put on another shirt since the incident at the horse race. Even with Toby's injuries, Abigail had struggled at the time to keep from openly admiring Justin's bare chest. Now she was grateful for his unannounced arrival at the back door.

"There's nothing we can do for you," Justin said. "Not at this moment."

Bailey and Smith turned to look at Justin. "And you are . . . ?" Bailey said.

"I am a friend of Mr. Johnson's. That's all you need to know." Justin turned slightly, revealing the pistol he'd been holding low, next to his leg.

"A friend of the Johnsons. How fortunate for you," Bailey said.

Smith scowled at Justin but looked to Bailey, apparently for instructions.

Justin held out his free hand, palm open and away from the house, inviting Bailey and Smith to leave. "If you have any business with Tobias Johnson, I'm certain he will contact you when he is able."

Abigail glanced behind her, hoping Toby's father or one of the servants would arrive. She couldn't explain the tension filling the air, and she feared the men might cause trouble. But Bailey backed down, even though Smith looked eager to start a fight.

"How right you are," Bailey said. "Come, Mr. Smith. We should let Master Tobias rest and make a full recovery." To Abigail's relief, the two men walked down the steps. Bailey paused and doffed his hat when he passed Justin. "We will inquire again when the master is better able to attend to business. Good day."

"Good day to you," Justin said.

Smith gave him a grim smile and kept walking.

Justin watched the two men go until they had crossed the Johnsons' back lawn and entered onto the tree-lined public lane bordering the rear of the property. Then he came up the steps and stood at the screened door.

"Thank you," Abigail said. "I can't imagine who those men are." She held the door open.

Justin came in. "As luck would have it, I saw them talking to Toby just before the race."

"Is that why you came armed?" She pointed at the pistol.

"What? This?" Justin held the pistol up at eye level and

examined it. "It's not loaded. I was just returning it to Mr. Johnson."

"Ah, yes," Abigail said. "Someone had to put down Toby's horse. It's so sad."

Justin set the pistol on a small table next to the divan. "An absolute waste. I hope I'm never required to perform that particular task again. How's Toby doing?"

"Pretty much the same." She smiled. "The doctor compliments you on your splinting skills and says you'd make him a good assistant, if you ever give up farming."

Justin placed a hand on Toby's forehead. "I'll consider it. There must be more profit in doctoring than farming, if you can put up with sick people." He smiled to show he was kidding.

"Better to put up with the sick than people like those men. Who were they?"

"I don't know, but I have my suspicions."

"And what are those?"

"As long as we've had horse racing, money has changed hands. I think those men were betting on the race."

"With Toby?" She looked down at her friend, whose sleep was troubled one again. "Do you think he owes those men money? That's horrible."

"I hope he doesn't," Justin said. "But men like that would not have come here so quickly to pay off their own debts. And how horrible the situation is would depend on how much money Toby may have lost."

She shook her head. "It's bad enough that he's lost the race and his horse, too. I can't imagine being in debt to gamblers." She sat and took one of Toby's hands in hers. "I'm going to sit with him awhile. It may be better if you aren't here when he wakes. You would remind him of his losses."

"Very well." Justin shrugged his shoulders and left.

Abigail looked down at Toby's placid face and wondered what kind of mischief he'd been up to.

Walter Sterling glanced over the top of the book he was reading when Justin came into the sitting room. The boy seemed worried, unable to decide whether to sit or pace the room.

"Good evening, Father."

"Good evening, son."

"What are you reading?"

He glanced at the cover of the tattered red book. "It's an ancient Greek tale. An adventure, written by a man named Homer."

Justin hesitated, interrupting his apparent self-absorption to look at his father. Walter smiled, but something worried him.

"An adventure," Justin said. "That's fine for the Greeks, but what can they tell us about the hardships of a farmer's life in rural Tennessee?"

"Oh, I don't know." Walter set the book in his lap. "Men have always been set upon by demons, some more exotic than others. Some are of their own making, and farmers are not immune."

"There's no need to go on an adventure to find those demons," Justin said. "And we'll never be free of them, I suppose."

"Probably not," he said. "But it's how we respond to the demons that marks us as men. Or, in the case of this story, how fathers relate to their sons and their demons."

"Your son hasn't done too well with his demons, lately." Justin dropped into a chair opposite him. "I should have won that race. I could have, too, if Toby hadn't taken a fall."

"No, you didn't win the county free-for-all, son, but you did something much more important. You helped your friend when he needed it. That should provide returns long after the excitement of winning a horse race has waned."

"Thank you, Father, but a single incident of helping Toby Johnson is akin to once helping the Queen of Egypt step out of her carriage. It's bound to get lost among the other trappings of the Johnsons' lives. Toby's broken leg will mend. In time it will be nothing more than a story he'll tell his children, nothing more than a momentary inconvenience in his comfortable life. But my coming to his aid may have resulted in a serious setback for the Sterling farm. Or at best it was an opportunity lost."

Walter picked up his pipe from a small table next to his chair and looked into the bowl. "These things, these demons if you will, happen from time to time. It's not the end of the world. We've bred some fine stock, in no small part due to your help." He knocked a few ashes from the bowl into a clay ashtray and started reloading the pipe with fresh tobacco. "There will be other races, not that it matters so much. Sooner or later men who look for horses like ours will find their way to our door. I have faith in that. As I have faith in you."

"Thank you, Father. I knew you would. I just wish there was something more I could do for you. For us." Justin waved a hand in the air, taking in the whole Sterling farm. "I feel like there's so much more we could have, but it remains out of reach."

"You're doing as much as any father can expect of a son. Perhaps our lot in life is set. And if that's true, we may never be as comfortable as the Johnsons or the Whitfields, but we're comfortable enough, God willing. And don't be fooled. Families who appear so much better off than others have their own problems, ones we poor Sterlings do not."

"Maybe so." Justin nodded. "But what I wouldn't give to have their problems, just for a day."

Walter looked a little more closely at his son. "Forgive me if I pry, but I suspect your concern over not winning the race has more to do with something else, something more personal than taking home the purse. Am I right?"

Justin's head shot up and he grinned. "You know me too well."

"It's the Whitfield girl, Abigail, who's got under your skin. I know."

Justin's grin turned into a rueful smile and Walter's suspicions were confirmed. He had been expecting this kind of trouble sooner or later.

Justin ran his fingers through his hair. "I suppose that's a tale as ancient as it is current. And, much to my dismay, the author, whoever he is, can't seem to write a happy ending. At least for me."

"And you believe that's because of a difference in wealth. That there is too much distance between us poor Sterlings and the Whitfield family, which lives high above us, metaphorically speaking, in a shining farm on a hill."

"Aye, that's the stopper. But even if it weren't, Abby herself causes me as much suffering as I can stand. One moment I see such a light in her eye—the spark of love, at least I hope—and I do everything I can to fan that spark into a flame." Justin clenched his fist. "Then she turns away, to Toby perhaps, or to the next man who approaches her, and she has no more time for me. I feel the floor fall away beneath my feet and I tumble into pitch darkness. How can one woman cause so much misery?"

"I know it won't help to point this out, but the aching heart in question is yours. So you may have some choice in the matter."

"So true. I would give everything I own to know that Abigail Whitfield's heart ached as much for me, even for the briefest moment, as mine does for her. Or, if it doesn't, to be free of this pain, once and for all."

"I am familiar with young Miss Whitfield, and you may underestimate the woman's feelings for you."

"What do you mean?" His son looked at him with cautious hope.

"I've seen the two of you together. I've surely seen the light in your eye when you're with her. And I've observed Abigail, too. She has her eye on you, of that I am sure."

"Is my interest in her a motive for revenge? Is that why she tortures me so?"

"In a sense, yes. She would not torture you if she did not feel favorably toward you. Unfortunately, she may not be able to do otherwise."

"How do you mean?"

"Abigail's life is not entirely her own. None of ours is." He set the book on a side table. "We all have obligations. Some are of our own doing, and some are like the demons of an adventure. And some of them are set upon us by our circumstances at birth."

"Now you speak of Henry Whitfield, surely a demon and the bane of my existence."

"Henry doesn't wish you ill. He simply wants the best of all things for his daughter. What father wouldn't?"

"Am I such a sorry prospect? No, don't answer that. I know my own worth. It's Henry who doesn't."

"If love for a woman were a measure of a man's worth, you, my son, would be wealthy indeed. But Henry must be concerned with more worldly matters. He cares for his family in the same way you and I and your mother do, each within our own means. In Henry's case, his means are substantial, and that's the standard by which he measures what's good for his daughter."

"And because of that I am doomed. Abby and I have no say in our fates, is that what you're telling me?"

"No, I hope that's not true. I'm merely telling you that Abi-

61

gail understands these things. She must be torn between her feelings for you and her love and respect for her father."

"And, being unable to express whatever those feelings are for me, much less to commit, she settles for torturing me."

Walter laughed. "What you think of as torture may simply be a test. Have you ever considered that?"

"She tests me? How much more testing do I need? How much more can I stand? Would she drive me to my knees before she can love me?"

He laughed again. "No, son. I'm sure that's not the case, but think of this. If you were Abigail Whitfield and you loved a poor farmer's son, what kind of man would that boy have to be to win her away from Henry Whitfield?"

Justin hung his head. "The man would have to be Agamemnon, leading an army of heroes who storm the high, forbidding walls of the Whitfield mansion."

"He'd have to be strong, that's true. As strong as his love."

Justin regarded him in silence. "That's what you mean by a test."

"Abigail Whitfield is not a flirtatious woman, as far as I can tell. If she had no interest in you, and you little in her, she'd have no reason to torment you so. More likely she would ignore you. As it is, the degree to which you are tormented might be proportional to her feelings for you, although about that I can only guess."

Justin grinned. "If that's true, Father, then Abigail Whitfield loves me more than the moon and stars, more than her next breath."

Walter struck a match and spoke between breaths as he lit his pipe. "Keep that in mind, son, when your heart aches. Do what you can, within reason, to pass the test, but be true to yourself."

"And if I fail the test and Henry wins?"

"Unlikely as it may seem to you now, you will continue to

live. And when the time is right, you will love again. More strongly than ever."

"Thank you, Father, but I will never know that second lover. I cannot fail whatever tests Abigail wants to set before me. I must not."

Justin leaped from his seat and strode from the room. Anne Sterling watched him go as she came into the room and looked at Walter.

"What have you been telling Justin?" she said. "He's got more energy in him now than I've seen in a fortnight."

"I was telling him stories," he said. "About when you and I were young."

CHAPTER NINE

May 1834

Abigail sat on a comfortable stuffed settee, knitting a forest-green sweater spread in her lap. Her hands worked swiftly, even though she had only recently learned the skill. She'd avoided knitting when she was younger, considering it "woman's work," or at least nothing that would help her raise horses. But, since she had grown older, she'd come to realize its practical value. Ridgetop was far from a large town like Nashville, and even farther from any real city like Louisville or Saint Louis. It seemed impossible to find quality clothing nearby, and when Abigail did find it, it was always expensive. True, her parents could afford to buy her nice clothes, nicer than many of the families in the valley, but she had no desire to set herself apart from her friends and neighbors by what she wore.

"Abigail, dear," her mother said from her seat at the rolltop desk. She lay down her quill pen and used both hands to tighten the already neat bundle of graying hair at the back of her head.

A familiar tone of parental concern in her mother's voice caused Abigail to take notice. She was immediately cautious.

"Yes, Mother," she said as innocently as she could. She didn't look up from her knitting. Her mother closed the ledger she was working in and watched Abigail with a thoughtful expression.

"Abigail," her mother said again. "It seems like only yesterday I was changing your diapers." She sighed a bit too dramatically.

"And now you've grown into such a beautiful young woman."

"Yes, Mother," she said. "Thank you for noticing." She still did not put down her knitting, but she glanced up and smiled at her mother in a way she hoped didn't look too patronizing.

"Abby dear," her mother said, switching to the more familiar name, which she normally would forgo.

Abigail braced herself.

"You have a birthday coming up," her mother said.

Now Abigail knew where her mother was going. It was a topic her mother raised more and more often lately. It was high time Abigail got married and started having grandchildren.

"Will you bake me a cake for my birthday this year?" Abigail stopped knitting briefly and looked up.

Henrietta folded her hands in her lap and smiled a patient, motherly smile. Perhaps she was glad she'd at least engaged her daughter in the conversation.

"Well," she said haltingly. "I suppose I can, but you're very much a grown woman now, so you shouldn't expect too much." Her smile still had that patient look about it.

"Yes," Abigail said. "Since I'm all grown up, Father will probably throw me out of the house and out into the world to fend for myself. Won't he?"

Henrietta chuckled and waved a hand dismissively at the comment.

"Oh, I won't mind," Abigail continued, "I can always move to Nashville and write poetry. I can take in laundry to support myself. It might be quite romantic, in a way."

"Now Abigail, you mustn't talk that way. Although I don't know if I've ever been able to stop you. You've had a mind of your own since you were old enough to know where the cookie jar sat."

"Thank you, Mother. I'll consider that a compliment."

"Well, you shouldn't. You are such a headstrong young lady,

and that won't help you . . . well, when it comes time for you to find a nice young man and settle down."

There it was. They had joined the familiar battle again, but Abigail decided not to confront her mother with the issue head-on.

"Oh, it shouldn't be any problem at all," she said in a distracted way, pretending to focus on some unseen stitch. "I always thought the nice young men were supposed to find me." She lowered her knitting to her lap and looked out the window. "This is the way I see it." She tried to sound as if she had given the problem quite a bit of thought. "One day I'll be traveling to Nashville for a lyceum, or to attend a fund-raising assembly for widows and orphans sponsored by the governor. Or whatever. My carriage will break down on the road. The wheel will fall off or something, right in the middle of nowhere. Anyway, my manservant, struggle as he might, will not be able to put the wheel back on.

"What are we to do? Well, just at that moment, a fine, strong gentleman will ride out of the woods on a great black stallion. He might be a highway bandit. I don't know, but when he spies me in my distress, he will be hopelessly smitten. He cannot help but offer assistance."

Henrietta laughed a quick high laugh and then discretely covered her mouth.

"So you see," Abigail continued. "This gentleman or bandit, again I don't know which, will strip off his coat and single-handedly lift my carriage—with me in it of course—right off the ground so that my manservant can put the wheel back on."

Abigail sighed, looking a little wistful. "Surely you know the rest. It's love at first sight. We'll ride away together on his horse and live happily ever after." She returned to her knitting, hoping she had blunted her mother's enthusiasm for any more discussion on the subject of marriage.

"My," her mother said. "That *is* a fanciful story. I'm sure I never taught you to think life was like that."

"Who said anything about *life*, Mother. I'm talking about *love*."

"Love is all well and good for stories and the like," her mother said. "But love is not something that just happens to you, young lady. In the practical world, you've got to find a gentleman who has the right, well . . . circumstances, and then love will follow in time."

Abigail knew that "circumstances" meant as much money and social position as possible.

"Like with you and father?" she asked.

"Exactly," her mother said firmly. But her eyes fluttered and she glanced out the window.

Abigail had never been given a full accounting of how her parents met, or what their lives had been like when they were younger, before they were married. But she couldn't imagine their lives had been anything more than what they were now, bereft of any drama.

"I was very lucky to meet a man as nice as your father," her mother said.

Indeed you were, Abigail agreed silently.

"And I want you to have the same benefits in life that I've enjoyed," her mother continued. "That's why your father and I are planning a little coming-out party for you. Of course, we don't need to call it a coming-out party. We can call it a birthday party."

Abigail dropped her knitting and gaped at her mother.

"What? Oh, Mother, you wouldn't."

"No need to thank me, dear. We intend to invite young men and women from all of the best families. I know young people love to dance, so we'll hire musicians. Margaret Anne will bake pies and it will be a wonderful gathering. Don't you agree?"

Abigail fought the urge to shout all her objections at once. Instead, she inspected her handiwork, calmed her tense stomach, and sighed.

"It would be nice to see my friends, I suppose," she allowed, "but you don't need to go to such trouble just for me, just because it's my birthday."

"It's no trouble at all, my dear." Henrietta smiled sweetly. "Besides, being in the country, as we are, you don't often have the opportunity to meet the right kind of . . . gentleman."

Realizing her mother was serious about her plans, Abigail set her knitting aside.

"Mother, I have no interest in picking a husband like an apple from a market basket!"

"But Abigail dear, you should be pleased you are able to do so. You're so fair and such a beautiful girl. Not every young lady is so lucky that they can choose the proper husband."

"Thank you, Mother, for saying so." Abigail rolled her eyes. She didn't think of herself as any better looking than other young women in the valley.

"Look at it this way," her mother said. "You certainly don't want to leave such an important decision to chance, do you?"

"But Mother, surely you wouldn't go about selecting a husband like you would a Thoroughbred horse. Examining his teeth, inspecting the curve of his back."

"You would be surprised at the similarities," Henrietta said. Her smile was wooden.

"Oh, Mother! I won't hear of it. I could no more marry a man I did not love than I could marry a horse."

"You are still young," her mother chided. "But you will not be young forever. I simply want to give you the opportunity to meet as many eligible young men as you can, and I think sponsoring a social occasion for the better families of Ridgetop is an excellent way to do it." She cocked an eyebrow at Abigail and crooked a finger to her chin.

"If you're really not ready for marriage," Henrietta said, "I suppose I shouldn't force it on you." She gave the appearance of losing interest in the conversation and started leafing through some papers on the desk. "Perhaps," she said after a moment, "we should consider your education first. We could always place you in the Ladies of Chastity School for young women in Saint Louis. Their curriculum is good, and I understand they have proven methods of instilling proper Christian ethics in their young protégés."

Abigail shrank back into her chair at the thought. Her mother's shift in tactics had caught her off guard. What young woman from Ridgetop hadn't dreamed of moving to a city like Saint Louis? But doing so under the stern and constant vigil of the celibate ladies of the church did not appeal to her. She was trapped, and discretion being the better part of valor, she decided a party might be the lesser of two evils.

"Oh, Mother," she said, once again trying to sound slightly distracted, as if she too were losing interest in the topic. "Do you think Father should raise a gazebo on the east lawn? I think it would look marvelous there, next to the pond. For the party, of course."

"Hmm, dear?" Henrietta mumbled. "Oh, that is a very good idea. I will ask him about it." She tried to hide her smile. "But now I think I'll put a bit of orange blossom in my tea and take a nap upstairs."

Justin stood next to his father in the middle of a crowd of people outside the courthouse, waiting by the veranda to hear the invited speaker. It seemed like most of the county's citizens had come out, and the afternoon weather had cooperated.

"I think you'll appreciate Mr. Clay's talk," Walter said. "He's a strong advocate for the western states, especially for agriculture."

Justin nodded. He read the newspapers and had heard of the notable Kentucky politician. He was more interested in Henry Clay's anti-slavery position than his support for agriculture. The Sterlings kept no slaves, but Justin never knew if that was because of his father's politics, or simply because they couldn't afford them. He believed it was the former.

"Does Mr. Clay still want to be the president?" Justin asked this as much to impress his father with his knowledge of the world as to needle him by suggesting that they should be skeptical of anything a politician said.

His father looked at him sideways with a raised eyebrow. "This country could do a lot worse than elect Henry Clay president."

Justin nodded again, but he was more interested in looking for Abigail Whitfield in the crowd, and seeing who she might have come with. Women weren't strangers to politicians' talks, but some men in the county discouraged them from participating. After all, they couldn't vote, and they had work to do in the home. Justin wasn't sure how Henry Whitfield felt about such things, but he knew Abby would want to attend Clay's talk. Such occasions were few and far between in Ridgetop.

The crowd burst into applause when Clay and a number of local officials came out of the courthouse and stood on the veranda. Clay raised his hands, and the murmuring crowd became quiet. He began his talk with something he called the "American System," which, he assured everyone, would maintain strong support for America's agricultural products overseas, products the citizens of Ridgetop produced. Justin listened with one ear. He scanned the crowd, seeing many familiar faces, but not the one face he longed to set eyes on. After fifteen minutes he gave up, but by then Mr. Clay had finished the essence of his talk and was entertaining questions. A familiar voice sounded from the other side of the crowd.

"Wouldn't this 'American Plan,' as you call it, raise all our taxes? And we have to pay for the same goods everyone else does, after all."

"That's Toby." Justin wondered when his friend had become so interested in current affairs. Perhaps he intended to go into politics, too. His friend was ambitious, and the Johnson family's wealth would support a campaign, but Justin wouldn't care for the career choice. He preferred the independence of farming and raising livestock.

"A good question, my friend." Ever the politician, Clay wasn't put off his stride by Toby's question. "A great American once said, 'nothing is certain in this world but death and taxes.' "

Most of the audience was familiar with the quote from Benjamin Franklin and laughed. Justin craned his neck to see Toby. He caught a glimpse of his friend, who was standing with Abby and her father. A needle of jealousy stabbed his chest, and his jaw clenched. How many times had Justin schemed to simply catch a glimpse of Abby from afar, while Toby appeared to enjoy the most casual acquaintance with the Whitfield family? No doubt he was trying to impress Abby by questioning Henry Clay.

"No one likes taxes, to be sure," Clay said. "But they pay for some fundamental services we all rely on, not the least of which is the very postal service Mr. Franklin created. But I anticipate great things for the American West. The more this country of ours grows, the more we will need railroads, canals, roads, and the like to make sure your crops can be shipped efficiently to the mills and factories in the east, and the hungry mouths waiting there." This met with scattered applause. "The beauty of federal taxes is that everyone in this great country will help pay to build those roads for you, and you, and you." Clay pointed to individuals in the audience and a few more people in the crowd applauded.

"Speaking of the west," someone called out to Clay. "What about Mexico?"

"Ah, Mexico." Clay stuck his thumbs under his braces. "There's a conflict brewing, if ever I saw one." Many in the audience grumbled their agreement. "That part of the continent we call Texas is already populated by any number of Americans, and more are on the way. Unfortunately, Mexico is not in a position to guarantee the safety of these settlers, or even maintain the rule of law. Some say there will be war. Personally, I don't believe that will be necessary, but if Mexico is incapable or unwilling, we should do everything we can to develop the nearly unlimited resources we could find there."

Justin turned to his father. "How can America do that without a war?"

"War isn't always the answer to a country's troubles," Walter said. "Mr. Pinckney kept us out of war with Spain not so long ago, and don't forget President Monroe, who gave us Louisiana. Now there was an international horse trader of some repute."

"Of course." Justin decided Clay was happy to be diverted from the subject of taxes, but Mexico was a topic of some fascination for Justin. He had read stories of the conquistadores of centuries past, and he'd often wondered what adventures lay west of Tennessee. Not that he ever thought he'd go there. A farmer was tied to his land, after all. Justin enjoyed the hard work. He had no qualms about carrying on the life his father had created.

Of course every aspect of that life would be nicer if he shared it with a woman like Abigail Whitfield. But the Whitfields enjoyed many of life's comforts, and Justin had difficulty envisioning Abby embracing the strenuous life of a poor farmer's wife. That, as much as anything else, prodded him to improve his family's condition in any way he could. Not so much to impress Abby. He wasn't sure how much comfort she required, but he struggled to think of ways to meet Henry Whitfield's demanding standards.

If Henry would ever give him the chance.

CHAPTER TEN

June 1834

Plans for Abigail's party proceeded apace, and she was not surprised to find that her mother had long ago ordered pastry flour, colored bunting, and other items from Nashville she thought necessary for the party. The date was set, or rather revealed, by her mother, and invitations were sent to better families throughout the county and beyond. Marshaling her troops, Henrietta assigned their servant Martha the responsibility of ensuring Abigail had a proper dress for the occasion. The few farmhands Henry could spare did their best to prepare the lawn and gardens surrounding the main house. Henry special-ordered cut lumber, and extra help had been hired to construct the gazebo Abigail saw rising by the fish pond.

She watched these preparations from her bedroom with great trepidation. She reviewed the list of invitees over and over again, inspecting the names and trying to decide with which of the young men her mother might try to match her. Josiah Daniels would be there, of course, but who would want to marry him? His family had been one of the first, and certainly one of the wealthiest, to settle in the valley. But Josiah had a fondness for cakes, and rumors claimed that, though he was only twenty-four years old, his girth had swelled such that he weighed two hundred and seventy-five pounds. Enough to crush an unfortunate bride.

Abigail shuddered and read down the list. The Matthews

twins had been invited. Jim and John were darling, but everyone knew they were sweet on the Toliver sisters, and who could tell them apart anyway?

She saw Tobias Johnson's name, and a warning beacon flashed in her mind. Tobias was considered one of the valley's most eligible bachelors. Even more telling was the fact that Toby's father, Thomas, had done business with her father for a number of years. They lived on neighboring farms, and Abigail knew her father would love to see their two families' lands united into an even greater holding. Undoubtedly Toby was her mother's principal target.

She gazed out the window again at the gazebo taking shape on the lawn. Toby was smart enough, she knew, and her girlfriends considered him good-looking. But Toby had been her friend for so long, she had never considered marrying him. On the other hand, they had many of the same interests. Her mother would say that was enough, and that eventually true love would grow. Abigail wasn't so sure.

Her gaze fell upon one of the workmen on the gazebo. He was the only young man among them. He worked bare-chested, and there was something familiar about his broad back and sinuously muscled arms. He lifted long beams with ease, handing them up to other workers higher in the frame of the structure. As she watched his agile movements and physical grace, a primal, animal attraction surged through her.

Then she realized she was staring at Justin Sterling.

Wait a minute. She couldn't remember seeing his name on the list of party guests. She scanned it quickly, running her finger down the smudged names her mother had penciled on the long, thin length of paper. Justin's name wasn't there.

Had there been a mistake? No, she knew there had not. Justin's family simply didn't have enough money and, therefore, social standing, for her mother to consider him a good match for her daughter. She tossed the list aside, leaned out the window, and watched Justin and the other workers.

It simply wasn't fair. If her mother intended to introduce her to men with whom she might consider marriage, then certainly Justin should be on the list. It was an injustice she would address herself, if necessary.

Sprinting from her bedroom, she raced down the broad, curving staircase and ran toward the kitchen. She burst through the kitchen door and ran straight to the water pump mounted next to the large metal sink. She snatched a bucket and ladle from their resting place, tossed the ladle into the bucket, set the bucket under the spout, and began pumping water. Margaret Anne, the Whitfields' cook, was just removing a tray of sourdough biscuits from the oven when she saw Abigail.

"Land sakes, child," Margaret Anne said. "Is the house a'fire? If so, that little bucket isn't going to help much."

Abigail laughed. Margaret Anne searched for an empty space on the counter on which to set her cooking sheet.

"No, Maggie," Abigail said. "The house is safe enough. I just thought the men working outside might need some refreshment. They look so hot out there."

"You're right about that," Margaret Anne said. "This Tennessee heat is enough to suffocate ordinary folks." She craned her neck and looked out the window at the gazebo, rising steadily on the lawn, and shook her head. "Why, I remember when your daddy and I lived in Virginia—" At that moment Margaret Anne saw the strapping young Justin Sterling among the workers. She turned away from the window and looked at Abigail, this time with a raised eyebrow. Abigail saw this and spoke first.

"Would you be kind enough to put some of your prize-winning biscuits in a basket for me?" she asked sweetly. "I'm certain the men will love them."

"You mean you're sure that Sterling boy will love them, don't you?" She gave Abigail a wry smile, but she started tossing some of the still warm biscuits into a basket.

"Whatever are you suggesting, Margaret Anne?"

"That innocent act isn't fool'n me none, young lady. And it isn't going to fool your mama long, neither. You start messing around with young bucks from the other side of the creek, and she'll pack you off to those Saint Louis church-women in a heartbeat."

"She'll have to catch me first, won't she?" Abigail plucked the basket of biscuits from Margaret Anne's hands and left through the kitchen door with loud, swishing skirts.

"Oh, she'll catch you, all right," Margaret Anne called after her. "She'll catch you good."

Justin Sterling drove another long nail home with the heavy sledge he held in his right hand. Between strokes, he watched Abigail out of the corner of his eye as she approached the skeleton of the gazebo. Blood raced through his veins and he marveled at how his heart took flight at the mere sight of her. How could one woman have such an effect on a man?

"Hello, strong yeomen!" Abigail called out when she drew near.

Justin detected a note of humor in her voice, and that she had diplomatically avoided using any term that would remind the men they were merely day laborers for her father.

"Hello, Miss Whitfield," one of the older workers said.

"I've brought you some refreshment," Abigail said. Then, to the men who had climbed up on the expanding structure, she said, "Please rest a minute. Come down and sample some of Margaret Anne's blue-ribbon biscuits."

They didn't need much encouragement, but Justin Sterling tried not to climb down any faster than the other men.

"You're doing good work," Abigail said. "The gazebo looks

wonderful." She handed the bucket and a stack of metal cups to the nearest man and let them help themselves to water. Then she began passing out the biscuits, working her way toward Justin as she did so.

When she finally stood in front of him, she said, "Hello, Justin. Do you think it will be finished in time for the party?"

Everyone in the valley had heard of the festivities her mother had planned, and Justin was no exception, even if he hadn't been invited. He looked back at the gazebo as if he were assessing their work for the first time.

"I think you'll be able to sit here in a day or two, Abby, and feed the ducks on your father's pond."

"That would be wonderful," She gave him an earnest look. "Have you received your invitation?"

"No, Abby." Justin smiled, but he looked down at his boots. "I can't say that I have. And I really don't think—"

"That's not good," she said, interrupting him. "I will have Martha deliver it to your mother this very afternoon." She spun on her heels and marched back toward the house without giving Justin a chance to answer.

Watching her go, Justin shook his head. He took a bite of biscuit and returned to work, but he spent the rest of the afternoon pondering what sort of trouble Abby Whitfield had in store for him.

"Walter!" Anne Sterling called to her husband as he came in the back door from the barn. "Walter, the Whitfields' servant just paid us a visit!"

"Well, that is impressive. Is Henry in some difficulty? Does he have a problem with us?"

"Oh, no," Anne said. She waved away Walter's dire thoughts with one hand. "Abigail has invited Justin to the party! Can you imagine that?"

"Abigail, you say." Walter rubbed his chin and looked over to Justin, who had just returned from working on the Whitfield gazebo. "What do you know about this, Justin?"

"No more than you," he said carefully.

Walter put his hands on his hips. "Has the spirit of democracy suddenly descended on Henry Whitfield's shoulders? Somehow I don't think so."

"Now Walter," Anne said. "You need to be less suspicious of Henry."

"Let me see the invitation," he said. She handed it to him and he saw that it was signed by Abigail, rather than Henrietta Whitfield. He looked at Anne and saw the quiet hope in her eyes. Obviously she was willing to overlook the irregularity in the invitation, and the implications it presented. He handed it back to her with a soft "Humph." If Anne thought Justin could rightfully attend a function sponsored by Henrietta Whitfield on the strength of Abigail's invitation, he would not interfere. He had no desire to argue social decorum with his wife, who undoubtedly knew more about the subject than he.

"Better make sure the boy has something decent to wear," he said, taking off his greatcoat.

Justin and his mother looked at each other with a wink and a smile.

CHAPTER ELEVEN

July 1834

From the comfort of her second-floor window, Henrietta Whitfield surveyed the finely dressed young men and women who mingled on the lawn and along the paths in the flower garden. Most of the valley's well-to-do families were represented. And why shouldn't they be? The Whitfields could be proud of the success they'd earned since she and Henry had come to Ridgetop. Any parent concerned about the security and future of their son, not to mention their whole family, would do well to marry their interests to those of the Whitfields. Careful, Henrietta, she chided herself. You're thinking like Henry now. She of all people should remember that Abigail's happiness mattered, too.

A burst of laughter rose from the brightly painted gazebo next to the pond. Henrietta was ready to pronounce the gathering a success, at least in terms of attendance, when she saw Justin Sterling riding a powerful black mare across the field that separated the Whitfields' farm from the creek, and the Sterling property. Did he intend to stop at the Whitfields?

He had not been invited to the party, of that she was sure. It had been a difficult decision, since Abigail seemed so enamored with the boy. And what woman, young or old, would not have been? His chestnut-brown hair, cut shoulder-length, flowed out behind his broad straight back as he rode, and even from this distance she could feel his smoldering dark eyes examining the party. The simple act of watching Justin drive his mount forward stirred untamed feelings at Henrietta's core that she had not experienced in decades, and she felt her face flush pink.

Oh, yes, she was well aware of Abigail's feelings for Justin, and why. But such moods were no longer hers to possess. Henry insisted the party was only an accommodation to their daughter, to make her feel as though she were included in the process. The ultimate objective was far too important to leave to the fickle whims of a young woman's yearning, or to her romantic ideas of love. Henry intended to find an appropriate mate for Abigail in spite of love. One who would be there to serve and protect her and her children, long after the fires of youthful passion were extinguished. Given her own past, how could Henrietta object?

Unfortunately, Justin Sterling, as strong and virile as he might be, would not be the chosen man. Undoubtedly Justin could provide Henrietta with many grandsons. But to what avail? The Sterlings might never achieve any comfortable financial independence. That would ensure the family remained forever beneath the status Henry sought to guarantee for Abigail.

And for himself, of course.

No, Justin Sterling's "situation" simply did not meet their requirements. More's the pity, she thought, but Henrietta would play her part. Uninvited as he might be, she would not refuse Justin her hospitality. No indeed. She would treat him as though he were her own son, returned from some faraway adventure, and receive him with open arms. After all, there were supple young ladies aplenty in the garden that day, all with sufficient charms to distract a young man in his sexual prime. Henrietta would make sure Justin met every one. She set a smile on her lips, gathered up her skirts, and descended the stairs to greet her new guest.

Justin slowed his mount to a walk as he drew near the Whitfields' vast trimmed lawn. The imposing, three-story red brick structure, with its white columned portico, always impressed him. It was by far the most elaborate and elegant house in the county, set on a low hill and surrounded by a field of grass, which Justin thought was an unnecessary extravagance. His own modest home would be dwarfed if placed next to such a palace. His pulse quickened when he saw the milling knots of men and women in the yard and garden. He fought the urge to search for Abby among the gaily dressed women. She would be there, of course, and he would see her soon enough. Before reaching the inner yard, he reined the horse toward a livery uniformed servant, Eric, who had come forward to receive him. He swung his right leg over the horse's back and dismounted.

"Good morning Justin," Eric said.

"Good morning Eric." He paused. When he handed Eric his reins, a wave of discomfort swept over him. The younger brother of a schoolmate, Eric was from a family not much different from his own, and the sight of his equal in a serving capacity reminded Justin that he was out of his element.

"You've got some balls on you, Justin." Eric grinned.

"Balls and an invitation."

"Lucky boy."

As Eric led his horse away, Justin resolved to remain on guard, lest he commit some horrible faux pas that would offend the Whitfields and alienate him from them forever. As if on cue, Henrietta Whitfield appeared in front of him.

"Good morning," she said.

She smiled so broadly, Justin decided the invitation he'd received must have been legitimate.

"Good morning, Mrs. Whitfield." He bowed as low as he could without falling forward and knocking her down. "Thank you so much for inviting me to Abigail's party." True, she had not written the invitation, but he calculated it best to credit her, as she *was* Abigail's mother, and the sponsor of the event.

"Not at all," Mrs. Whitfield said, unfurling her fan for emphasis. "We're always happy to receive a gentleman as charming as you. And how is your sweet mother Anne?" She offered her elbow and, when he took it, she guided him toward the party.

"She is very well, thank you. I will be sure to tell her you asked."

"You are such a good young man." She beamed at him. "You'll find many of your friends here." And then with a wink she added, "There are some pretty young ladies who want very much to talk to you."

He could not help but be impressed by his reception. She made him feel as welcome as a cousin from Virginia she hadn't seen in years.

As they strolled through the garden, he did see many young men and women he recognized, including Toby, who was entertaining a knot of partygoers near the gazebo. One young woman in a hat glanced at him around Toby. Was it Abigail? He didn't get a good enough look. He considered nudging Mrs. Whitfield that way, but Henrietta took him in a different direction.

"Let's get you some iced punch," she said. "Then there are some people I'd like you to meet."

It continued like that for thirty minutes more. The punch tasted cool and sweet, and Justin luxuriated in the ice. Tables to which Mrs. Whitfield escorted him were piled high with rare delicacies, sandwiches, and cakes, the likes of which Justin had never seen. The attention Abigail's mother lavished on him continued to surprise him. What had he done to merit such thoughtfulness?

Finally, with a firm grip on his arm, she guided him to a delicate young woman who sat off by herself on a short white bench beneath a towering green oak tree. Her long brunette hair fell luxuriously over the shoulders of her sunburst yellow gown. The spread of her skirts nearly covered the bench, which was only long enough for two to occupy.

"Sally Marston," Henrietta said as they approached. "I'd like you to meet Justin Sterling."

Sally's eyes fluttered briefly at Justin, who felt a warm flush of embarrassment at the young woman's sweetness.

"Pleased to meet you," Justin said a little haltingly. She looked familiar, like a girl he'd known all his life who'd become a woman when he wasn't looking. He had been too distracted by looking for Abigail to remember the girl's name.

"Oh, we've met." Sally smiled. "And I'm pleased to see you again. You live west of the confluence at Elk Creek, do you not?" Her voice betrayed no notion that many of the less socially important families homesteaded in that direction.

"Yes," Justin admitted. He quickly rummaged through his mind to find some qualifying characteristic of his family's that would explain why they had settled where they had, but he didn't have to.

"We live that way, too," Sally said. "But much farther away."

"Of course. Your father operates the ferry landing."

"Jacob Marston, yes. Would you like to sit with me a spell?" She brushed her skirts to one side, revealing just enough of the bench for him to sit down.

Justin had no reason to dislike Sally Marston, but he hadn't planned on spending his afternoon on the edge of the party—and away from Abby. He looked at Mrs. Whitfield for help, but Henrietta released his arm and said, "How very nice of you, Sally. I'll go check on the other guests. You two enjoy yourselves!"

Henrietta smiled and left Justin standing by the bench, trying not to look uncomfortable. He gawked at the space Sally had cleared for him. Pretty as she was, his chest ached at the thought of being trapped with her under the shady oak. But what could he do? It would be the height of rudeness to excuse himself and walk away, especially after Mrs. Whitfield had introduced them. He sighed and sat down heavily next to Sally. They smiled at each other and an awkward silence fell between them. He took a sip of punch to buy some time, but as he was drinking Abby appeared in front of him, seemingly out of thin air.

"Sally. Justin. Are you enjoying yourselves?"

Justin was so startled, he stood straight up and choked on a swallow of punch. He placed his hand over his mouth to keep from spraying Abby as he coughed.

"My," Abigail said. "It's a good thing we're not serving anything stronger than punch."

Sally laughed, but in the back of his mind Justin could tell that she wasn't entirely happy to have been interrupted by Abby.

"Forgive me, please," Justin said when he had recovered. He looked down into Abby's impossibly green eyes and felt the familiar surge of raw desire sweep through him. It was such a palpable sensation, he felt sure the woman must be able to see it, and he blushed.

"So, you've only been here a few minutes and you're already apologizing," said a new but familiar voice. It was Toby. "I must know what for, since Justin Sterling seldom does anything he needs to be sorry for."

Toby had appeared as suddenly as Abby had, and now stood a little too closely beside her for Justin's comfort.

"Hello, Justin," Toby said before Justin could answer. He extended his hand. "How are you?"

"Aside from trying to breathe my punch, I suppose I'm fine, thank you." Justin shook Toby's hand, but he thought the gesture a little too formal, coming from his lifelong friend.

"I saw you standing alone with these two delightful young

85

ladies," Tobias said, "and I thought it a shame that you should hoard them all for yourself." He took Abby's hands in his.

Toby had referred to both girls, but he beamed at Abby, and Justin could tell his compliment was meant for her entertainment. Surely the women could tell that also. He glanced at Sally, whose stoic smile showed no trace of embarrassment.

"Actually," Justin said, "there seem to be plenty of ladies to go 'round." As he spoke, Sally stood up and clasped the crook of his arm, which he raised reflexively for her benefit.

"Good," Toby answered quickly, "I'm glad you said that, because really I need to speak to Abby here about a matter of some importance."

She looked at him quizzically. Noticing her expression, Toby said, "Oh, all right. It's her mother, actually. She wants Abby to show me where the pall-mall equipment is. We're starting a match."

Mother, Abby thought, as she let Tobias lead her away. "I'll be back," she called over her shoulder.

Justin stood for a moment, watching them go, then glanced at Sally as though he'd forgotten she was there. He smiled at her sheepishly.

"I'm sorry," he said.

"No, I'm sorry," Sally said. "For you. Come. Sit down again and tell me all about it, as if I didn't already know." She sat back down on the bench and patted the seat beside her. Justin dutifully joined her.

"Is it that obvious?" he asked, sipping more punch.

"Well," she said with mock seriousness. "No more so than a puppy dog gazing at a fresh bone."

He gave her a quick smile and hung his head.

"In all honesty," she said. "I knew all about it before we were introduced."

"How?"

"You don't think I was invited to Mrs. Henrietta Whitfield's birthday party for her only daughter, Abby, because my father operates the ferry landing at Wilkinson's Corner, now do you? No, it's because I'm a friend of the poor girl's, whether her mother likes it or not."

"I see," Justin said, rolling his cup of punch between the fingers of both hands. "I guess that's the only reason I'm here too."

"It's a pretty good reason," Sally said. "But in your case, I'm sure Mrs. Whitfield is less than pleased."

Justin realized then why Henrietta had personally escorted him through much of the party. Her attentions were intended only to keep him away from Abby, and it looked as though she had succeeded.

"Damn the Whitfields," he muttered. "And damn all rich people wherever they are." He stretched his long legs out in front of him and leaned back against the bench.

"You're only saying that because you're not one of them," Sally said.

"And they never let me forget it."

"I don't know," she said. "Someday you might marry a pretty young rich girl, and then where will you be?"

"I will have died and gone to heaven before Henry Whitfield will let that come to pass." He scuffed at the grass with his boot.

"Don't be so sure," she said. "I happen to know that Abby is quite fond of you."

Justin let his skepticism show on his face.

"I should know," she said, smiling. "I really am her friend, after all. And girlfriends talk about these things. Believe me, she has an eye on you."

Justin's disbelief turned once again to hope, and he looked across the lawn at the milling crowd of gaily dressed young men and women. Abby was nowhere to be seen.

"Then again," Sally continued, "she seems to see something in Tobias Johnson, too."

Justin gave her a frustrated glance.

"I don't know why," she said slowly. "But it might have something to do with the fact that he's rich, and not so bad looking on top of that."

Justin laughed. Truly he had been acting like a puppy worrying a bone. He could see that now, but he couldn't help it. He would have given all of the Whitfields' riches and those of every other family represented at their party for the chance to make Abby love him. He wondered how much the simple, unfortunate fact of his birth would ultimately thwart him from reaching the only goal that meant anything to him.

"Come on now, and take my arm," Sally said as she stood up from the bench. "Let's us poor folk mingle with the idle rich and see what trouble we can cause."

The afternoon wore on, and standing around in the heat in his best coat and breeches wasn't Justin's idea of fun, although he was grateful for the shade of the gazebo he had helped build. Meanwhile, Tobias kept Abigail engaged in a seemingly endless round of pall-mall games, in which the winners of one game were obliged to play the next challengers. Justin wasn't sure enough of the rules of the old game to try to play, but he watched Abby from the corner of his eye whenever the conversation slackened and gave him the opportunity. Abby seemed to know he was watching, as she glanced at him occasionally, too. Meanwhile, Justin found Sally's company agreeable enough, and there were other friends with whom he shared news and stories. None of the young men and woman ignored him or treated him with disrespect, and Justin had hope that prejudice on the basis of social standing might die out with his parents' generation.

All the while, each new rivulet of sweat that tickled its way down his back magnified his impatience at not being able to talk to Abby. Eventually, the energy of the party started to wane. A few of the invited guests made their apologies and departed. The remaining young men and women seemed as worn out by the heat and gaiety as Justin. They remained out of politeness, it seemed, and Justin was beginning to think he no longer had the patience to outwait the other young men who showed an interest in Abby. The lawn games finally ended, and the competitors made their way into the shade of the gazebo and looked for a cool drink.

Tobias stood next to Justin.

"You have a knack for pall-mall," Justin said.

"I love winning, that I won't deny. But the truth be known, I lost that last round on purpose, just to get it over with."

"I can't imagine how you managed all this time in the heat." Justin wiped at his brow.

"I'm a wreck, but you look as though you've been swimming in the creek with your clothes on."

"I wish I had."

At that moment a young lady in a powder-blue dress collapsed onto a bench, nearly fainting. Abigail bent to help her, holding out a cup of water while another girl fanned the poor woman. Everyone seemed at wits' end, but the young lady's condition and Toby's last remark gave Justin an idea.

"Toby," he said. "Are you up for some different fun?"

"Anything to get my mind off the heat."

"Come with me." With Tobias in tow, he made his way to the side of the gazebo that overhung the edge of the fish pond. He turned to face the remaining guests and raised his hands.

"Excuse me! One moment, please!" he said, getting everyone's attention. Abby watched him with caution and curiosity written on her face.

"We are all suffering from the afternoon heat and humidity," he said. "And for myself, I've had quite enough of this stifling cravat." He elbowed Tobias to follow his lead and swiftly stripped the tie from his neck. Then he tossed it over his shoulder into the pond.

"Me, too!" Toby did the same, much to the laughter of the guests. Soon all of the men were tearing at their necks to rid themselves of the offending neckties.

"And while we're at it," Justin said. "My feet are roasting in these boots like game hens in the oven." Justin danced on one leg and then another until he had pulled his boots off and he stood in his stocking feet. Toby and the other men followed suit as soon as they realized what Justin was doing.

"Now then, without a tie and boots, surely we no longer need these heavy jackets to maintain decorum." The women were all laughing as men's jackets quickly littered the floor of the gazebo. Abigail smiled in disbelief, and even the woman who'd nearly fainted had recovered enough to watch the show. But Justin wasn't finished.

"Now then, don't we look like a silly bunch of fools, standing around in the heat when there's a cool bath waiting for us, right here at our feet?" He gestured at the fish pond, then turned about and dove headfirst into the water.

"He's made a very good point, don't you think?" Tobias said. He jumped in after Justin.

Screams of laughter filled the gazebo as every man who remained at the party ran forward and jumped or dove into the water.

Abigail's party had quickly come to an end after Justin's stunt. The only thing that saved him from Henry's wrath was that Tobias and every other man remaining at the party had jumped into the pond, too. Even so, Justin got more than one irritated glance from Henrietta as the men dried themselves off, dressed, and took their leave. Justin much preferred the looks of amusement and appreciation he'd received from Abby. He still hadn't talked to her at any length, or been alone with her; Henrietta had made sure of that. What the future would bring, he had no idea, but damn the consequences. He considered the party a success. Even so, he didn't expect to be invited to the Whitfield farm again anytime soon.

Two weeks later, he welcomed the escape from his chores, not to mention the questions of his parents, to indulge in one of his favorite activities, deer hunting. The hunt had a practical purpose, as it put meat on the table for his family, and he knew his brief sojourn into the quiet forest would help him sort out his thoughts about life and Abby. The young Whitfield was never far from his mind and, given the unspoken purpose of Abby's party, he felt more pressure than ever to find some means of winning her hand. He had to act, and that meant revealing the true depth of his feelings to Abigail. It was time.

Having made the decision to talk to Abigail, he felt liberated—no, exhilarated—by the idea. She already knew something of how he felt, of course. Only a blind man could not have seen the way he mooned at her when she was near. But he would finally tell her outright, and knowing this, he felt a great weight suddenly lift from his shoulders. Unfortunately, as soon as that weight was gone, another one took its place. What would Abby say if he made his desire plain? He thought she felt the same, but that might only be his earnest wish. And even if she returned his affection, there would still be her parents to deal with. He hadn't done anything lately to improve his relationship with them. He shook his head to clear it, then tried to put aside such thoughts and focus on the immediate task at hand.

He brushed quietly through the lower branches of a copse of pine trees, advancing a dozen steps, no more, before stopping.

He waited, his senses alert for any movement, any sound or subtle change in the color or pattern of the woodland canvas spread before him.

He remembered the day he talked with Abby outside the store in Ridgetop. He played the conversation over in his mind for the thousandth time, searching for every shred of significance in the words Abby had spoken. She had been coy, it was true, but she had been coy as long as he'd known her. Yet she encouraged him, too. He was not mistaken about that, even though she had never confessed her own feelings, and that uncertainty unsettled him whenever he considered it.

He stood motionless for a full three minutes. Seeing nothing move, he stepped forward carefully, avoiding twigs and dried leaves. He wouldn't put his full weight on his leading foot until he knew he had not stepped on anything that would snap or make a sudden noise and reveal his presence.

Carefully stalking through the trees, he felt his uncertainty about Abby grow in proportion to his desire to tell her how he felt. The woman puzzled him. She could have any beau she wanted, and not just from the Ridgetop Valley, so why should she want him? He had visions of Abby traveling to New York, Paris, and other exotic locations he'd only read about. In each scene, finely dressed men with trimmed moustaches hung on her every word, laughing at her humor, holding her hand. They drank wine and danced every evening, and for the thousandth time he silently cursed his family's poor circumstances.

Then he chuckled at himself. The wealthy men in his visions never received any more commitment from Abby than he ever had. For him at least, she always left the possibilities open. The delicate dream, which she could crush at any time with a single word, had always been left secure. And that fact encouraged him, driving him on.

Once again he tried to clear his thoughts. He checked the

flash pan of the musket one more time, but he could no more rid his mind of Abby than he could will himself to stop breathing.

Standing motionless, he watched unblinking as a large buck stepped cautiously into a clearing, almost thirty yards away. The animal's nose twitched as it sampled the air for any dangerous scent, but the soft breeze on his cheek told Justin he was upwind of the buck. He might not be seen as long as he didn't move and give away his position.

The buck took two more careful steps. Without looking down, Justin slowly felt the breech lock of his musket with his thumb, confirming that the weapon was cocked and ready to fire. Still he waited, not yet lifting the heavy gun to his shoulder.

The buck bent its head down tentatively, still looking up, as if it anticipated some unseen terror. Justin was that terror, but he felt no regret over the role he played in the unfolding scene. He was as much a part of the natural order as the deer he was about to kill.

The buck's antlers swung low as it bit a mouthful of the sweet grass at its feet. At virtually the same instant, Justin raised the musket to his shoulder. The smooth wooden stock and weight of the weapon felt familiar in Justin's hands. He looked at the deer over the small metal bead at the end of his gun's long barrel. He could shoot it at any time. Instead, he hesitated, watching the animal, studying its behavior to learn all he could before he ended its life. Sunlight glinted through trees and played patterns across the animal's brown fur. Justin practically felt the soft texture of the fur as it ruffled in the breeze.

At the instant his finger tightened on the trigger, Justin thought about the softness of Abigail Whitfield's skin. He envisioned stroking Abby's delicate forearm, the smooth alabaster wonder of it, soft as deer's fur. Rather than smoothly pull the trigger, his finger quivered. The hammer shot forward, striking flint against steel and igniting the powder in the breech as the gun fired. His hesitation had been infinitesimally small, but it was enough to send his shot wide of its mark. Through a cloud of smoke, he saw a flash of red blossom on the deer's flank behind where he had judged the heart to be. The animal dropped to its knees from the impact of the shot, but immediately regained its footing and limped gamely away into the underbrush.

"Damn," he muttered.

He gave up any pretense of silence and crashed through the trees and bushes to follow the deer. Its wound might eventually prove fatal, but it could take some time. He followed the deer to end its suffering as soon as he could. Unfortunately, if his round had not crippled the deer, it might take hours, even days, to track the animal and finish the job. It was not a task he would enjoy, but he could not let the deer suffer needlessly simply because it might be difficult to follow it.

Rushing to the spot of trampled grass where the buck had been grazing, he saw drops of blood. He knew then that tracking the animal would not take long. He stalked through the trees in the direction the deer had disappeared and found more blood on the lower branches and leaves. The deer too had given up any pretense of secrecy and, listening carefully, Justin heard it smashing through the underbrush in front of him.

As he followed, Justin poured a measure of gunpowder down the long barrel of his musket. Then he rammed another lead ball and wad home and renewed the charge in the pan of the breech lock. Glancing around, he found himself on the edge of another clearing. Through the trees he saw what must have been one of Henry Whitfield's pastures. A dozen or so cattle milled about in the distance, but their heads were up and looking at a rider coming into the pasture from Justin's right, about two hundred yards away. He recognized Toby's riding coat and the dusky gray roan he'd owned for several years. Toby held a section of rope in one hand, which he spun at the milling cattle, herding them toward a gate in the fence some distance away.

Toby rode back and forth, directing the cattle and punctuating his movements with an occasional whistle or shout. Justin almost called out to Toby, but he hesitated. Something about the scene struck Justin as odd. It wasn't simply that Toby was herding cattle on Henry Whitfield's pasture. It wasn't the strangeness of seeing Toby; it was what he heard. Toby's shouts and whistles were muted, almost whispered, as though he didn't want to unduly disturb the cattle.

Justin stood still and watched a moment longer as Toby cut one cow from the herd and guided it toward a gate in Henry's fence. He stepped farther back into the woods until he was sure he couldn't be seen if his friend happened to look in his direction. Whatever Toby was doing with Henry's cattle wasn't his business. But seeing his friend on the Whitfield farm and remembering how he'd clung to Abby at her party made him cautious. Perhaps it was too soon to confess his love for Abigail. He might look the fool if he did so without first learning how she felt about him. Especially if she were letting Tobias court her.

He turned away and studied the ground for signs of the wounded deer. He would not go home until he found it and put it out of its misery.

CHAPTER TWELVE

September 13, 1834

With fall coming on, Abigail dared to hope her parents had given up their plan to marry her to a carefully selected, so-called suitable mate. Until Elly, her trusted servant, knocked on her bedroom door. She looked worried.

"Your parents are in the family room. They sent me to tell you they want to talk to you."

"What?" Abigail wasn't accustomed to receiving such a formal summons. "What's that all about?"

"My guess is they've got something important to say, Miss Abby. I think it's about you know what." Elly gestured as though she were slipping a ring on her finger. A wedding ring. Abigail sighed. As with most of her troubles, she had confided in Elly her struggle for the right to choose her own husband. Elly's instincts were usually right. Her parents must have come to some decision.

"How awful could it be, Miss Abby? Maybe they picked a handsome one for you."

"Maybe I will become the Queen of England."

Elly laughed. "Don't forget to take me with you when you move to the palace."

When she entered the sitting room, Abigail found her parents waiting near the fire in the hearth. Her mother sat in a straight-backed chair, while her father stood behind her, with one hand on her shoulder. They looked like they were posing for an artist, waiting to have their portrait painted. The fact that her parents were both watching her when she entered was unsettling. She expected Henry to be at his desk fretting over the farm's ledgers, while her mother attended to correspondence.

"Hello, Abigail," her father said. "Please sit down."

She obliged, choosing one of the small stuffed chairs with white doilies on their arms and pinned on their backs that sat about the room.

"What may I do for you, Father? Mother?"

Her father glanced at the ceiling and appeared momentarily uncomfortable, or no longer sure of what he was going to say.

"Abigail, dear," he started. "I hope we provided you with some level of entertainment at your recent social event."

"Entertainment?"

"With your coming-out. I mean the birthday party. And the, uh . . . young men."

"Oh, yes, the party." Abigail folded her hands together in her lap. She half-heartedly searched for some way to deflect what she suspected was coming. "I enjoyed myself thoroughly. I appreciate all you and Mother have done for me. I do."

"Well, yes," Henry said. "You know there was a more practical purpose behind all of our efforts."

"A practical purpose for the party?" She feigned innocent confusion. Any hope that her parents had given up finding her a husband were dashed. They were sticking to their plan. Her mind raced as she searched for some defense, but she couldn't think of any. "You wish to see me married, I know."

"Yes!" Her father sighed, grateful the subject had finally been broached.

"Fulton Pierce seems like a very nice man," her mother said. "Don't you think?"

"Yes, I like Fulton, but he's so thin." It was all she could think of. "Hardly as big around as one of my knitting needles. A stiff wind might blow him into the next valley. Then where would I be?"

"His family owns half the cattle in Livingston County." Henry's jaw was set. "They would be a very good match."

"Would I be marrying the cattle or the family?" she smiled. "In any case, I understand Fulton has been in, uh, discussions with Emily Brown's family."

"Oh?" Her father seemed uncertain again, probably because Wooford Pierce, Fulton's father, did a fair amount of business with Henry, and neither man would want to disrupt that relationship.

"They make such a darling couple," she added.

Silence interrupted the discussion. Apparently her parents had settled on Fulton as the husband of choice, and they hadn't examined many alternatives.

"Well, what about Harrington Jones?" her mother asked.

"Mother, you can't be serious. Harrington is fifteen, no, sixteen years my senior. Besides that, he's got to be twenty stone if he's a pound. Can you imagine that man . . . and me . . . ?"

"Abby," her mother said. "Please don't use that kind of language—"

"It's not about that," her father said.

"Perhaps not for you, but it is for me."

Her mother's cheeks turned pink, and she fanned herself with a handkerchief.

Her father started pacing about the room. "Abby, dear. You're seventeen years old, if I'm not mistaken."

"Eighteen, actually."

Her father stopped pacing. "Good Lord. Well, at any rate, it is high time you were married. You can see that, can't you? We can't have you living in our house forever as a spinster. There are any number of decent, honorable young men in the county or beyond, if necessary, who would make a perfectly good match for you."

"That all depends on how you define 'perfect,' doesn't it?"

"All a man needs is the right, well, circumstances to be a suitable match."

"And what would I need?"

"Don't be so particular. What more would you need?"

"Father, I hope to have some say in whom I marry."

"Certainly. Of course, dear. We have always listened to your concerns."

"My concerns? How comforting to know." She sighed.

Her father looked briefly at the ceiling again. "Abby, dear, we want the best for you. You know that, but I feel this is a matter that may be coming to a head."

"Coming to a head? What kind of wedding plans come to a head?"

"Stop this!" Her father scowled. "You know what I mean. We will let you know when your mother and I have reached a decision."

The finality of her father's statement so shocked Abigail that she reacted immediately, instinctively, and she wasn't sure what she was saying until the words spilled out of her mouth.

"Very well, if you insist. I choose Tobias Johnson."

Her father froze and she could see a smile forming on her mother's lips, so she held up her hands to stop them from reacting any further. "I choose Tobias, but not for marriage. At least not immediately. This is the nineteenth century, after all, and I insist on having a say in whom I marry. And, in order to be sure of my match, I must know more about the man first."

"You've known Tobias since you were a child," her mother said.

"Known him as a friend, yes. But I need to learn the temper of the man under different circumstances. Different stresses, as it were. Ones that you wouldn't find in a casual friendship. Only then will I know if he will be a suitable husband, someone I'd want to spend the rest of my life with. To have children with."

"How on earth are you going to know that, Abigail?" Her father's face had turned crimson. "Do you want to have a trial marriage? Sign a contract, perhaps?"

"I would do it the very same way you would, Father. The same way you have with Thomas Johnson. By going into business with him."

"What?"

"Yes. It's no secret that I want to raise horses. The Johnsons have a successful farm, although Toby isn't principally in charge of it. I think he would enjoy starting a business with me to raise horses of our own. It would give him some practical business experience, and I would learn more about him."

"Do you have any idea what you'd be getting into?" Her father asked. "It's not like planning a spring social, you know."

"Exactly my point. Marriage isn't a spring social, either. It's serious business. For a wife, what more serious a business can there be?"

Her mother smiled. "Henry, I think Abigail has a good idea."

"Pish and tosh!" Henry threw his hands in the air. "I've never heard of such a thing."

"Don't worry, Father. It shouldn't be long before Tobias and I know each other well enough. Anyway, that's my condition. If Tobias and I can be successful business partners, we're bound to be compatible as man and wife. If that's what I want."

"Now you want to put conditions on marriage?" Her father shook his head.

But her mother looked as though she enjoyed the idea more and more. "Henry, think of how often you have described your business affairs to me as a marriage, good or bad."

"Yes, dear, but that's different."

"I don't see that it's so different. Except for having children, of course." Henrietta stood and faced her husband. "I think even you would want to know more about your business partners if you expected to have children with them."

"Unbelievable! Completely unbelievable." Henry glared at Abigail and her mother in turn, then stalked from the room muttering to himself.

Henrietta's smile sparkled as Abigail had seldom seen it. She wagged a finger at Abigail. "I don't know where you came up with this remarkable idea, dear, but I've always said there's more than a little of your father in you."

"Really?" Abigail couldn't imagine the two of them being more different.

Abigail sat at her dressing table, studying her face in the candlelit reflection of the mirror. Yes, she had become a woman, no doubt about it. Well into the age for marrying and having children. Why, then, did she object to her parents' insistence that she do just that? Was it only because it should be her decision, and she hadn't yet been able to make it? When it came to suitors, her life was an embarrassment of riches. The party had proven that. But she feared being chained to a loveless marriage, and the business with Toby was all she could think of under pressure. She knew she was only buying time. Her parents would expect her to marry Toby as soon as the business was successful, if not before.

An image of Justin Sterling, bare-chested and jumping into the fish pond, came to mind and she smiled. She would love to go into business with Justin, but her father would have none of that.

She felt the trap of her own making starting to close around her, and she suddenly wanted to get out of the house. She'd go for an evening stroll to clear her head. She snatched up a shawl and started to leave her room but stopped and looked back at the dressing table. She'd forgotten to blow out her candle. Sitting next to it, glinting in the reflection of the candle's flame, was the small, chrome pocket pistol her father had given her. He said she should keep it with her if she insisted on taking evening walks. She never thought she'd need it. Now the idea of having it gave her comfort. She slipped it carefully into her small wool purse, blew out the candle, and left.

CHAPTER THIRTEEN

New Year's Day 1835

From his comfortable chair near the crackling hearth, Justin sipped from a cup of rum and nog and listened to his neighbors' friendly talk. He always looked forward to the Johnsons' New Year's gathering. The annual party provided welcome relief from the quiet isolation of winter, and through the blending of many voices, he picked out bits and pieces of many conversations. There were discussions of new farming techniques someone intended to try in the spring, rumors about who was courting whom during the fallow season, and general good-natured revelry.

Justin noticed with interest a sprig of mistletoe hanging from the wooden beam separating the large living room from an equally large and open dining room. He wondered if Abby would let him catch her underneath it and speculated on how much scandal it would cause if he kissed her. It would be an appropriate prelude to confessing his love.

He cautioned himself against acting rashly. Abby appeared nervous enough for some reason. She had left the gathering and was off somewhere in the kitchen, helping Mrs. Johnson's servants, who provided a seemingly endless supply of cookies and punch. Abby looked resplendent in her wool skirt and high-necked blouse, which, to his mind, barely concealed the swell of her breasts. To Justin, who had imbibed more than one cup of nog, the anticipation of seeing her again made him carefully monitor the doorway leading to the kitchen.

However, it was Tobias and his father who appeared in the doorway first. They worked their way, arm in arm, through the knots of gathered friends who greeted them. Justin's gaze settled on Toby's smile. Seldom had he seen such self-satisfaction. It occurred to him that Toby knew something. Something important.

Abby came into the room wiping her hands on a towel, which she set on a serving tray. She looked less than satisfied, as if some sort of burden weighed on her shoulders. She smiled politely and followed Toby and his father into the living room. The sight of her so close behind Toby alarmed Justin. Perhaps the look on Toby's face had something to do with Abigail. He did not have to wait long to find out.

Toby tapped on the side of his brandy snifter with a silver spoon to get the attention of the gathered neighbors. "Listen to me everybody. I have wonderful news." Tobias smiled as though he were a ten-year-old again at Christmas. "This spring Abigail Whitfield and I will start our own enterprise. A sort of business, you could say."

The hairs on the back of Justin's neck stood on end.

Abby flashed a reproachful look at Toby. Had she not wanted him to reveal their plans?

"My goodness," Toby's mother said. "What sort of business?"

By way of answering, Tobias raised his snifter and said, a bit melodramatically, "Ladies and gentleman, I give you the Johnson-Whitfield horse-breeding consortium."

Oohs and aahs spread through the group. Everyone drank to their good luck. Justin was relieved that the business wasn't marriage, but it was as close as a couple could get without tying the knot.

"Yes," Toby said. "I have spoken with my father, and of course to Mr. Whitfield"—a nod of the brandy snifter in the direction of Henry, who held no glass. "And we've decided to quarter the horses in the old Thompson barn, down by the river. We chose it because it's about halfway between our two farms. And it's the only barn available for now. It will have to be rebuilt, I imagine, but it will do until the venture can move on to a bigger and better location."

He beamed at Abigail and grasped her shoulder awkwardly but enthusiastically, as if he had just announced that they were engaged to be married.

"How extraordinary," one of the older gentlemen said.

"Between the two of you, I'm sure no luck will be needed," Henrietta Whitfield said. The satisfied look on Henrietta's face told Justin all he needed to know. Undoubtedly she'd been planning something like this since Abby's party, if not before. If so, the scheme had taken shape nicely. The only thing left for Abby and Toby would be marriage. Justin suddenly felt like an awkward stranger in the house.

The younger men in the room were excited by the news and shot questions at Tobias, to see if he was serious and to gauge whether the plan could actually succeed. Abby stood to the side, and Justin noticed that all of their questions were aimed at Toby, not her.

"How many horses?" one asked.

"A half-dozen or so to begin with," Tobias admitted. "We'll start out quite modestly, but when we are successful, who knows?"

Other questions followed, and, as she stood to one side, Abigail was relieved they were directed at Toby, and not her. She knew that Toby, as a man, was expected to control the business. Her intentions weren't important to the men in the room. Yes, she had always wanted to raise horses, and going into business with Toby might be the most expedient route to that goal, but the arrangement did something else. It would turn away any number of men who might want to court her or ask for her hand in marriage. And, because her parents assumed marriage to Toby would eventually follow, they would no longer pressure her to select another mate who met their rather narrow requirements. It was an awkward delaying tactic that would have to suffice until the business failed or she could explain why marriage to Toby wouldn't work.

She searched the faces of her friends and relatives and saw that their reactions were, for the most part, just as she had predicted. Some of the older men looked askance at Henry, obviously wondering at the prudence of letting a young lady take part in the less-than-genteel practice of raising horses. Henry said nothing, but gently raised the palms of his hands, as if to signal that his daughter's participation was only a matter of youthful enthusiasm, which would fade in time and in the face of hard work. Abigail relished the idea of mortifying the old men further by proving her father wrong.

Then her gaze fell upon Justin. His eyes were fixed on the cup he held in his lap. Had the boldness of her enterprise impressed him? It didn't look so. Something else shown on his face. Disappointment? Sadness? Of course, she realized that he, too, must think there was more to her plans than a business or her love of horses.

A wave of regret swept over her. At that moment she was tempted to stand up, stop the chattering crowd, and announce, "Toby and I are not going to be married!" She would have shouted it, but would anyone believe her?

What could she do to disabuse Justin or anyone else of the notion that her intentions were not ultimately romantic? After all, what young lady would think twice about marrying Tobias Johnson? He stood tall, and he had turned his share of the heads of the women he passed on the road. Perhaps she really should consider marrying Toby. Much as she hated to admit it, a woman could do much worse.

But the decision should be hers. She bristled at the idea that, because she was a woman, she couldn't go into business with a man without marrying him. Why should she have to justify her actions, even to Justin? She would decide whom to marry in her own good time. For now, she would work hard to create the financial independence she might need if she truly were to decide whom she should marry.

A few high clouds were scudding across the blue winter sky, but they gave no hint that bad weather might be on the way. Abby sat, bundled in her sheepskin coat under an ancient, gnarled oak tree that had given her shade since her mother had brought her here as a child. All of the important events of her life had unfolded on the stage the view before her presented. From the oak she looked north, as she usually did, down across her father's pastures and fields, into the distance. How many times had she admired this view without realizing those lands in the distance that made the view so spectacular were the rolling acres owned by the Sterlings? Now their neatly plowed rows, waiting for spring corn and tobacco, called to her as if they, not the Whitfield property, were her home.

Salty tears formed in the corners of her eyes. Some part of her had hoped—no, secretly prayed—that nothing in her life would ever change. That she could stay a single girl, a girl of some privilege, yes, but still a girl, forever. If she never grew up, she could continue to receive the admiring glances of the young men of the valley, never refusing their attention, but never forced to pick and choose among them. To settle for the awful permanence of one.

All of that had been a foolish childhood notion. A silly dream. Sooner or later she would be required to awaken and take her place in life, probably alongside a man she'd never intended to marry. Never intended to choose. To promise to love and obey him, then bear him children and her father grandchildren.

"Men!" she growled.

She reached down with both hands and dug her fingers into the soil on either side of her. It was familiar Whitfield soil, but it was cold between her fingers and gave her no comfort.

Justin considered hiding the clay jug of sour mash when his father came into the kitchen, but by that time he no longer cared.

"You're into your cups a mite early, are you not?" Walter asked.

"What of it? A man's got a right to take a drink, no matter the hour."

"Aye, and you are a man, now, Justin. But along with being grown comes the wisdom of knowing when to drink. And how much."

"Wisdom has nothing to do with me or my drink." Justin raised the mug and finished the remaining liquor in two swallows. He let the mug bang down onto the table and wiped his mouth with the back of his hand.

"Well, now," Walter said. "I may be old, but I still have a modicum of wisdom, or so your mother tells me. And if not wisdom, I do have some experience. Is there anything I can do for you, something you won't find at the bottom of your cup?"

"You can put a musket ball between my eyes and put me out of my misery. Or, better yet, put one between Henry Whitfield's eyes."

"Ah, now I understand. It's about young Abigail, isn't it? That girl has a sparkle in her eye and a skip in her step, that's true."

"I love her, Father, and there is no chance in heaven or on earth that Henry will let me marry her. He's put Abigail in business with Tobias Johnson."

"So I've heard."

"It's just a first step toward marriage."

"Has she told you that?"

"No. But everyone knows it's true. Besides, Henry won't let me get near enough to talk to her."

"It's a shame. You and Abby have been close since you were no higher than a wagon axle."

"A lot of good that has done us." Justin eyed the jug of whiskey, but decided against pouring himself any more while his father was in the kitchen.

"I am truly sorry, son."

"There's nothing for you to be sorry about, Father."

"There you're wrong."

He looked at his father. "You had nothing to do with it. It's all that high-and-mighty Henry's doing."

"I'm sorry I haven't had the Johnsons' resources, son. I'm sorry a mere Sterling isn't good enough for the Whitfield clan."

"We're honest farmers," Justin said. "We work the land as hard as Whitfield—harder, since we can't hire the hands Henry can. How does that make us less of a family than his?"

Walter sat down at the table opposite him. "You may not believe it, son, but Henry Whitfield has as much respect for you as any man."

"Then he has no respect for any man."

Walter reached for a cup and poured himself a short measure of whiskey. "The thing is, Henry isn't refusing to let you marry Abigail because he lacks respect for you."

"No? He's just doing it for sport then? This is how he gets his entertainment, ruining the lives of two people, and one his daughter."

"Quite the contrary." Walter sipped the whiskey, savoring it. "He wants the very best for Abigail, the same as you. It's nothing personal to Henry, but it's precisely to ensure that Abigail's life doesn't come to ruin that he won't let you marry her."

"He has no idea what's best for Abigail. Why shouldn't she marry the man she loves?"

"Has she said she loves you, then? I hadn't heard that."

"No, not in so many words." He pointed at his father. "But I can tell."

"Love is a wonderful thing, Justin, but it won't pay the miller, or the farrier, or bring in the crop in the fall."

"Money? That's what everyone says it comes down to, but I don't think so. It's more to do with Henry himself, and his sin of pride. He can't imagine his precious daughter marrying below her station."

"Son, I think we should stick to the facts as we know them. And, as far as you and I know, Abigail is only going into business with Toby. She hasn't agreed to marry him."

"It's only a matter of time."

"Then I suggest we let some time pass before we lose faith."

CHAPTER FOURTEEN

September 1835

Spring had come and gone and summer would soon follow. The horse barn was finally built, but to Abigail's frustration, Tobias appeared unconcerned about making further plans for the new horse farm. He seemed to think plans were unnecessary, or else they would take care of themselves, and he was in no hurry. Abigail knew that if they were to start the business, they needed to purchase horses from the auctions in Kentucky. But the summer slid by too and Abigail knew they had lost the season. She did nothing to make her anger and frustration known, lest Toby or her father decide she should give up the enterprise as an unnecessary trifle. She was determined to see her own plans through and have Tobias acquire the necessary stock.

At the critical moment, however, Tobias came down with a flu and was quarantined at the Johnson home. He would not be able to travel for several weeks. With this disappointing news, Abigail sat in the family room, knitting and wondering how they could keep from losing another year. Her mother sat in a comfortable chair near the fireplace, reading correspondence from relatives. Her father was working in one of the barns.

"Oh, my." Henrietta set down the letter she'd been reading and looked at Abigail. "It seems that your Aunt Tilda in Louisville has taken ill."

"I hope she doesn't have the same illness as Tobias. It may not be serious, but he has taken to bed and will be weak for some time."

"Tilda is said to have the grippe. From her letter it appears she's in a fair bit of pain."

"How awful." Abigail set aside her knitting. "Will Aunt Tilda suffer this affliction very long?"

"The surgeons don't know. From her letter I assume she'll recover in due time, but the poor dear is a bit older than I am, and she has always been a frail one, even as a child. She does have a penchant for drama, though, so she may not be as sick as she describes, but now that your Uncle Arnold has passed away, I wish I could be there for her."

"Yes, of course. I hope there is someone in Louisville who can help her." Even as Abigail said this, a plan took form in her mind.

She had wanted to take advantage of whatever momentum she and Toby still had after they announced their plans. If preparations continued to stall for whatever reason, she feared that Toby, or more likely her father, might change his mind and simply insist that the two of them marry. Abigail was willing to play the game, so long as marriage remained only an unspoken assumption, one that could be put off for the indefinite future. If marriage weren't presumed to be in the offing, Toby's father might question the wisdom of his son for continuing a business with a woman. Abigail wanted to take concrete steps as soon as possible to prevent any second-guessing. A successful business might continue on its own, even if it became clear that no marriage would follow.

But with Toby lying sick in bed, there wasn't anyone who could travel to the Kentucky horse farms to purchase new stock. That might delay her plans another year or more, and a year could bring many unpredictable changes.

She took her leave from her mother and found her father in the horse barn, giving orders to a few of the hired men. The workers left to go about their tasks, and she waited until her father turned away to catch his attention.

"Hello dear." He coiled a length of rope as he spoke.

"Hello, Father. Have you heard of Toby Johnson's illness?"

"Yes, of course. He has a flu, doesn't he?"

"It may be that. It seems to linger, leaving him weak."

"He's a strong young man. Don't you worry, dear. God willing, he'll be up and around in no time. You'll see." He briefly patted her arm.

"Yes, I hope so, and we should be glad of that. But I'm concerned about the timing of his illness."

"The timing?"

"Yes. As you know, the auctions will begin soon in Kentucky. Toby was hoping to go there to purchase a few foals and several brood mares for our enterprise. But now . . ."

"But now he can't. Is that what you mean? Such are the uncertainties of any business, I suppose." Henry appeared unconcerned, or ready for her to call the whole venture off.

"Yes," she said. "But I was hoping we could find a substitute. Someone who could go to Kentucky on our behalf."

Henry lifted the coil of rope onto a wall peg and looked at her. "A substitute?"

"Yes. Someone who is knowledgeable of horses, and who can purchase good stock."

"Of course. But who would that be? I suppose we could contact one of the firms I sometimes deal with in Louisville—"

"Oh, no, Father. I wouldn't want some stodgy old breeding firm in Louisville picking out my horses. I'd want someone whose opinion I can trust. It would have to be someone I know personally. An expert, perhaps, like you." She added that last bit of flattery on a whim. She knew her father would never consider taking a lengthy trip away from the farm in the midst of harvest, especially for something he considered frivolous.

"Me? I couldn't possibly. I have too many responsibilities here." He waved his arm, taking in the barn and the whole farm.

"I suppose that's true. Then I will have to look for someone else. But it will be hard to find anyone with your knowledge of horses, Father."

"True enough. I'm sorry I can't go myself. You let me know if anyone suitable comes to mind. If not, then perhaps next year, eh?" Henry gave her a knowing smile, one that wished her "good luck" on such an impossible task.

"Thank you, Father. I will let you know when I have arranged for a substitute." With that she spun on her heels and left the barn.

Her father hadn't suggested the name of anyone in particular who might go to Kentucky, undoubtedly because he didn't take her venture seriously. Even so, Abigail hoped her last statement made it clear that he had effectively given his permission for her to find someone else to make the trip. She already had someone specific in mind. The perfect candidate.

It wasn't until the following Sunday that Abigail was able to speak to Justin, and then only after church services. She found him near the church corral, where he was preparing to leave. She walked up to him casually, with her hands clasped behind her, as though she had no specific purpose in mind.

"Hello, Justin Sterling," she said.

"Hello, Abigail Whitfield." He looked up from inspecting his saddle and seemed pleased, but not surprised, to see her.

"It's a fine day, isn't it?" She studied the blue sky overhead.

"Yes it is. And your father gave us a fine Sunday service. Did he not?"

She wondered why he referred to her father's service. The topic of Henry's sermon was clarity of purpose. The purpose being to live an honest, Christian life. Perhaps Justin was being

114

pleasant, or maybe he wanted her to get to the point.

"Father has a way with words."

"Aye, he does, and with everything he puts his mind to."

"Yes, of course." She was struggling for a way to pose her question, but Justin provided the opening himself.

"Congratulations on your new venture," he said. "I'm sure you and Toby will make fine partners." The look on his face didn't match his congratulatory words. If only Justin had the financial means to help her, there would be no question in her mind whom she'd rather have as a partner. In business or otherwise.

She looked down at the ground. "Thank you, but things are not beginning as well as they might."

"How's that? I'd have thought a Whitfield and Johnson enterprise would be nothing but a roaring success."

"And it will be. It will be." She reached out and touched him briefly on the arm. "It's just that Toby isn't well, at the moment."

"So I've heard. I missed him at service."

"Yes, well. His illness isn't too serious, but it means we have no one who can travel to Kentucky to acquire horse stock."

"That is a problem." He cocked his broad-brimmed hat back on his head and smiled as if he enjoyed the idea that her business might fail before it got off the ground. "You can't start a horse farm without horses. That much I know."

She ignored his sarcasm. "I knew you'd understand. And that's why I was hoping you could help us." She looked into his eyes, gauging his reaction.

Silent for a moment, he appeared to freeze. Then he looked down at this boots, thinking.

"What did you have in mind?"

"Simply this. I want you go to Kentucky in Toby's stead and purchase our stock at auction."

"Me? Truly?"

"It's only going to be a small operation at first, so we'll only need a few horses. Half a dozen, perhaps."

"If you're speaking of Fayette County, that's not a small journey, especially for a few horses."

"We can pay you, of course. Quite well, actually." She had no real idea whether Justin could be spared by his family for such a task, but she intended to make it worthwhile for them if he'd agree to go. She feared his thoughtful silence meant he was trying to decide how to politely reject her request, so she pressed ahead. "Father thinks one of his old crony firms in Kentucky can do the job, but I know you, and there's really no one else whose opinion I'd trust about horses, and—"

"Abby," he said. "Do you see this corral?" He hooked his gloved thumb at the wooden rails and milling horses within.

"Of course." The way he'd interrupted, she was sure he meant to refuse her. She felt somewhat ashamed to assume he could be employed so easily. She was so close to accomplishing her goals, but she couldn't insist that Justin help. "Look, if you don't think—"

"Do you remember standing with me at this corral, on that very rail, when we were but children?"

"Yes, I suppose, but . . ." She rose up a little on her toes. What sort of reproachful lesson was he going to give her?

"When we stood there years ago, you told me all about your dream, and your wish to raise horses when you were grown."

How sweet of him to remember. She felt her cheeks flush pink and she turned slightly to look at the railing. She still remembered the comforting feel of his arms and chest when she hugged him.

"I was impressed," he said. "Don't get me wrong. At the time, I didn't believe it was possible for a slip of a girl to have such dreams, but I was impressed anyway."

"Why, thank you." She wished she knew what point he was trying to make.

"And now you are a grown woman, Abigail Whitfield, and I am still very much impressed with you. With all of you, including your dreams." His gaze took her in from head to foot, lingering in certain places. She teetered between appreciating his compliments and still fearing his ultimate rejection.

He tossed the reins over his horse's neck. "And, more importantly, if you remember that one particular Sunday so long ago, then you'll remember that I promised to help you."

A smile crept to her lips.

"Now, I guess it's time for me to keep that promise."

"Oh, thank you!" She threw her arms around his neck and gave him a hug. In his surprise, he stood stiffly still, just as he had when they were children, but then he slipped his arms around the small of her back and pulled her tightly to him.

"Abigail!" Henry stood near the church steps, next to the family surrey in which Henrietta already sat.

Unbelievable, Justin thought. Whitfield had interrupted them once again, just as he had so many years ago. Back then it had cost Abigail two more years before she had a horse of her own, or so Justin thought. Maybe this time things would be different.

"Come away, Abigail. We are leaving."

"I'm coming, Father. Thank you," she said again to Justin. "We will talk about the particulars very soon. I am so happy. And don't worry about Father. I'll find a way to break the news to him gently." She kissed him quickly on the cheek and walked toward the surrey.

Justin couldn't help but notice the scowl on Henry's face.

"What?" Henry Whitfield almost choked on his tea. "You're not serious."

"I am perfectly serious." Abigail crossed her arms. She

117

expected resistance, but not such a strong reaction. "You said I could find someone to go in place of Toby—or you—and I have."

"But Justin Sterling?"

"And what is wrong with Justin Sterling?" She took a sip of her own tea, chamomile, and tried to stay calm.

"He's but a boy, not much older than you."

"He's as old as Tobias, with whom I'm raising the horses. You do remember that, don't you?"

"Yes, of course, but—"

"I don't think there's a 'but' that applies here, Father. If we are going into business, I need—and Toby needs—someone to go to Kentucky for our stock. You've seen the horses the Sterlings breed. Clearly Justin knows a bangtail from a two-year-old."

"Well, yes, but—"

"No buts, please. If you truly wish this enterprise to be a success, we'll need horses this year. Justin Sterling is the person I've employed to get them." She hoped referring to Justin as an employee would signal to her father that she hadn't chosen Justin simply because he was a friend. Or, heaven forbid, because she was attracted to him. She also counted on her father's presumption that a failure of the business might also call into question any matrimony.

Her father ran his fingers through his thinning gray hair. "I only want the best for you, dear. You know that. But I don't know if Walter can spare Justin at this time of year. Harvest season is nearly upon us, and—"

"I've promised Mr. Sterling that Justin will receive enough compensation to offset his absence from the farm for a few weeks."

"You have?" Henry's look of disbelief slowly turned to a grin. "Well, then. I guess you've thought of everything."

CHAPTER FIFTEEN

Early October 1835

Four days after Justin left Ridgetop to travel to Kentucky, Abigail sat with her parents in the family room, knitting. Her mother was reading a book, while her father perused a week-old edition of the *Louisville Gazette* newspaper. When they spoke, the conversation consisted mostly of plans for the coming holidays.

Her father looked up from his newspaper. "I see that civilization has finally come to Tennessee."

"It's about time, I think. In what way?" Her mother didn't look up. She was clearly skeptical.

"Someone has started riverboat service on the Cumberland and Tennessee rivers. They say the service is first class. Apparently you can travel all the way to Cincinnati. Or the other way to New Orleans, if you care to."

"Imagine that," her mother said.

Abigail watched her mother's reaction carefully. Henrietta, the homebody, had seen enough travel in her life, just by coming to Ridgetop. The only travel she might consider at her age would take her back to Virginia and to civilization as she knew it. Even that was questionable, now that Ridgetop was home. Abigail had read the same newspaper article earlier in the day. New riverboat service perfectly complemented her plan, but she hadn't said anything to her parents. She wanted them to believe her idea, when she revealed it, was spontaneously conceived.

"Have you received any more news from Aunt Tilda?" Abigail asked her mother.

"Nothing since her last letter. But you know how hard it is to get any news in Ridgetop. Perhaps riverboat service will improve that."

"I hope poor Tilda is feeling better," Abigail said.

"As do I, dear. As do I."

Abigail let a minute or two pass in silence.

"Didn't Uncle Thurston's brother die of the grippe?"

"Uncle Thurston?" Her mother looked up from her book. "Yes, I believe he did. His oldest son, Alva, did, too, if I recall. A nasty business, the grippe. And they were all alone on that farm of theirs. It was so terrible."

Terrible, Abigail knew, because Thurston lay dead in his farmhouse for more than a week before anyone found him.

After another minute of silence, Abigail said, "I am so looking forward to spring. It seems a year that we've been cooped up in this old house."

"Yes, dear." Her mother looked at her over the top of her half-frame spectacles. "I imagine you'll be getting into all manner of trouble with your friends when the days turn warmer."

"Oh, I don't know. I'm older now, Mother, and more mature. And there's the business to think of."

Her mother glanced at her again, but this time said nothing.

Abigail decided it was time to strike. Once again she spoke casually, without looking up from her knitting. "I do worry about Aunt Tilda, though, all alone in Louisville. I wouldn't want the poor woman to end up like Uncle Thurston."

"Please don't say that." Her mother didn't like to think about such grizzly things.

"Oh, I know! Mother. Father. I have a wonderful idea." She put down her knitting. "I shall travel to Louisville on the new riverboat and look after Aunt Tilda myself. Even if she's past her most serious illness, she's bound to need assistance with her household chores. Don't you think?"

"Oh, my." Her mother put her hand to her mouth. "Louisville is so far away."

"Not anymore." Her father slapped the newspaper with one hand. "They say it's only three days up the river. Two in the other direction."

Her mother gave Henry a "don't encourage her" glance and said, "It's bound to be dangerous. What kind of person travels on a riverboat?"

Her father set the newspaper down, as if to hide it from Abigail. "Your mother is right. You shouldn't travel alone, even on a riverboat." He looked at his wife, hoping she realized he supported her. Henrietta gave him a stiff smile.

"I'll take Elly with me," Abigail said. "We should be fine." Abigail felt her secrets were safe with Elly, who was only a few years older than she. Elly had been a close companion for Abigail as they grew up together, and she and Elly had spent many hours in Abigail's room talking about the boys in Ridgetop County.

"I just don't know, dear." Her mother shook her head. "I don't like the idea at all."

"Surely you wouldn't begrudge Aunt Tilda a little aid in her recuperation, would you?" Abigail looked at her mother with pleading eyes. "She'll be so happy to see me, I know. And I her. Don't you think?"

Her mother looked at the ceiling, or perhaps to the Lord in heaven for support, but Abigail felt her mother's resistance weakening.

After two more days of on-and-off discussion, Abigail finally prevailed. It turned out that a local farmer, Jules Compton, was

121

traveling by boat to Louisville himself. He said he'd be glad to accompany Abigail and her servant.

For Justin, getting away from the insular community of Ridgetop and his chores was well worth the long journey on horseback to northern Kentucky. He had read about Lexington and other faraway places in books and the occasional newspaper, but he never expected to get the chance to visit them. Not that Fayette County was as distant or exotic as London, or even Texas, but he took in every detail of what he saw along the way.

The time alone also gave him a chance to think. The news that Abigail and Toby were going into business together was a hard blow, but eventually he realized it wasn't the end of the world. Not yet, anyway. He was surprised that Henry had agreed to the business, but no doubt he thought it the first step in a more permanent joining of the Johnson and Whitfield families. Surely Abby realized the danger of her bargain, but to what extent did she agree with the underlying presumption? He couldn't believe she did, or at least he didn't want to. Abigail Whitfield knew her own mind, and she'd rather spend time with her horses than with any man Justin knew, including Toby. No doubt she was using Tobias to get her father to agree to the enterprise. Still, Abby's dream was strong enough. She might be willing to pay the price of marriage to seal the deal. As his father had said, only time would tell.

In spite of everything, the fact that Abby had asked for his help gave him hope. Perhaps this was one of the tests his father had spoken of. And it was fortunate that he'd had his father's timely counsel. On hearing the news of his friends' business, Justin was utterly dismayed. He wanted to seize Abigail by the shoulders and shake some sense into her. On the other hand, if she was indeed willing to marry Toby, then Justin's understanding of her feelings for him, or at least his fervent hopes, were simply illusions and always had been. He refused to believe he had been mistaken about Abby for so long. But for now, at least, he intended to keep his emotions anchored and his sails furled until he knew which way the wind blew.

Pondering life's unexpected turns, Justin rode steadily through woodlands and gently rolling hills that gradually gave way to Kentucky's open green pastures, the color of which reminded him of Abby's eyes. Whitewashed fences ran for miles in every direction. On each farm he passed there stood a house bigger and more impressive than the Whitfields', if such a thing was possible. At one of the smaller mansions he asked for directions, only to learn from the occupants that he'd stopped at the servants' quarters. His head swam at the thought of such wealth. If these were the farms of Kentucky, he couldn't imagine what the city of Lexington looked like. It was reputed to have a population of nearly 7,000 people.

After seeing the county's farms, he was ready to think the residents of Lexington lived on fluffy white clouds and traveled by magic carpet, as in the stories of the *Arabian Nights' Entertainment.* The reality turned out to be less impressive than what he'd imagined. Lexington was firmly anchored to the ground. Houses on the periphery of town were substantial, but more modest than those of the wealthy horse farms. Most of the streets were no more than muddy lanes running between the houses and businesses, but closer to the center of the city the streets had been cobbled, making travel easier. Three- and four-story brick houses stood shoulder-to-shoulder, with a bakery, wheelwright, butcher's shop, or some other business on every corner. Justin had never seen so many people in one place. How could they live in such crowded conditions? Where were they all going? Except for the tradesmen, most of the residents he encountered were dressed in clothing Justin would only have worn to church on Sunday, not the sturdy leather and wool workaday clothing of a farmer. More than a few men he saw reminded Justin of Hutchison Bailey, both in their manner of dress, and in the unfriendly glances they gave him. They looked silly in their pantaloons, elaborate cravats, and beaver-skin top hats. Surely Justin looked every inch the country bumpkin to these city men, dressed as he was in his buckskins.

The women were a different story. They wore graceful dresses, long enough to cover their ankles, with elaborately decorated shoulders. Most wore hats of many styles and colors, but they still carried parasols to shade them from the sun. They wore their hair gathered at the top or sides of their head, often rolled into decorative braids or other shapes, and to Justin they could have been goddesses descended from Mount Olympus. Would Abby ever want to live in such a city? What would she think of the outfits these city women wore, outfits he could never afford to buy her?

More than one woman on the street gave Justin an appreciative look, much to the dismay of their gentleman companions. He wasn't sure what it was they found so interesting, but he intended to find a decent shirt and jacket as soon as he could and change out of his traveling clothes.

He left the center of Lexington and found lodging in a road house near Richmond. He was more comfortable there, where he could learn about the available stock and take advantage of auctions near both towns.

A week later, Justin sat in a Lexington sale barn with other interested bidders, listening to the singsong cadence of the auctioneer, who encouraged higher and higher bids. A superb Arabian caught his eye as it was led into the ring. If he could acquire the animal for a reasonable price, he'd have seven exceptional horses, enough for Abby and Tobias. The bidding came fast, but each new offer was topped by a gentleman,

124

whom, he was told, had come from Louisiana by riverboat. From the man's beaver-skin top hat, brocade vest, and plum-colored jacket, Justin assumed he had money. Justin's first few bids nearly exhausted his remaining budget. But in his mind's eye, he could see Abby galloping the Arabian over open fields like the ones outside Lexington, with her red hair flowing behind her in the wind. With that image in mind, Justin intended to pay for the Arabian with his own money if he could.

He raised two fingers, agreeing to pay twenty-five dollars. The auctioneer barely interrupted his song enough to recognize Justin's bid. He continued, encouraging someone to top it, but the other men in the room fell silent. The gentleman from Louisiana held his fist to his chin, thinking hard. Silently, Justin prayed that the southerner would concede. The auctioneer's voice changed pitch, indicating that bidding would close. At "going once," the Louisianan bid thirty dollars. Justin was crushed. He could not afford a further bid, even with his own money. The auctioneer's cadence slowed. Even he knew the bidding couldn't go much higher. He looked at Justin one last time. Defeated, Justin set his jaw and shook his head. The auctioneer nodded and started to bring the bidding to a close. At "going twice," a woman called from the back of the room. "Thirty-five dollars!"

Surprised, even the auctioneer skipped a beat, but he acknowledged the woman's bid and took up his chant again, albeit at a slower pace. Odd as it was for a woman to attend an auction, much less to bid, every man in the room turned to see who she was. She stood by herself in the last and highest row of the elevated seats. A teal-colored cloak covered her shoulders, and her face was hidden in the shadow of a hood. But red hair spilled from the corners of the hood and Justin's jaw dropped. Abigail Whitfield was the bidder.

The gentleman from Louisiana tipped his hat and bowed to

Abigail. Reluctantly, he shook his head for the auctioneer and the hammer slammed down, ending the bidding. Abby had her Arabian. A new horse of lesser quality was led into the arena and the auction continued. Abigail motioned for Justin to meet her at the entrance to the barn, and he made his way in that direction.

When they met, he took off his hat and slapped his thigh with it. "Abigail Whitfield, what in the world are you doing here?"

"I could see your resolve weakening back there." She gestured in the direction of the arena. "And I couldn't let the Arabian get away." She smiled to show she was kidding.

"It wasn't my resolve weakening, it was my purse, but I can't imagine a better turn of events. How did you—?"

"The riverboat to Louisville." She tilted her head coyly, reveling in Justin's astonishment at her presence so far from home. "I went there to visit an ailing aunt. And, as long as I was nearby, I took a coach to Lexington. I thought I'd check up on you, to see whether you'd taken my father's money and sneaked off to Boston."

"I was tempted to, of course. But knowing your volatile temper, I'd have needed a steamship to the Orient to get far enough away. And your father wasn't quite that generous."

"You know me too well." She threw back her hood.

"But not nearly as well as I thought." Justin's appreciative gaze took her in from head to toe, causing her to look away.

"Perhaps we can remedy your unfamiliarity," she said. "I intend to go with you when you take the stock home."

"What? What of your sick aunt?"

"If Aunt Tilda were any more fit, she'd be swinging from the parlor chandelier. We had a very nice visit, and now I want to accompany my investment, and you, back to Tennessee."

"Are you sure?"

"Of course. Someone has to make certain you complete your task."

"Abby. The trip home will not be as easy as a riverboat cruise. I've seven horses and two fillies to shepherd all the way to Ridgetop."

"Then you could use some help, couldn't you?"

"Perhaps, but you haven't eaten my cooking."

"I know how to catch—and cook—a fish, if you are so miserable a chef."

"I'll be living in a tent for at least a week."

"You?" She examined her fingernails. "Have you forgotten your manners?"

"No, of course not." He rolled his eyes. "It's big enough to sleep four, but I'll be sleeping under a tree for a week, not in the tent."

"That's better."

"Your father will kill us anyway."

"He might."

"And Toby. What will Toby think?"

"Toby doesn't own me. Not yet, anyway. Besides, Elly will be with us. She can attest that you kept your hands to yourself."

"I'm doomed either way, since Henry would fault me if I abandoned you in Lexington."

"It would be remiss of you at that, now that you know I'm here."

"God, Abby, it's good to see you. Worth every blow your father will strike on my poor, weathered brow."

"Such a poor brow." She put a hand on his forehead. "I'll make sure my father behaves. Now let's go collect my horses."

CHAPTER SIXTEEN

Lexington, Kentucky, Mid-November 1835

Few preparations for the return journey were necessary, other than purchasing additional flour, some salted meat, and a few extra blankets. Justin was ready to leave Fayette County in two days. By that time Elly had taken ill, and Abigail decided her servant should return to Ridgetop on the steamboat. Neither Justin nor Abigail wanted to delay the return trip or take the chance of contracting Elly's illness. Neither had the funds at hand to buy passage on the boat for all three people and the horses. More importantly, Abigail hoped that, if Elly arrived home first and brought the news that she was returning with Justin and the horses, enough time might pass to dampen her father's inevitable anger before she finally arrived.

Justin was not disappointed to have only one, not two, women to look after on the ride home. It would be the first time in his life that he'd be alone with Abby for more than a few minutes. He looked forward to the intimacy and feared it at the same time. What would they talk about? Would they get tired of each other's company? Justin couldn't imagine he'd ever tire of Abby, but he'd never entertained a woman for so long, and he didn't know what kind of attention she would require, especially if her future lay with Toby.

Two days later, Abigail sat on a folding stool in front of the canvas tent, pretending to read from a small bible her mother had insisted she take on the trip to Kentucky. Surreptitiously, she watched Justin tend to the horses, framed as he was by the blood-red setting sun. They were camped in a grassy meadow, next to a small river, and, although the setting was idyllic, dark clouds pressed on the horizon and promised that bad weather would soon be on them. She wondered if Justin noticed. After all, he hadn't appeared to notice her much in the last two days. He attended to all her needs, to be sure, but that wasn't the kind of attention she sought or expected.

He had started their journey as a perfect gentleman, but did he have to remain one? Unfortunately, his maddening deference had opened an awkward distance between them. She had known Justin Sterling most of her life, and she had never felt uncomfortable with him. But now he no longer spoke to her with the alluring charm she was used to. As pleasant as he'd been, he was clearly ill at ease, and that surprised her. Whatever the cause, she had to get to the bottom of it.

Abigail had always been drawn to the subtle desire that smoldered behind Justin's otherwise steady gaze. She enjoyed it, needed it, but she always kept a respectful distance. Justin could be teased, but he wasn't attracted to casual flirting. She couldn't lead him by the nose down a garden path, like most of the other young men who paraded to her family's farm to try to court her. As clear as his desire for her might be, he would have her only on his terms. No other man challenged her so, and she did not know what to make of it. Until now. Now it was if a veil had been taken from her eyes, letting her finally see the depth and sincerity of Justin's feelings. For as long as she had known him, his love for her had never wavered. It had been steady as rock, but it was a rock to which she was never chained. His love wasn't possessive. It left her free to pursue whatever life, or man, she wanted, while Justin waited patiently for her to come to him. When she was ready.

Recent events had impressed on Abigail the need to make certain decisions in her life, if she wasn't going to let others make them for her. But now Justin's gentlemanly demeanor seemed to close a door. Perhaps he behaved so because her father had hired him. He was, after all, an employee, practically her servant. Though nothing about him was or could be servile, the distance between them had been growing.

She watched him, in his sheepskin coat, as he fed the picketed horses, moving among the animals with an ease born of a lifetime of familiarity with their needs. Normally she would have helped, but Justin seemed not to need or want it. For all intents and purposes, he had settled into a role as Abigail Whitfield's hired man, and the thought disturbed her. She couldn't read Justin's thoughts, but he couldn't be happy as anyone's servant.

He lifted a heavy bucket of oats and passed it back and forth among the hungry charges. With his broad back and sinewed arms flexing, he stroked the animal's necks and withers, clucking and cooing as he attended them. He was at home with the horses, and they with him. This sparked a small ember of jealousy in Abigail, and not because she, too, wanted to be at ease with horses. She would be, if her plans with Toby succeeded. She would also gain a measure of independence few young women in Tennessee ever experienced, or wanted to experience.

She stood up and tossed the bible behind her into the tent. She walked over to the line of tethered horses and picked up a currying brush, then began stroking the flanks of a mare who stood between her and Justin. The animal's flanks quivered. Justin dropped the hoof he'd been inspecting, stood up, and looked at her over the back of the mare.

"Have you decided to get more experience before you go into business?" he asked.

She felt the blood rush to her cheeks, but she knew he was joking and kept her sudden anger in check. "I don't pay my employees to question me," she said with a smirk.

"Sorry. I thought your father had hired me."

She almost threw the brush at him, but stopped herself. Their harsh exchange surprised her, even though it was meant in jest. Did he still resent her business with Toby? She stepped around the rear end of the horse, trailing her hand along the animal's back, to make sure she didn't frighten it. She looked down at Justin, who scraped at another of the horse's hooves with an iron pick.

"Tell me truthfully, Justin. Do you begrudge me the right to go into business?"

Justin continued inspecting the hoof a few seconds more. Then he let the horse drop its hoof and stood up.

"No," he said. "You're a free woman, and . . ." His voice trailed off and he looked away from her and back to the horses.

"And what?"

"I've got work to do, Abby, and I have no wish to debate the merits of the Whitfields' plans."

"The Whitfields' plans?" She pressed him. "Don't forget Toby and the Johnsons. Do you resent that our families have the resources to support an enterprise?"

"If I did, I would not say it."

"Well, they do," she said. "And I am sorry the Sterlings have been visited by misfortune and poor times."

"As am I," he said with discomfort.

He turned to face the horses and Abigail suddenly felt ashamed to have confronted him.

"Justin, it's not my fault that I am well born, and I do not apologize for it. If I am to be successful, I will have to use my family's wealth."

Justin turned to face her. "I've never begrudged you the Whit-

131

fields' wealth, you know that," he said hotly. "If you were poor as field mice, and I were the sultan of Arabia, I would gladly lavish riches on you. As poor as I am—"

"So that's it," she cut in. "Because you would lavish riches on me if you could, you feel the Whitfields should return the sentiment. Or perhaps Toby Johnson."

"No! You don't understand." He threw down the pick he had been using on the horses' hooves and took a step backward, but his anger appeared to abate. He held his hands up in frustration. "You, you're a woman. Sometimes I wish you *were* Toby Johnson, and we could settle things with our fists until one of us says 'uncle.' "

Her anger vanished, too, and she laughed out loud.

"The Whitfields owe me nothing," he said. "And I certainly don't expect—"

Lightning struck a tree less than thirty yards from where they stood. The crack of splintering wood and a deafening concussion seemed to finish Justin's statement for him.

A muffled cry escaped Abigail's throat. For a fraction of a second they stood still as statues, but the shrieks of the frightened horses brought them back to their senses. The animals reared and jerked against the ropes that staked them to the ground. Another bolt of lightning flashed. Justin lunged at her, catching her about the waist and propelling her away from the colliding, thrashing animals. They tumbled together onto the ground away from the horses' trampling hooves.

She came to rest on her back, reclining on her elbows. Justin was on his stomach, lying next to her. From the looks of it, they could have been enjoying an afternoon picnic, rather than having escaped being crushed by horses. The surprise and incongruity of it made her giddy with laughter. Justin laughed too, and laid his arm over her stomach.

"Are you all right?" he asked.

The glint in Justin's eyes told her he was asking about more than her physical condition. She didn't have time to answer. A gust of wind brought a heavy sheet of cold rain pounding ferociously over them. Laughing again, they leaped to their feet and raced for the protection of the tent.

"Check the fastening holds!" Justin shouted. Abigail complied, knowing that if the tent went down, they would spend a miserable night under wet canvas. Bracing themselves in the wind, they secured the tent from collapsing and were quickly soaked.

Once inside the canvas shelter, they threw off their coats, but their wet clothing clung to their skin and did nothing to disguise Abigail's gooseflesh or the smooth hardness of Justin's chest.

She rubbed at her crossed arms. "Come here and keep me warm."

Justin put his arms around her and held her tight.

"That's better." Her hands roamed over his back.

Justin bent his head and she met his lips in a hungry kiss, but their mouths were blocked by locks of wet hair. Without letting go of each other, they tossed and shook their heads to clear away the sopping strands. After each shake they kissed again, but somehow a persistent string of hair intruded on each kiss. She laughed at their efforts and started to pull away, but he held on to her.

"After all of the obstacles I've faced in my life, and all the measures I've taken to win your heart, Abby, I will not let a bit of hair stop me from kissing you. I'll shave my head bald in the morning, if I must."

"Don't you dare. Old age will take your beautiful hair soon enough. Until then it's mine, wet or dry." She poked him in the ribs and he flinched enough to let go of her.

She brushed his hair away from his face and they kissed again. Her body ached for Justin, but she resisted the urge to hurry.

She wanted to savor each moment, each movement as it unfolded, and remember it forever. When she sensed some restraint in his kisses, one last, lingering shred of uncertainty crept over her. Should she make love to this man, this friend whom she'd known all her life? The single act would change their lives forever. But if they didn't make love now, when? Would there ever be another chance? Her uncertainty drifted away like a storm warning that lingered in the air after the seas had calmed.

As if on cue, the rain pelting against the canvas overhead began to slacken. Pale moonlight daubed the inside of the tent with a chalky white glow. Making love to Justin Sterling would simply be the most perfect, truthful thing she'd ever done in her life. More than that, at that moment she needed Justin's body more than she needed her next breath.

But Justin broke off his kisses and drew back slightly. The look in his eyes also questioned how far they could let things go.

"Abby . . ."

"Hush." She put one hand his cheek. "You have always been a gentleman, Justin Sterling. Frustratingly so, at times. But tonight I trust you will not be sleeping under a tree."

He laughed. "If that's the case, dear Abby, we should get you out of these wet clothes."

"My thoughts exactly."

Quickly, but with the utmost care, they undid each other's buttons, ties, and fastenings. As soon as a layer of clothing came loose, she or Justin would shuck it off and toss it into a growing heap in one corner of the tent. Finally, there was nothing covering their slick, wet skin. In the dim, moonlit tent, they tenderly held each other. Abigail savored the long-awaited sight of the body she had dreamed about so often. She wasn't disappointed. Years of hard work had chiseled Justin's arms, legs, and chest in ways Abigail had only seen in pictures of ancient Greek sculptures. She didn't need to look at his beckoning sex, but he gently moaned when she cradled its firmness in her hands. She felt a moist, undeniable warmth between her legs, but her skin prickled in the chill of the air, sending her nipples erect.

"Where is your blanket?" he asked. "I need you lying down."

She unrolled a blanket on top of the other bedding and, with shallow, quick breaths, they lay down together. She on her back, he on one elbow next to her. When he reached over her shoulder to pull her to him, his hand bumped something solid, covered in fabric. He picked up a small wool purse to move it and a chrome-barreled pocket pistol fell out onto her stomach with a heavy plop.

"Whoa! What's this?" He held up the tiny gun and admired it in the pale moonlight.

"It's just something for protection."

"It's a pretty little thing, but are you expecting trouble?"

"Of the worst kind." She grinned. "My father gave me that. I like to take walks in the evening, and he feels better knowing I have it."

"Henry's hand stays me even here," he muttered.

"Now is not a good time to mention my father."

"You are right, of course. I will focus on a matter of greater importance."

She took the gun out of his hand and set it down beside her. "I promise not to use this, at least not tonight."

"Indeed. Give me a few minutes to experience heaven first, before you send me there." He smoothed his hand lightly over her belly, lingering on her breasts and her neck, then kissed her tenderly, brushing his lips over hers. She teased him, running her tongue lightly over his lips, but she gave a soft, pleasurable moan when he finally rose up over her. As he did so, he pushed the small pistol to a far corner of the tent with his left hand.

"I am yours," she whispered. "I have always been yours."
"And I intend to keep you that way."

CHAPTER SEVENTEEN

The Following Day, 1835

Bright sunlight lit the inside of the tent when Abigail's eyes fluttered open in the morning. She smiled and stretched her arms over her head, until the cool air on her skin reminded her she was naked. She pulled the blanket up to cover her bare breasts. Justin wasn't lying beside her, but the scent of coffee boiling over a fire wafted to her nose. Her smile broadened when memories of the night before flashed through her mind. She'd never expected love to be so fulfilling, so unlike anything she'd ever experienced. She sighed at the new, satisfying comfort of it. A milestone had been passed, and nothing could have made her happier. But her smile quickly disappeared when she realized the implications of what they'd done.

She was going into business with Toby Johnson, and her parents expected the two of them to marry. She needed to disabuse her parents of that idea, if she could, as soon as possible. Justin would believe, and rightly so, that their lovemaking signaled a commitment. She wanted as much herself, but what would she tell her parents? Any hint of what had happened the night before would certainly terminate her father's support for her horse farm. He might throw her out of the house altogether. That would resolve the matter once and for all, but Abigail wished she could make her parents understand her love for Justin without putting an end to her business with Toby, much less destroying her relationship with her family. She had to make them see reason, but it wouldn't be easy. She resolved to bide her time and bring her parents around gradually to the idea that marrying Justin was the right thing to do. Even so, the joy and happiness at the wonderful love she'd reveled in earlier slid away. It was quickly replaced by an inky black cloud that covered her hopes with trepidation and fear.

She sat up and gathered the scattered pieces of her clothing together to dress. The tent flap was closed but, given what had transpired the night before, Justin might come into the tent unannounced. Once she'd dressed and tied her boots, she took a deep breath, opened the tent flap, and stepped into the chill morning air. The coffee pot was indeed boiling, and there were two metal cups set on a rock next to the fire to warm. But Justin wasn't there. She looked back and forth, thinking at first that he might have left camp altogether and gone down the trail, leaving the fallen woman to her own fate. But no; he was brushing the horses and readying them for the day. She picked up a cloth lying next to the cups and used it as a hot pad to pull the coffee pot away from the fire.

"Are you ready for a cup?" She waved one of the tin cups in the air for Justin to see.

He glanced her way and nodded. Then he gathered up his equipment and walked over to her.

"Good morning," he said.

"Good morning to you." She brushed her hair back with one hand and held out a steaming cup of coffee to him, which he accepted. She was suddenly conscious that her hair must be a mess and her clothing as rumpled as the bedding she'd slept in. She felt her cheeks heat as she refastened her blouse where she'd missed a buttonhole. Then she brushed a few bits of grass away from her skirt. Justin wasn't quite smiling, and she couldn't tell from the tone of his voice what mood he was in.

He sipped the coffee, his suddenly playful eyes watching her over the rim of his cup. "You look as though you slept in a barrel last night."

She put a hand on her hip, pretending offense, and opened her mouth to object, but he continued.

"As bed-tossed and disheveled as you are, you are a delight to my eyes this morning."

She was caught off guard and her mouth hung open.

He grinned and glanced at the trees around them. "The gentle, doe-eyed fawn and all of the colorful birds of this forest are quiet this morning. They're in awe, I think, and silenced in the presence of your unnatural beauty." He swept his free hand around to encompass their surroundings. "As for myself, I could not be happier if every morning of my life I met you in the same, truly dreadful condition in which you stand before me now."

She finally laughed.

"Did you sleep well?" he asked.

"Never better." She wanted to kiss him. She wanted to drag him back to the tent before breakfast, but dismay still held her and swamped her desire for him. "Justin, there is something I need to tell you."

"Trust me," he said. "I learned all I needed to know last night." His eyes twinkled as he sipped again, but she could see his neck and shoulders stiffen.

"No, you didn't." She gave him a grim smile, and the playful light in his eyes was gone in an instant. "Justin, all you learned last night is the simple truth, which is that I love you. I think I have always loved you. I always will."

"You said as much last night. You said it simply, that's true, but with great eloquence." But his lips pursed, as he knew another shoe was about to drop. "There is nothing more I need to hear."

"I wish that were so, but now I must tell you the complicated truth that follows us into the light of day." She looked down at her boots. "As much as I love you, my life is not my own. Not yet, anyway."

Justin froze, then tossed the remaining coffee from his cup into the fire and looked away at the trees. "What's that sound? Did you hear it? I think it was your father's voice."

"Aye, it was. And, for the moment, at least, I can't say no to him. But I will. I promise you—"

"Stop. Say no more." He tossed the empty cup onto a rations bag on the ground. "I think I know the rest of this complicated truth. Henry Whitfield doesn't believe I'd make a worthy husband for his daughter." He put his clenched fists on his hips.

"My father's opinions are old-fashioned and he is narrow of mind. But he intends well and I love him in spite of his shortcomings."

"Henry is my demise."

"You are plenty good enough for Father, and he knows it. He simply resists accepting it, but I will sway his feelings. And Mother will support me."

"Your mother has been kind to me. But to live with Henry, she must be a saint. I hope he appreciates her."

"Mother has her own way with my father."

Justin looked over her shoulder, as if he wanted to travel on down the road and leave the discussion behind.

"I appreciate your honesty, but I'm not sure I've ever seen Henry change his mind about anything. If I'm not good enough in his eyes, I'm not good enough."

"Few if any men are, but you're very well good enough for me." She touched his arm and gave him a wan smile.

He covered her hand with his own. "If there were anything I could do to satisfy Henry, I'd do it. You know that."

"I do." She stepped closer and placed a soft kiss on his lips. He hesitated at first, then he wrapped her in his arms and kissed her with such strength and tenderness it was as if he'd never get the chance again.

To Abigail's frustration, Justin appeared resigned once again to losing her. Each evening, once they'd stopped for the day, Justin would tend to the horses, then build a fire and prepare a simple meal for the two of them. She helped when she could, but Justin didn't ask for any assistance. After their meal, Justin kept watch until well after she had retired to the tent. He slept outside, under a tree, if he slept at all, and he was up and preparing breakfast before she awoke. Then they resumed their journey with little or no conversation. Much less any ardent kisses between new lovers.

To a stranger, Justin might appear to have forgotten about the one night of passion they'd shared, but Abigail knew that wasn't what caused him to keep his distance. If Henry would never let him marry her, Justin wouldn't torture himself further by taking what love and passion she could give him in the little time they had left together. He was reluctant even to discuss the situation. Better to forget what he might never know again. She couldn't convince him that her father hadn't betrothed her to Tobias, so she redoubled her commitment to changing her father's mind about Justin. In the meantime, Justin had withdrawn to save himself, and her, from further pain and frustration, until such a day that their love might be legitimate. If that day could ever come.

Justin once again treated her with respect and friendship, but he would barely return a kiss on the cheek or clasp her hand when she placed hers gently on his. He wouldn't shrink from these familiarities, but wouldn't commit to any gesture that hinted at more than a casual relationship. Even so, Abigail still saw the desire burning in Justin's eyes, and the frustration that tensed the muscles in his neck and shoulders, even if he were remarking on something as insignificant as the bright coloring on the blue jays they saw chattering in the trees. His emotional distance anguished her. She wanted to pour her heart out to him, to make him love her again. Instead, she wept alone in the tent, then steeled herself to accept Justin's attitude as the best course of action, at least until she convinced her father she must marry for love and nothing else.

The remainder of the journey passed without incident, save one. When they were but one day's travel from home, they encountered a handful of game-hunting Cherokee Indians on the road. They eyed each other warily, waiting to see if the other would give way, until Justin greeted them and offered tobacco. Not wishing to give offense, the Cherokee offered Justin a portion of dried beef and invited him and Abby to rest a few minutes while they smoked. Their chief, no older than Justin, had worked as a guide for white settlers and spoke some English. His name was Atohi. While everyone sat beneath a spreading oak tree, Atohi leaned over and spoke to Justin, but well within Abigail's hearing.

"Please tell me."

"Tell you what?" Justin asked.

"How many horses will you take for your woman?"

Justin nearly burst out in laughter, but he turned away from Atohi and looked at Abby to hide his face. When he'd controlled his reaction, he spoke calmly to the chief.

"Atohi, you have an excellent eye for women." He gestured at Abby. "This particular woman is not mine. She is the daughter of a white chief where I live. She is worth many horses."

"I will give you six," Atohi said.

Justin put his hand to his chin, appearing to consider the offer.

"*Justin*, what are you doing?" she said. "Please don't—"

"Be quiet." Justin raised his hand to stop her. Then, to Atohi he said, "As you can see, this woman's hips are strong. She is

142

young, and she will provide a man with many children."

Atohi nodded, clearly impressed. "I will give you eight horses."

"*Juss-tinnn!*" Abigail knew Justin wasn't happy with her but couldn't believe he would sell her to a band of wandering Indians.

"Your offer is very generous," Justin said. "Especially since this woman's tongue is as strong as her hips."

"A woman's tongue can be trained." Atohi smiled. "But not as easily as a horse can be trained."

Justin allowed himself the slightest chuckle and nodded appreciatively at Atohi's joke, but he slipped into a more serious demeanor. "The white chief whose daughter this is has been offered fifty horses. I would dishonor him if I accepted any less."

"Justin! How dare you!" she hissed. "My father will have you shot!"

Atohi's eyes grew wide, but he looked over at Abby and openly studied her hair, her breasts, and her hips. He glanced at the anger in her eyes and her clenched jaw and pursed lips more than once.

"I understand what you say," he said, finally. "She is a great prize, that's true. But I do not have fifty horses with me that I can give the white chief."

"I am disappointed, but I, too, understand." Justin nodded. "Let us say nothing more of this woman." He dismissed Abby with a wave of his hand. "May we meet again on some other day when we are better able to trade."

"Yes, may we meet again and trade." They shook hands, officially ending the negotiation, and Atohi focused on his pipe. Justin chewed on a piece of dried beef.

Abigail sat in silence with her arms crossed and refused to look at either of them. She couldn't tell whether the chief was disappointed or relieved at having failed to purchase her, but then she realized Justin couldn't have refused to negotiate. It would have been rude and brought dishonor on the chief in front of his men. If that happened, the chief might have chosen to take her by force to salvage his pride, and she and Justin were outnumbered by the well-armed Indians. It was only by her own loud objections and Justin blaming her father for setting too high a price that he'd been able to negotiate an honorable conclusion for both sides.

Atohi's pipe had gone out. He turned the bowl over and knocked out spent ash. Justin saw this and remembered a plug of tobacco his father had given him to compare with what he found in Kentucky. He hadn't smoked it or any of his tobacco because Abigail was with him.

"Atohi, please take this." He pulled the plug of tobacco and his knife from his shoulder bag. He deftly cut off a short length and held it out to Atohi, but the Indian stared at his knife.

"Where did you obtain this?" He pointed at the blade.

Justin looked at the knife, too, wondering what sparked the Indian's interest. "It was a gift," he said. "From an Indian boy. In return for a small act of friendship."

Atohi's eyes grew wide. "The spirits weave a very small web."

Justin gave him a questioning look.

"The gift was from me," Atohi gave Justin a quick bow of his head.

"Yes?" Justin thought Atohi might be boasting. The knife had nothing special about it, other than its Indian design and the manner in which Justin had acquired it. It must look no different than a thousand other Indian knives.

"It was a time of great hunger for us," Atohi said. "The gift of your fish was much appreciated."

"It was you!" Justin grinned. "I'm glad I have finally met you, Atohi."

They clasped arms and Atohi smiled. "Now that I know who

you are, I know the white chief whose daughter this is. I wish great luck upon the man who desires to make this woman one of his wives." He winked at Justin.

"You are a wise man, Atohi. A very wise man indeed." Justin struck a match and helped the Indian light his pipe.

As soon as it seemed proper, Abigail and Justin said goodbye to Atohi and his band, and they each continued on their way. Once they were out of sight of the natives, Abigail gave Justin a stern, angry look.

"Why would you even *consider* trading me to Indians?" She slapped him on the shoulder.

"Why not? Imagine how relieved your parents would be to learn that you'd finally found a husband."

They both burst out laughing.

When they finally reached Ridgetop, Justin was stopped at the Whitfield fence line by some of Henry's waiting farmhands. He turned over the horses to them but, notwithstanding Abby's disbelief and outrage, Justin was forbidden to come any farther onto Whitfield land. Moreover, the men said Justin was forbidden to see her at all from that day forth. Contrary to Abigail's prediction, her father had been stewing in his anger as he waited for his daughter to arrive home. He blamed Justin for taking her with him rather than seeing that she traveled by the safer, swifter, steamboat.

Given the level of her father's anger, Abigail thought it best not to confront him immediately with the fact that she was in love with Justin. Her father needed time to accept that no harm had come to her during the journey, and that his anger was unjustified. Once he had calmed down, she would remind him that Justin was an honorable man and convince him Justin was worthy of her hand. Thankfully, no one pressed her with questions about what happened on the journey home.

In those drowsy moments in bed each night before she was

quite asleep, she imagined eloping with Justin. If she resorted to that desperate plan, she might never have the wedding she'd always hoped for, but she would be happy anyway. Her mother would help her, she felt sure. Either way, if she and Justin were living on the Sterling farm, practically next door to her parents, eventually they would be forced to accept Justin as her husband. Surely in time her father's opinions would soften, when he saw how well Justin treated her. When the grandchildren came. When . . .

The anticipation of a confrontation with her father often gave her nightmares, one of which suddenly came true.

CHAPTER EIGHTEEN

Ridgetop, Tennessee, Late November 1835

Abigail remained firm, but tried not to raise her voice. She hoped to end the conversation with her parents as quickly as possible. "You act as though I went into business with Toby to breed children, not horses, but I do not recall seeing marriage recitals in the terms of our contract."

Her father set down his quill pen and looked at his daughter. "Don't patronize me, Abigail. You know why we agreed to let you raise horses with Tobias Johnson. You simply needed time to get accustomed to the idea of marriage."

"What I *need* is the right to make up own mind."

"What is so awful about Tobias Johnson?" her mother asked. "You've been the best of friends all your lives."

"It's simple, Mother." Abigail waved her hands in the air in frustration. "A friend he may be, but I do not love Tobias Johnson and, therefore, I do not wish to marry him. Would Father marry one of his Louisville lawyers, just because they have a business arrangement?"

"Abigail! Don't talk to your mother like that."

Henrietta hid a smile behind the book she'd been reading.

"I am sorry, Father, but the comparison is apt."

"Look, Abigail. Your mother and I are not getting any younger and, yes, we would dearly love grandchildren. But there is a more immediate concern, and that is preserving and continuing what we have built in Ridgetop."

147

"What you've *built*? Will your barns and fields disappear if I do not marry Toby? Will the crops stop growing?"

Her father stood up from his desk and put his hands on his hips. He spoke through clenched teeth, and Abigail had never seen him so angry, at least not with her. She sat back in her chair, instinctively moving away from the controlled rage she saw in his eyes.

"Your mother and I have given you a good life, Abigail, and we've asked very little in return. We are dealing with concerns here, real concerns, that are much greater than your romantic concept of love. Even so, we've given you plenty of time to decide things for yourself. And you haven't."

Abigail didn't think she had been allowed to decide anything. She opened her mouth to speak, but her father held up his hand and stopped her.

"Now it must end. In this one matter, Abigail, you will not, you cannot, disobey me. I know what's best for you, even if you cannot see it for yourself. The marriage will take place. I have arranged it with Thomas Johnson. That is the end of this discussion as far as I am concerned. Henrietta, see if you can talk some sense into your daughter, as I cannot." With that he stalked from the room.

Abigail and her mother looked at each other in silence, listening to Henry's heavy footfalls as he mounted the back stairs to the master bedroom.

"Can you talk to him for me?" She pleaded. "I simply cannot marry Toby Johnson."

"And why not?" Her mother took a deep breath. "Tobias is not an un-handsome man, you know. I dare say he's better looking than many other men in the county. Any number of girls would leap at the opportunity to become Mrs. Tobias Johnson."

Abigail's shoulders sagged and she put a hand on the arm of

her chair for support. "Would you have me enter into a loveless marriage, simply to satisfy Father's financial plans?"

"Abigail, you may not realize this, but I know a thing or two about love. In spite of what you may read in your novels, love is not something that springs forth on a whim. It does not burst into flames when you're in the arms of a handsome stranger."

"I don't require a stranger, just some passion. Some fire." She thought of her night with Justin.

"True love is not a fire burning in your heart," her mother said. "That kind of love isn't, well, it isn't real. It isn't lasting. True love is something you need to earn and work to achieve with a man. Even though you've known Toby most of your life, you will learn many more things about him and yourself the longer you are together. You will grow close and in the end, you will know real love."

"In the end? You mean love is a reward I will earn after suffering a lifetime of a man's peculiar habits, the way he picks his teeth after he's eaten his evening meal? The way he mounts me in bed?"

"Abigail! Love is much more than intercourse. You know that."

"Yes, but why have intercourse at all with a man you don't love? Oh, don't answer. It's to birth children or, as Father believes, to preserve an estate. I truly am being bred to Tobias Johnson." She put her head in her hands and fought back tears.

Her mother stiffened. "If you prefer to see it that way, you may. But I hope you can get accustomed to the idea of a practical marriage. Think of it as a wonderful opportunity."

"Mother. I must tell you, I love another. With all my heart."

Her mother gave her a stern, knowing look that suddenly softened.

"It's Justin, isn't it?"

"Of course." She hadn't meant to mention Justin. She only

meant to put off her parents' insistence that she marry Toby, or anyone else of their choosing. But, having confessed her love for Justin, she knew it felt right.

"I'm not surprised." Her mother wrung her hands. "I wish there was something I could do, but I'm sorry. Your father will never accept Justin."

"But he must." She pounded her fists on the arms of the chair. "Don't you see? Marrying Toby Johnson will be the death of me."

Her mother gave a surprisingly deep sigh of resignation and spoke in a near whisper. "Believe it or not, I know something about lost love, too. But Tobias isn't so bad as you make him sound. Your father has made up his mind, and we're going to have to make the best of it."

With that she rose from her chair, plucked up her skirts, and followed her husband up the stairs.

CHAPTER NINETEEN

December 15, 1835

"Unbelievable." Sally Marston set her cup on its saucer, and Abigail couldn't tell if the look her friend gave her was more pity, sympathy, or concern.

They were alone in the tea shop, except for Mrs. Wilkins, the proprietress. Abigail had just told Sally in whispered tones of her trip back from Kentucky, and of her forced engagement to Tobias Johnson.

"It's going to be an awful Christmas without Justin," Abigail said.

"What are you going to do?"

"I am at my wits' end. My father has me watched every minute of the day."

"That would explain the servant waiting for you in front of the livery?"

Abigail nodded. "He is to accompany me wherever I go, and I am forbidden to speak to Justin or even ride in the direction of the Sterling farm. It was all I could do to meet you for tea."

"I can talk to Justin if you like."

"No." Abigail shook her head. "Please tell no one, especially not Justin. The engagement hasn't been announced, and I am determined to change my father's mind. If I can't, I will escape in the night and seek refuge at the Sterling farm."

"How romantic!"

"How desperate. Justin knows my father is angry, but we

both hope things will work out before it's too late. Until then, if Justin finds out I'm nearly a prisoner, he'll come charging into my house with a shotgun."

"That could be very romantic, too. Assuming it's not you who gets shot."

Abigail chuckled. "I'll get to talk to Justin soon enough."

"And what will you tell him?"

Abigail sighed. "I don't know, but I want to talk sense into my father. Make him see that I can't marry Toby."

"And what about Tobias. Is he looking forward to the, well, arrangement?"

"Truly, I have no idea. I haven't spoken to him, either, since my father's decision, but he must know about it. Toby's father is as old-fashioned as mine, so Toby may have no more choice in the matter than I. He was happy enough to go into business with me, but I've not otherwise encouraged him."

"Suppose he tells Justin?"

"He might. He and Justin have been so competitive over the years. Toby might believe he's won something from Justin if he's in possession of Justin's lover." Abigail put her head in her hands. "Sally, am I headed for disaster?"

"All the more reason for you to quickly come to terms with your father."

Abigail nodded. As she bit into a cookie, she glanced up at a stranger who came through the door of the tea shop. His high boots clomped across the wooden floor, and his shoulder-length, graying red hair flowed from beneath a broad-brimmed hat. He was an interesting character who, Abigail judged, wasn't quite as old as her father, but perhaps a little older than her mother. Dust spotted his greatcoat, and he had two or three days' growth of rust-colored but graying beard, not unusual for a man who had traveled some distance. He walked directly to the counter, set a large leather valise on the floor, and placed both hands flat on the zinc countertop in front of Mrs. Wilkins.

"Good day, madam," he said in greeting.

"Good day to you, sir. How may I be of service?"

"Would you be kind enough to give me directions to the Whitfield farm?"

"Oh, my," Abigail whispered. She held her half-eaten cookie in the air with one hand and held her other hand up to quiet Sally. But Sally, too, had heard the man's request and turned in her seat to look at him.

"I might give you directions," Mrs. Wilkins said. "But if it's a Whitfield you're looking for, perhaps Miss Abigail Whitfield can help you." She gestured in Abigail's direction with her palm up.

"Abigail . . . Whitfield? How fortunate." The man sounded uncertain of her name, and Abigail didn't recognize him, but when he turned to look at her, a smile came to his lips and a vague light of familiarity shone in his eyes. He approached their table and bowed slightly. "Pardon me ladies, please." Looking at Abigail, he said, "Abigail is a fine name, and, if I may speak so boldly, you appear to be a fine young lady."

She set down her cup and exchanged a questioning look with Sally. Ridgetop got its share of salesmen, traders, and other travelers, but Abigail hadn't met many who asked for her family's farm by name, and then complimented her for no apparent reason. She felt the need for caution.

"Please forgive me," she said. "I don't believe I have ever made your acquaintance."

"No, of course not." The man's smile faded. "It is I who should ask your forgiveness. And no, we have never met, but I would recognize you anywhere." He held his palms out as if he were admiring a fine painting. "My name is Browning. Archibald Browning."

The name wasn't familiar to Abigail, although she knew she had relatives whom she'd never met, mostly in the east.

"This is Miss Sally Marston." She gestured at her friend.

Browning doffed his dusty hat, but he only glanced at Sally and said, "A pleasure to meet you." His gaze fixed on Abigail again.

If he were interested only in meeting young ladies, Sally was as good-looking as any girl in the valley. But the man was particularly interested in Abigail, which both piqued Abby's curiosity and heightened her apprehension.

"I am a surveyor by trade," Browning said. "Have been most of my life. I work out of Virginia, and in all these years I have never traveled to this part of Tennessee until now. I am in charge of a team sent here to map the area for the government in Washington."

"Welcome to Ridgetop, Mr. Browning." Sally smiled at him, then looked at Abigail with a slightly raised eyebrow, as if to say, "What's this all about?"

"Thank you, miss." Browning glanced at Sally with some concern, as though she were a problem, but he spoke again to Abigail.

"You *are* the daughter of Henrietta Whitfield, are you not?"

"Yes, she is my mother." The man's interest in her mother, or any of her family, seemed odd and, because he was a stranger, misplaced.

"You have Henrietta's eyes," Browning said.

A chill swept down the back of Abigail's neck, in spite of the overheated tea shop. "Do you know my mother?" She thought it time Browning got to the point of their conversation.

"Yes . . . well, no," Browning said. He seemed unsure of himself again. "I mean, I knew your mother a long time ago. We were very close, but we fell out of touch. I haven't spoken to her in many years."

That seemed innocent enough to her. "Perhaps you'd like to come to the farm. I'm sure Mother would be delighted to meet an old friend."

Browning frowned. "I would enjoy that, I would. But I think it's quite fortunate that I've found you here first."

"Oh?" That raised Abigail's eyebrows and brought back her apprehension.

"Perhaps I might talk to you," he said. "Alone." He glanced at Sally. "I have . . . well, a bit of news that I feel only you should hear before anyone else."

"Very well." Sally patted Abigail's hand and rose from the table. "I should be going anyway. I expect we will continue our conversation soon."

Abigail didn't want Sally to leave, but it didn't look as though Browning would talk to her if she stayed. Sally gave her a knowing smile and a wink. She'd want to hear all about Mr. Browning later.

"Good day, Mr. Browning."

"Good day, miss."

Browning watched Sally leave, then glanced around the shop and spied Mrs. Wilkins watching them.

"There is a bench outside," he said. "Under a lovely old oak. It's a fine December day. Let's go sit outside and get some fresh air, shall we?"

"Very well." Abigail reached for her coat, which Browning helped her put on. She wasn't seriously concerned for her safety; the bench sat in full view of the open front door of the tea shop and Mrs. Wilkins. Browning seemed harmless enough, and he would hardly do anything untoward in such a public place, especially with one of her father's servants watching them. Even if he did, Abigail still carried the pocket pistol in her purse. In any case, whatever Browning wanted to talk about might at least be a diversion from worrying about her future. She rose from the table and Browning offered her his arm. She noticed

Mrs. Wilkins's curious look as Browning escorted her out the door.

"It's all right," she said to the proprietress as they passed the front counter. "We'll be chatting just outside, and one of my father's servants is waiting for me nearby."

Mrs. Wilkins nodded, but gave her a stern "watch yourself young lady" look anyway.

Outside, a comfortable whitewashed bench surrounded the trunk of the tree, allowing travelers to rest while facing in any direction. No one else occupied the bench when Abigail and Browning sat down. She made sure there was at least two feet between their legs and waved at the waiting servant, who had nearly dozed off atop a barrel at the livery.

"Well, now. What bit of news do you bring from Virginia?" Her voice cracked, and she wished for a glass of water.

Browning looked her in the eye. "There is nothing to be gained by putting off the most important fact, and I am sorry if this startles you, but it's just this. I am your father."

She gaped at the man, then laughed out loud. "You make fun of me! Nothing could be more preposterous." But she glanced again at Browning's graying red hair. His stern eyes, pale but almost as green as hers, told her the man did not intend to be lighthearted.

"No, I am in earnest. I am your father. I've waited a long, long time to tell you this, and I can explain myself if you'll permit me."

She remembered to breathe and put one hand lightly over her beating heart. "I don't know what you mean, or how what you say could be true."

"I know this . . . this news comes as a shock, but it's an undeniable fact."

The chocolate nonpareil sugar cookies in Abigail's stomach

turned flip-flops. Who was this man? Was he touched in the head?

"Surely you don't expect me to believe such nonsense." Feeling her cheeks heat with embarrassment, she gathered up her skirt to leave, but Browning put a hand gently on her arm, stopping her.

"Of course you disbelieve me, but before you go, tell me this. Does your mother still have a slight scar on her thigh, close to her right hip? It's reminiscent of a small red rose, if I recall."

Browning removed his hand, but Abigail froze. She had seen her mother's odd scar on several occasions when she was younger. She had almost forgotten the mark, a silent witness to some long-ago injury Abigail never knew of, and never thought to ask about. If Browning were not a physician and had firsthand knowledge of the scar, he must have seen it under the most intimate of circumstances.

"You've just heard someone's odd story," she said. "And I would not reveal anything about my mother's limbs to a stranger."

"As well you should not." Browning grinned. "But your protest falls short." He gently wagged a finger at her. "I see in your eyes that you know of the scar, and you may believe me."

She shook her head. "I admit nothing. I will listen a moment longer, but then I must be going."

"Fair enough. I can tell you the story of how I met your mother, if you care to hear it."

How could she not? She sat back and glanced at the waiting servant. Then she judged the distance between the bench and the door to the tea shop, should she need to leave in haste. "You seem to mean no harm, but you must know that I don't believe a word you've said so far. Even so, I'll listen to your fantasy a few minutes more."

"Oh, it was like a fantasy for me, I assure you. But real, so real."

For the next half hour, Archibald Browning wove a story for Abigail that turned everything she knew about her family upside down.

"I met your mother more than thirty years ago," he said. "It was in December of 1799. We were quite young, and our families had traveled to Mount Vernon to attend the funeral of George Washington. It was an emotional time for everyone, as you can imagine."

"It must have been." Abigail set her jaw but tried not to show any reaction. She remembered little of her life before her parents brought her to Ridgetop from Virginia. She had heard her mother's stories about Washington's funeral, but she refused to believe whatever this strange man said, even if he knew certain things about her mother. Still, she felt compelled to listen.

"I spied your mother immediately at the reception," Browning continued, "and I made it a point to speak to her. I think she saw the sparkle in my eye, and perhaps the emotions of that sad event helped move things along, but she and I talked much longer than I'd hoped was possible. Afterward, I made it a point to correspond with her. I became a young civil servant with an uncertain future, but I kept up my correspondence as it was the best way to press my cause without drawing any harsh judgment from her father. He undoubtedly felt his daughter would forget all about me after the funeral and nothing would come of it. He was wrong. Henrietta eventually told him of my letters. He didn't entirely approve, but at long last he agreed to let me come calling."

If Browning were inventing a story, it was as good as any novel Abigail had read. It reminded her of the far-fetched romantic tales she'd told her mother, of how Abigail would meet the love of her life. She was starting to feel a little sympathy for Mr. Browning whom, she decided, must have struck a fine figure as a younger man.

"I was in love as I'd never been before," he said. "And I believed the feeling was mutual. Even so, I was uncertain how to go about wooing Henrietta. Eventually I convinced her father I had credentials enough to be an adequate suitor. I'm sad to say it took a number of years before he realized I was serious and he accepted me. Sadder still, it was only a few months after that when I learned that my work would take me away from Virginia, and from my love, for an extended period of time. We had talked of marriage secretly, of course, but I wasn't sure when I'd return. Henrietta wanted to go with me, and I was sorely tempted, but I could hardly take her. The frontier was dangerous, unsettled territory, after all."

"Of course. You might have been forced to trade her to Indians for a horse or something," she said.

"How's that?"

"Nothing, really. Just a story of my own. Go on, please."

Abigail could hardly believe her mother had taken such a lover as Browning, given the practical explanation of love her mother had given her. Had her mother once experienced such romantic passion as to consider following a man west? She had come as far as Ridgetop, but was Browning certain he was talking about *her* mother?

"You see the trouble," Browning said. "If you've been in love, you know that such a separation would be the finest of tortures."

Suddenly it didn't matter whether Browning's story was true. Sympathetic tears threatened to sting her eyes. Were the tears for Browning, or for herself and Justin?

"I am sorry if my story affects you so," he said. "I have carried it in my heart for so many years, I know no other way to tell it."

Abigail nodded and dabbed at her eyes with a kerchief.

"Please go on."

"As the day of my departure approached, we could no longer restrain ourselves." Browning looked away delicately for a moment. "To put it politely, love overcame caution. Some weeks after I was gone, Henrietta learned she was with child."

Thus, Abigail thought, Mr. Browning would have me believe I was conceived.

"I see," she said. "But the sequence of events as you tell them doesn't prove anything."

"It proves we were foolish. Or I was, at least. I accept all the blame. We told ourselves we'd marry as soon as I returned. I wrote her letters almost every day, but what could I do with them? There was no postal service on the frontier. I was constantly on the move, and communications of any kind were problematic. Receiving a letter was impossible. Unknown to me, Henrietta's condition, her pregnancy, progressed. All the while she had little news of me. What could she do?"

"What did she do?" Abigail now needed to know.

Browning leaned back against the oak. "Henry Whitfield had his eye on Henrietta even then. He was a young man of means, but he was the second son of a Virginia plantation owner with a questionable inheritance."

Poor Henry. No wonder he feared for his estate. Still, Abigail could hardly believe what she was hearing. "And so my father stepped in?"

"Not immediately. Henrietta expected me to return. I desperately wanted to, of course. In spite of the efforts of Henrietta's family to keep the scandal secret, Henry learned of her condition. And of my prolonged absence. Needless to say, my reputation grew more questionable with each passing day. Eventually, Henrietta agreed to marry, and Henry took her with him here to Tennessee, where no one would be the wiser. Henrietta must have assumed I'd given up. Or worse, that I'd been scalped by Indians. They married quickly, but given Henrietta's delicate state, they didn't leave for Tennessee until well after you were born."

Abigail had only vague memories of Virginia, and of the long journey west.

"When I returned to Virginia and found out what had happened, I was devastated. It was much too late for me to intervene. They had been gone for some time, and I felt it best not to disrupt Henrietta's life any further."

Browning looked away at the sky. His gaze softened, and he spoke to himself as much as to Abigail. "I pined to see her. To speak to her or just to hold her hand. The idea that I had fathered a child I might never see tortured me until I considered, well, ending my own miserable life. It was over anyway, as far as I was concerned. They say time heals all wounds, but that's not entirely true. The scars on my heart have never healed, although I've learned to live with the pain."

"You poor man," she said. But Abigail wasn't ready to accept that Browning was talking about her mother, or her. Not without some further independent corroboration.

"I was absolutely the poorest," he said. "Oh, I pulled myself together and buried myself in my work. But life had lost its meaning. I hadn't planned to come to Ridgetop. In truth, I've done everything I could to stay away, but my work has finally forced me. I'm here now, and I wonder if enough time has passed for the wounds I'd caused Henrietta to be healed. Or, if not healed, perhaps your mother is capable of forgiving me." He pointed at the tea shop. "I was asking for directions to your farm, but dare I make contact with your mother? Even now I'm not sure."

Abigail didn't know what to say. If Browning was a charlatan, coming to her home would confirm whether his story was true. But if his story was true, what chaos would his appearance cause? She sat quietly on the bench, her head bowed, examining the red and brown colors of the fallen leaves at her feet, conscious that Browning studied her almost without blinking, as if to memorize every detail of the daughter he had never before seen. She couldn't deny some physical resemblance between herself and this man, but what she should do with Browning's story she had no idea.

"Is your mother well?" Browning asked.

"Yes, yes." She looked up and brushed the hair from her eyes, red hair and green eyes this man would have her believe she inherited from him. "I cannot tell you she is ready or even willing to see you."

Browning's fists clenched, and she felt a stab of sympathy for him. As touching as Browning's tale was, it might still be the invented musings of a master storyteller. Or he could be talking about another woman entirely.

She sat up straighter. "Of course Mother and, uh, Father, have never discussed any of this with me, even if what you say is true."

"Of course. And I suppose there's no reason for you to believe me, or to want to believe me."

"It *is* a fantastic story, to be sure. Have you never married? Is there no other family in your life?" She held fast to the idea that this man would go away. Her life could go on with its own complications, which were enough without any question of her parentage.

"There is no one else. I pledged I would stay true to Henrietta, and I have. Whether that's due to my own fortitude or by mere chance, I cannot say, but I have never met anyone I loved as much as her. Unfortunately for me, every woman I've met since has suffered by the comparison."

A smile crept to Abigail's lips. She'd never heard anyone, including her father, speak of her mother in such dramatic and ardent terms. She almost wished Browning's story were true, and that she could reunite her mother with her long-lost love. But people change, and Abigail had never heard any hint of such a morally questionable incident in her mother's past.

"Aren't you worried that, after so much time, my mother may no longer live up to your image of her? And what of my father? He would look askance at a competitor for his wife's affections, even if the question has long been put to rest." As she said this, Abigail remembered an old saying, that unrequited love is the strongest of all. But had Browning's love been unrequited? How would her mother react if Browning came back into her life, even for a day?

Browning nodded his agreement with Abigail's reservations. "Henrietta is no longer young, I know, and neither am I. For better or worse, our lives and our emotions have seasoned with passing time, but what I saw in your mother, those special qualities I fell in love with, they're far more than physical beauty. And those good qualities are ones that time could not erode."

"Not time," Abigail whispered, "but apparently you haven't met my father."

Browning gave her a sideways look. "Mr. Whitfield has not treated her well?"

"Better than well," Abigail said. "She wants for nothing, and Henry loves her, in his way, but I have never heard him express his feelings for my mother with quite the ardor I hear from you."

Browning smiled. "No man could, I dare say."

"Archibald. May I call you Archibald?"

"I don't expect you to call me father, but my friends call me Archie."

"Archie then. You must accept that your presence at my home would create a monstrous disruption. Even more than your claim to be my father would in me, if I let it."

163

Browning lowered his head. "Yes. And as much as I still love Henrietta, I am prepared that she might refuse to see me. I cannot blame her, and I truly do not wish to disrupt her comfortable life. Or Henry's or yours, for that matter. It was almost too fortunate for me to meet you here by this accident. To finally see my daughter fully grown and so beautiful."

"Please, sir. Archie. I hardly know you."

"Much to my sorrow."

To her own surprise, Abigail placed her hand on Browning's arm. "Archie. I can't tell you whether I believe your story or not. I can't even say whether I want to believe you. But I hear the suffering in your voice and, as Henry has said many times at Sunday services, there is truth in suffering. But I can't believe my mother is ready to see you, and so unexpectedly."

"I understand. I had only hoped, but I knew this might be the case." He reached into his coat and withdrew a worn, wrinkled letter envelope. "I've written to Henrietta many times over the years, but never dared to post my feverish ramblings." He placed the envelope in her lap. "This is a more thoughtful recitation of my feelings. I should not ask this of you, but would you do me the very great favor of delivering it to your mother personally?"

She clutched the worn paper and felt the thickness of the sheets within. "I have listened to your story, and I admit a certain sympathy for you. But on your claim that you are my father, I have no response. As for this . . ." She held up the envelope and stared at it.

"I can't expect you to believe me at once," he said. "I don't expect you to greet me with open arms and toss out your family history. We all have our own lives, and they must go on as they were. As for the truth of what I've told you, only your mother can confirm it. But you need not deliver that letter today. Wait as long as you feel you must. Do so at a time of your choosing.

Do it when it might best suit your mother."

"After Henry is gone, perhaps?"

"If you so desire." He shook his head. "Once again, I don't expect your mother to leave Henry. I only want her to know I did not abandon her. That I still love her to this day. What she does with that knowledge is entirely up to her. I have not asked anything of her in this writing. I only express my loss and my sorrow at the unexpected turns our lives have taken. And I ask her to forgive me."

Abigail felt tears well in her eyes again. She couldn't help but compare Browning's love with what she felt for Justin. Her greatest fear at that moment was that her own love might never be realized, either, with Justin at her side. "I feel sorry for you," she said. "To have suffered all these years. I will take this, but I don't know if I can deliver it, or when. I can't make you any promises."

"I understand."

She tapped the envelope. "Does this provide a means by which my mother can reply to you, if she chooses?"

"Yes. And my work crew may overwinter in the county, but if I never hear from Henrietta, at least I'll know she has finally learned how I feel. That's all I can ask."

Browning stood up as Abigail, too, rose from the bench. She turned to him and held out her hand, which he shook warmly. She glanced at the tea shop, then at a few scudding winter clouds overhead. She felt as if all of these things should have utterly changed by what she'd just heard.

"You tell a very interesting story, Archie. And your appearance has provided me with an unusually interesting morning."

He bowed. "Whether you believe me or not, it was a pleasure to finally meet you, Abigail. A very great pleasure indeed." He smiled at her as only a father could, and she warmed a little under his gaze. She stared at him for a moment, trying to decide if the man actually could be her real father.

And, if he was, what did that mean for her?

CHAPTER TWENTY

January 1836

The sun had not yet risen above the horizon, but neither that nor a persistent drizzle kept Justin from setting out. He kissed his mother on the cheek and shook his father's hand, then he mounted the horse he'd packed and had ready since shortly after midnight.

He had learned about Abigail's betrothal in a note from Tobias. His first instinct had been to ride to the Whitfield farm, to confront Abigail and find out if the news was true. He had no qualms about fighting his way past Henry's farmhands or Henry himself, but Abigail's silence and her absence since they'd returned from Kentucky said enough. Perhaps Henry had forbidden her to speak to him, but surely she could have found a way. And what if she had? What could she say that would make any difference? Henry's plans included no accommodation for their love. There was no point in humiliating himself and casting a pall over the two families' arrangements by creating a disturbance and insisting he hear the awful news directly from Abigail's lips. He could not bear that anyway.

He wanted to get as far away from Ridgetop as he could before the light of day. He reined his horse onto a little-used path westward, through the woods. For some distance it would take him along the creek near the Whitfield and Johnson farms, and he wanted to leave those behind before anyone saw him. He didn't want to speak to anyone or have to explain where he was going. He didn't know himself where he was going. He was pretty sure his father hadn't believed his explanation, that he'd find work in Saint Louis helping load and unload the new steamboats plying the great rivers of the west. Saint Louis wasn't far enough away for Justin. He needed to find solace in a place where few people lived. He would ride all the way to China, if necessary.

It was to Walter's credit that he hadn't tried to stop him. His father knew how much Justin suffered, knew he could never live in the same county as Abigail Whitfield if she were married to anyone else, much less his friend, Toby. Did she have any romantic feelings for Toby at all? Justin doubted it. He doubted whether Abigail was willing to pay so dear a price for her dream of raising horses. But everyone had assumed the horse farm was simply a first step toward marriage. Now, even though Abigail had denied it, it had come to pass. If Abby wasn't in love with Toby, what did it matter? Emotions carried little weight with Henry Whitfield. All he saw was a man's wealth, and how that could benefit him and his family. Well, damn Henry Whitfield and damn all rich people, wherever they were. Justin would have nothing more to do with them.

In spite of everything, Justin still had a vague notion that he could ride south, maybe strike it rich in a Mexican silver mine. In a year or two, Abby's marriage to Toby surely would have fallen apart. Then perhaps . . . but no. By that time they'd have at least one child and, if nothing else, that would ensure the marriage continued, even if the participants no longer enjoyed each other's company.

Day broke as gloomy as Justin's heart. The light, freezing drizzle continued, creating a fog that further limited his ability to see very far ahead. It didn't matter. He would be seeing a strange new country soon enough. Maybe he'd encounter hostile Indians. He imagined the stories people would tell, years from then, of Justin Sterling, Indian fighter from Ridgetop, Tennessee. Maybe Abigail's children would idolize him. How would she feel about that? She might rue the day she married Toby, instead of him.

He reined his horse to a stop on the sandy shoulder of the creek to let his horse drink. As he sat there in his misery, a cow bearing the Whitfield brand appeared out of the fog on the other side of the creek. It walked down to the water to drink opposite his horse. Justin thought he had ridden beyond the Whitfield farm, but he hadn't paid much attention. He wondered if this was where he and Abigail played hide-and-seek when they were children. Near the place where Toby had found the mysterious three-sided stone. Funny, he hadn't thought of that old stone in years.

He started out of his reverie when a man's low whistle pierced the fog, followed by a too-quiet "Yee-hah!"

Justin recognized Toby's voice, but something about it was wrong. He must be herding some of Whitfield's cattle, but why, and why so early in the morning? His friend had not developed a habit of rising early to work, especially on a cold winter morning. In any case, Justin had no desire to talk to Toby. He reined his horse away from the creek and rode a few yards into the woods. He stopped behind a full-grown oak surrounded by thick underbrush. From there he watched as Toby appeared out of the fog on horseback, swinging a length of rope as a whip to retrieve the thirsty cow.

"Get outta there, you miserable brute!"

True to form, Toby wasn't happy working cattle so early in the morning. Justin was tempted to call out to his friend, maybe give him a hand or say goodbye, but something stopped him again. Toby kept his voice too quiet for herding cattle, especially for someone not happy at his work. His friend lashed at the cow with the rope until the beast raised its head and ran to join the others, which Justin saw plodding along in the still dim light. Toby yanked on his horse's reins to turn it back to the pasture. He applied his spurs and galloped away, looking over his shoulder more than once, as if he had misplaced other cattle along the creek. Justin would worry about that, too, if he were responsible for Henry Whitfield's herd. Toby disappeared back into the fog, but Justin could still hear his friend's voice, urging the small herd forward.

"Get along, you damned swine. Move!"

Toby acted like a man in a great hurry, but he didn't sound like one. Justin assumed he wanted to get his chores for Henry Whitfield over as quickly as possible, since the Whitfield servants were probably frying up hotcakes and boiling coffee for Toby's breakfast. But the quietness of Toby's voice struck Justin as odd. Sound carried farther through a fog but, even though this section of the creek ran almost a mile from the Whitfield's house, Toby might not want to disturb anyone still sleeping, especially his future father-in-law. How considerate. Justin was almost thankful it was Toby and not him herding Henry's cattle so early in the morning. The old man would surely be a hard taskmaster.

He shook his head. The sight of Tobias Johnson working Whitfield cattle was an appropriate image for Justin's last memory of Ridgetop. If Toby's connections to the Whitfield family were already that strong, all the better that Justin should be moving on.

"Good luck, my friend," Justin said to the fog. He walked his horse back to the trail and continued his journey.

As it turned out, the sight of Tobias herding cattle would not be Justin's last memory of Ridgetop. Somewhat later that morning, he passed Mr. Bailey and Mr. Smith on the road making haste toward Ridgetop in a buckboard wagon loaded with supplies of some kind. The two men did not appear to recognize

Justin. They gave him no greeting, paid him no mind, and hurried on their way.

And Justin was fine with that.

CHAPTER TWENTY-ONE

January 1836

From the bay window in her bedroom, Abigail watched her father and Toby ride toward the house from a cattle barn. They had been out to the pastures all morning, longer than usual and, according to Elly, Henry had been riding in the forest and fields beyond the Whitfield property. Something was amiss, which wouldn't help her father's mood. His anger never seemed to abate. It seethed below the surface of his outwardly calm demeanor, as if he expected, rightly, that Abigail wasn't through arguing that she should choose her own husband. She hadn't told her mother about Browning or his letter, which she had carefully hidden in a shoebox in the back of an armoire. News of Browning's presence was bound to make her father's attitude still worse.

Since her father would not see reason, Abigail had resigned herself to fleeing to the Sterling farm and to Justin. She had been calculating what to take with her, and how to deal with her parents once they found out, when she heard of her father's strange activities in the field. Now that he was returning, she went down to the kitchen, where she knew the men would enter the house, to see what the matter was.

"Father?" He came through the kitchen door and strode past her without taking off his greatcoat or hat and headed toward his first-floor office. Toby came in behind him and gave her the briefest hug, which she did not return.

"What's the matter?" she asked him.

"It looks like a few cattle are missing." He hung his hat and scarf on the hooks by the door, as if he already lived in the Whitfield house.

"A few? Father wouldn't be so distracted by a few missing cattle."

"Twenty-six at last count."

"Twenty-six? That's more than could wander off."

"The fences are all up and in good repair. It looks like the cattle were stolen."

"Oh, my. That won't sit well with Father."

"No, dear. I'd better go help him." He briefly put his hands on Abigail's arms, then left.

It was not quite an intimate gesture, but it annoyed her, since it presumed his status as her husband-to-be. She found it difficult to think of Toby in a romantic way, but who was she kidding? The arrangement was entirely financial. Toby had been her friend since she was a little girl, but he was always more like an irksome brother than a potential mate. He had never expressed any serious romantic intentions toward her in all that time. Why should he now?

She shook her head in frustration and followed Toby to her father's office, where she overheard the men's conversation as she approached.

"It's as though they disappeared into thin air," her father said. He sat with his elbows on his desk and ran his fingers through his hair with both hands.

"Cattle don't disappear," Toby said.

Henry looked up. "You think they were stolen?"

"Well, you've spoken to the neighbors yourself. None of them has seen twenty-six cattle idling down the road unattended. And none of the fencing has been breached."

"None of my neighbors would do such a thing. Of that I am

173

sure. Besides, no one would be foolish enough to sell cattle with the Whitfield brand to anyone within one hundred miles of Ridgetop."

Toby noticed Abigail but turned away and looked out the window. "Then perhaps it was someone who is traveling farther than one hundred miles. Who do we know who has left Ridgetop recently who'd have the skill to spirit away twenty-six cattle?"

Her father's head snapped up. "Are you accusing Justin Sterling?"

"What?" Abigail wasn't sure she'd heard correctly. "Is Justin gone? Where? When?"

To her surprise, her father's gaze softened, slipping suddenly from anger and concern to caution.

"Aye, he's gone. Yesterday morning."

"Where? Where has he gone? Tell me!"

"We don't know. And if you ask me—"

"Abigail," Tobias broke in. "Isn't it obvious? He no longer wants to live in Ridgetop. Near us."

"How can that be?" She clutched her chest as an icicle of fear pierced her heart. "Why didn't you tell me?" How could Justin leave? The answer was obvious. Justin knew of her betrothal, and, in her caution, she had taken too long to stand up to her parents. Now, for all Justin knew, she had abandoned him.

"We have no need of Justin Sterling," her father said. He looked at Tobias. "Not anymore."

"But Justin may have needed your cattle," Tobias said.

"I don't know why he'd steal them. Of all people." Henry placed his hands flat on the desk.

Abigail couldn't stand any more of this discussion. Justin was missing, and now he was being called a thief. "Tell me you're not accusing Justin Sterling."

Her father frowned. "It does seem hard to believe."

Tobias raised his hands in supplication. "I don't like it any more than you do, but we must remain objective and consider where the facts lead us."

Henry scowled. "I admit I can't think of anything else."

"You can't mean what you say," she insisted. "Not Justin."

Toby turned to Abigail with his arms crossed. "You know Justin wouldn't be happy with our engagement."

"But that's no reason to—"

"The cattle disappeared on the very day Justin left Ridgetop, and he left without so much as a fare-thee-well to you or me or anyone else I am aware of."

Her father's fists clenched. "I've always thought that Sterling boy would bring me trouble, one way or the other." He glared at Abigail.

She raised her hands to her ears in frustration. "I can't believe what I'm hearing. There is no more honest man in his county than Justin Sterling. You know that, and yet you would believe the worst of him, simply because you haven't thought of any other reason why a few cattle might be missing. It's too convenient."

"Twenty-six is more than a few cattle," Tobias said. "You said so yourself."

"I'm afraid Tobias has a point, my dear." Her father leaned back in his chair. "I wish it were otherwise, but there doesn't appear to be any other plausible explanation."

"You have always had a fondness for Justin," Toby said to her. "It may be difficult for you to see the truth."

"How could believe this of your lifelong friend?"

Tobias looked out the window again. "It breaks my heart, to be sure, but who knows what a man is capable of when jealousy overcomes him?"

"What else could account for the coincidence?" her father said again, almost to himself.

"Perhaps this was Justin's revenge on you, Henry, for cutting Justin off and allowing Abigail to marry me."

"Allowing?" She almost reached for the ashtray on her father's desk to throw at Tobias, but one controversy was enough for the moment. "Please tell me. Where has Justin gone?"

"That's just it," Tobias said. "He's told no one. No one I've spoken to, anyway. Maybe his parents know, but a cattle thief wouldn't tell anybody where he was going, would he? And twenty-six cattle would bring a pretty penny, enough for Justin to make a fresh start, wherever he's gone."

Her father shook his head slightly, as if he couldn't believe this turn of events. But his faraway gaze hardened. "It's a hanging offense," he muttered.

"If he is ever caught." Tobias looked at Abigail. "He's had almost two days' head start. He could be anywhere between here and the Mississippi River. If indeed he went in that way."

"It's hard for a man to disappear forever, especially with twenty-six cattle." Her father put his hand to his chin.

"Oh, but we don't really know where Justin's gone," Toby said. "If the authorities went looking for him, he could have them riding in circles."

Her father came to his feet. "Walter Sterling will know where his boy has gone, and I'll wring it out of him if I must."

"But with two days' lead, how will you ever catch him?" Toby asked.

Toby's tone had changed, Abigail noticed. Why, after indicting Justin of theft, did he now seem willing to let the matter drop?

Her father pulled a map from a bin against the wall and unrolled it on top of his desk. "He can't move very quickly herding cattle by himself, and he couldn't possibly have sold the animals so quickly. With a good horse, I could catch him."

The look on her father's face so horrified her that she leaned against the doorframe for support. "What will you do then? Will you bring Justin home?"

"Home?" Henry barked. "That won't be necessary. If there are no local authorities to arrest him or to stop me, I'll hang him from the nearest oak tree."

"Hang him?" Toby appeared to blanch at the idea of a summary execution of his old friend.

"Father, you wouldn't do that." Abigail's voice trembled. "Not without giving Justin a proper trial."

"His offense is clear, Abigail, especially if I find him with my cattle. That's all the evidence any court of law would need." He folded the map and left it in front of him on the desk, presumably to take with him on the chase.

"I can't believe I'm hearing this. Toby? Would you let my father take the law into his own hands?" She glared at her future husband, challenging him to speak up.

He put his hands in his pockets and looked at the floor. "Your father is right, Abby, at least in principle. Blind justice would not be kind if Justin is caught with contraband cattle. What's more, I don't see how you and I can be happily married as long as this sad matter is hanging over our heads. But I have an idea." He looked up, almost smiling. "In order to bring the question of Justin's guilt or innocent to a swift and appropriate conclusion, I shall go with Henry to ensure that Justin is given the treatment he deserves."

"You?"

"Yes. The quicker I may return to you, dear, so we can be married and resume our contented lives." He turned to her father. "I'll go pack a horse at once." He patted her shoulder and left the room.

Rather than feel comforted, Abigail thought she might faint. Could Justin really be a cattle thief, to be hanged on sight like a common criminal?

"Father," she said.

"Now is not the time." He stood up and left the office.

At morning's first light, Abigail pleaded with her father one last time, clinging to his leg as he sat on his horse. But Henry had made up his mind, and he and Tobias rode away. They took with them a farmhand named Douglas. Later that day, Abigail sat in the family room, filled with dread, with her knitting lying unattended in her lap. Her mother sat opposite her, reading a book.

"Where do you think Justin is?" Abigail asked.

Her mother looked at her over the top of her half-rimmed reading glasses.

"I understand your distraction, dear, but we must go on living normal lives, at least until your father returns and we know more than we do now."

Abigail slapped at the knitting yarn in frustration. "I know all I need to know, and so should Father. Justin Sterling could not have stolen his cattle. There must be some other explanation, but that will do Justin no good should Father catch him."

"The rigors of traveling on horseback will cool Henry's anger before he finds Justin. He'll have time to think things through, and he won't act rashly. I'm sure."

"He's already acted rashly, assuming Justin is guilty without any adequate proof."

"I find it hard to believe myself. But if it's true . . ."

"It's *not* true, Mother! You know Justin Sterling. How could you believe such a thing of him?"

"I am familiar with the boy, of course, and I still give him the benefit of the doubt. But I've lived much longer than you, Abby, long enough to realize we don't always know people as well as we think we do."

"That may be true, Mother, but not about Justin." She

178

thought of Archie Browning, his claims, and the letter still hidden in her shoebox. Did she know her own mother as well as she thought? How could she confirm Browning's story without revealing too much?

"Do you have any dark secrets, Mother?"

"Me? I dare say not. I haven't had any secrets for a long, long time."

"But you did keep secrets once, didn't you? Does Father know any of them?"

"The problem with secrets is that, over time, they become harder and harder to keep." Her mother looked at her again over her glasses, sending a quick shaft of guilt though Abigail's chest. "It's better not to try."

"I agree, of course."

"I am an open book to your father, and very grateful that I have no secrets from him."

"Have you kept any secrets from me?" She asked this as innocently as she could.

Her mother gave her another stern, appraising look. "If I have kept any secrets from you, it was for your own good, and you shouldn't inquire further." She looked back down at her book, closing the discussion. Clearly her mother wasn't going to say anything about her past without being confronted by Browning or his letter.

Abigail wondered if Browning was still working in the area. He did say he might overwinter in the county. Perhaps she could arrange an accidental meeting between her mother and the man, such as she'd had at the tea shop. But she couldn't think of that until Justin had returned safely. Her thoughts turned dismal and she dwelled on the worst possible outcomes. Travel to the west was dangerous, and there was a chance that neither her father nor Toby would return. Then she and her mother would be left without a husband or a father. Trying to knit while she waited for news of Justin's fate was simply too difficult.

"Mother, do you suppose Aunt Tilda is still well?"

Her mother didn't bother to glance up from her book. "I'll not fall for that ruse again, Abigail." She remained calm, but her voice was cold as a stone. "Aunt Tilda can very well look out for herself."

Abigail felt her cheeks flush. She couldn't sit at home with her fate and Justin's hanging in the balance. She couldn't. If her father was bent on punishing Justin, she had to do something to stop him. But what? She set aside her knitting.

"I'm feeling a bit of headache, Mother. I think I'll go to my room and lie down for a few minutes." Her mother nodded but said nothing, assuming perhaps that Abigail's exit was due to the scolding she'd just received.

CHAPTER TWENTY-TWO

Arkansas Territory, Late January 1836

Justin considered himself lucky to find the roadside inn at the height of the storm, even though he'd already been soaked through by the driving rain, which threatened to turn to snow. The inn was a two-story, whitewashed building with a broad, covered porch, complete with thin columns, imitations of the much grander columns he'd seen on the palatial mansions in Kentucky.

His horse was safety stabled, and now Justin sat at a small table in the public room of the inn, near a crackling fire in the hearth. He ordered a cup of corn whiskey and a small bowl of stew from a man in a soiled apron who looked him over once or twice, but didn't ask any questions. Justin wondered what Henry Whitfield would think of him ordering alcohol to drink with his dinner. Then he banished the thought. He might never see Henry Whitfield again, and that suited him fine.

The stew arrived, but before he took up his spoon, he held his hands over the steaming bowl to warm them. He didn't know what meat the stew had been made of, but it tasted good, and it was his first hot meal since leaving home. It and the whiskey warmed him from the inside.

With his first sip of the liquor, he glanced around at the dozen or so others who had taken refuge at the inn. They looked like the usual mix of men. There were those who looked like they worked the land, with a few hunters and some traveling men of commerce thrown in, literally, he assumed, when the storm arose. The only woman appeared to be the proprietor's wife, a stocky matron in an apron, her graying hair tied back and out of the way as she worked behind the counter at a cooking fire. No one paid him much mind.

He had a vague idea that he was somewhere in the territory of Arkansas. Its rolling, wooded hills reminded him of Tennessee. It was a place he thought he might settle and look for work, but it reminded him too much of home. And it wasn't far enough away at that. If he got homesick, he could return to Ridgetop without much difficulty. He wanted to eliminate returning home as a possibility, and he wouldn't stop moving until he found a land so utterly strange and challenging that it would make him forget Abigail Whitfield forever. Not that he believed such a place existed.

After he'd eaten his stew and drunk most of the whiskey, he fell into a mild stupor. He considered ordering more drink, that being preferable to going back outside, into the storm, and he wasn't prepared to pay the price of a room. But his clothes were still wet and he couldn't spend the night outside without freezing to death. He wondered if the owner would let him sleep in the stable with his horse. He drained the last few drops of whiskey from his cup and knew if he ordered another, he might spend the night under the table. He gathered up his musket and saddlebag and looked around the room for the proprietor, to ask about a place to stay the night.

Just then one of the men sitting at the next table with two other men spoke to him. "From where do you hail, friend?" The man wore buckskins, like Justin, but also a tall hat, similar to those Justin had seen in Louisville, but this one made of a coarser pelt than beaver. It looked like cattle hide. The man struck Justin as not much older than he, but a rough-looking character, a frontiersman.

"I'm a Tennessean," Justin said. "Or I was."

"We, too!" the man said, gesturing at his friends. "The name's Bayliss. Joseph Bayliss. Late of Montgomery County."

"I'm Justin Sterling. From Ridgetop." He shook hands with Bayliss.

"We're all traveling to Texas," Bayliss said. The other two men at the table nodded their heads in a way that confirmed they were determined to make the long journey. In his idle moments as a youth, Justin had wondered about Texas and Mexico and what kinds of adventures a man could have there, but they remained the settings of tall stories and too far away for serious consideration. Now nothing stood in his way.

"What takes you to the Mexican territories?" he asked. He wasn't eager to make friends with these strangers, but he was less eager still to leave the warmth of the fire.

"Mexican?" Bayliss asked. "It won't be part of Mexico for long. Shoot, the Mexicans can hardly call it their own now. I here tell there are more Yankees in the territory than Mexicans." The other men muttered their agreement. "As it is, changing the name on a map is about all it'd take to make the territory independent. We want to be there when it happens, to make a new start."

Justin could sympathize with anyone making a new start. If what these men said was true, there might be all manner of prospects for a young man from Tennessee in a new, independent territory. "Do they run cattle in Texas?" he asked.

"Do they run cattle in Texas?" Bayliss slapped his knee and laughed out loud. "Hell, the Texicans practically invented cattle. You ever hear of the Texas longhorn?"

"I can't say that I have."

"Well the Spanish brought 'em over a couple of hundred years ago. You haven't seen cattle until you've seen a longhorn. They've got points nearly six feet apart." Bayliss spread his

183

arms wide for emphasis. "They can run all day on a thimble of water, but you won't find a finer cut of meat on the hoof, even in Tennessee."

Justin was intrigued. "What's your destination in Texas?"

"The politicians is all asking for people to settle as far south as they can git 'em, to solidify their claim on the country. We're aiming to find land in Béxar, near the San Antonio River. Plenty of open range there for cattle, if that's what interests you. And if you'll pardon me for say'n so, you don't look like a man with any pressing business."

"I'm not in any hurry, that's true."

"Well, then. If you've got no better offer, we could use another hand, if you've got a strong back and a mind to see new country. You interested in going with us?"

This query took Justin by surprise. He assumed he'd travel the west like a wandering hermit, with no other goal than to be alone in his misery. To leave Abigail behind and ramble the earth until lightning struck or Indians took his scalp. He only had a vague notion that, sooner or later, he'd need to get on with life. What that meant he hadn't yet visualized, but the unexpected offer of traveling to Texas could be an opportunity provided by the good Lord, as Henry might say. The men at the table looked a little rough around the edges, but no more so than he, after days on the road. They seemed friendly enough, and traveling with a group would be much safer than traveling alone.

Bayliss gestured at the belongings Justin held in his arms. "If it helps you decide, we have a room here, paid in full. It ain't King Solomon's temple, mind you, but you'd be welcome to a share of the floor."

Lightning flashed outside, close enough to light up the slats of the shuttered windows. Thunder rumbled over the sound of pounding rain.

"Many thanks, Mr. Bayliss." Justin set down his musket and saddlebag. "I guess I'm bound for Texas."

The morning after her father and Tobias left, Abigail woke up in bed with a start. She'd been dreaming about Justin and her father. In her dream her father was furious. He insisted that she marry Justin and nobody else, but Justin was having nothing of it. The angrier her father got, the more Justin refused her. Between the two men she felt utterly helpless and confused. But that wasn't what woke her up. It was the undeniable and irresistible sensation that she was about to be sick to her stomach. She threw back her covers, reached down, and slid the pan out from under the bed. She leaned over the side of the bed just in the nick of time, and promptly emptied the contents of her stomach. Then she lay back on her bed sheets and gasped for breath.

Slowly, the wave of nausea passed. Had she come down with the flu? She put a hand to her forehead but her skin felt normal, neither too hot nor too cold. Certainly she hadn't any fever. She thought back to dinner the night before, but she hadn't eaten much at all, much less anything that might have upset her stomach.

After a few seconds, a cold realization dawned on her. Her time of month had not come as scheduled, but its tardiness hadn't seriously concerned her. A woman's bodily rhythms were never as accurate as a clock and, ignoring the obvious, when she thought of it at all, she had blamed her failed period on her emotional crisis. But a chill swept down her spine, which couldn't be blamed on the nip in the morning air. It was too soon to be sure, but she might be pregnant. She tried to remember how long it had been since she and Justin slept together in the tent. The timing was right.

Thunder and lighting! She was going to be a mother. The idea of being with child filled her with glee and dread, all at the same time. Glee because she would be carrying Justin's child. Dread with the fear that her father would find out. And find out he must, sooner or later. But not until he returned with Justin. *If* he returned with Justin. Her father had sworn he would hang Justin as soon as he found him, if there were no authorities capable of taking Justin into custody. Surely he wouldn't hang Justin if he knew he was the father of his grandchild. But it might be weeks before her father returned and she learned the fate of her lover. How could she wait? She thought of Archie Browning's unfortunate story.

No, she wouldn't wait. The only sure way of saving Justin was to find her father before he and Toby found Justin. What else could she do? They'd only been gone a day. She would go after them. She tumbled out of bed and scrambled for traveling clothes from her wardrobe. She looked at frilly dresses and threw them aside. She needed clothing suitable for riding, camping, and herding cattle, if she must. She looked for her leather and wool outfits and began to make a mental list of the provisions she'd need, at least until she caught up with her father. She wanted her pocket gun, powder, and ball. And food for perhaps a week. But what was she going to tell her mother?

CHAPTER TWENTY-THREE

Early February 1836

Her mother would be beside herself, anxious with fear, but Abigail was determined. She would not wait patiently to learn whether her father and Tobias had hanged Justin. The only thing that might dampen her mother's panic and keep her from sending the sheriff after her was if she knew Abigail wasn't alone, and the only person who might agree to go with her was Elly. She found the servant in the kitchen, eating breakfast.

"Elly, when you're done, can you come up to my room? I've something I wish to discuss with you."

Elly had just bitten into a biscuit, but she stopped chewing and looked at Abigail. "Have I done something wrong?"

"No, no, nothing like that." She put a reassuring hand on Elly's forearm. "It's Justin. I want to talk to you about Justin."

Elly started chewing again. "Isn't that terrible, what he did with Mr. Whitfield's cattle?"

"You don't really believe he did that, do you?"

"No, I don't. But Mr. Whitfield and Tobias Johnson, they're mad as bees at a bear who's stole their honey."

"That's right. And it's that I want to talk to you about."

Elly put down her biscuit and pointed to the door. "Let's go."

Once they were safely in Abigail's room, she locked the door and told Elly to sit in the bay window, as far away from the door and any prying ears as one could get in her bedroom. Abigail sat next to her.

"It's this," she said. "My father is so mad, like you said, I'm afraid he'll do something terrible to Justin."

"That'd be awful," Elly said. "But what can we do?"

"If we were there when Father finds Justin, I don't think he'd do anything . . . too rash."

"You mean he won't string poor Justin up from a tree first thing?"

"Exactly. He'd be required to turn Justin over to the law for a proper trial."

"That's nice, but . . . wait a minute. Are you saying what I think you're thinking?"

"Yes. I need you to go with me."

"Lordy, Abby. Your father would skin me alive and make himself a pair of boots if I let you go after him."

"I won't let him do that. You know I won't. This is too important." She stood up and paced the room with her arms crossed. "Father's only been gone a day or so. Three men can't travel that fast, especially if they're looking to follow Justin and they don't know exactly where he is. We should be able to catch up with them pretty quickly if we leave right away." She stopped pacing in front of Elly and dropped to her knees. "I need you, Elly. Justin needs you. When you think about it, my father needs you to keep him from doing something awful. Please say you'll go with me."

The look in Elly's eyes shifted from concern to absolute wonder. She grinned. "Go with you? Lordy. I guess I could use vacation."

"Thank you!" Abigail stood up. "Go pack a bag. Find your best boots. Get some bread and cheese from the kitchen. I'll make ready a pair of horses and find my pistol."

"A pistol! This is going to be some vacation. What are you going to tell your mother?"

Abigail paused. "I don't know, but I'm not going to let her stop me. We'll leave at first light, before Mother is awake and can send the farmhands after us."

"You'd better leave her a note. She's going to be sick with worry about you."

"A note, of course." She glanced at the armoire where she'd hidden the letter from Archie Browning. "I'll leave her more than a note, and I'll distract her with a bit of news. Now, get going."

Elly leaped from the seat and sprinted to the door. Abigail ran after her and put a hand on her shoulder.

"Not so quickly, Elly. We don't want anyone to ask questions. And don't tell anybody what we're doing. Nobody at all. I need you to keep this our secret."

"Cross my heart, Abby." She passed her fingers over her chest in an "x"; then she composed herself and calmly reached for the door latch. "Until tomorrow morning then, Miss Abigail. Good day." She curtsied slightly and left the room.

Abigail sat down at her desk and penned a note to her mother. *Dear Mother,* it said. *Elly and I have gone for a ride. My aim is to find Father and Tobias. I cannot in good conscience let Father harm Justin on the basis of mere allegations of thievery. You and I know Justin Sterling would never do such a thing. Please do not worry about me. As you have pointed out many times, I am a grown woman. We should find Father in one or two days and, if we do not, I will return immediately. When I find Father, I will send Elly back with word for you. Although I do not believe I will be in any serious danger, if something should happen to me, I wish you to have the letter which accompanies this note. It is from a man named Archibald Browning, who says he knows you well. I haven't given it to you before this because I do not know the truth of what Mr. Browning says, and it may cause you some unease. I have no opinion about Browning's story, and I pass judgment on no one, least of all you.*

Please know that I love you and Father dearly. Until I return, Abigail Louise Whitfield.

She felt compelled to sign the note with her full name, to emphasize that she still considered Henry to be her father, in spite of Browning's claims. And because using her full name sounded more adult. She folded the note in half and placed it with the letter. She looked at the clock and mentally reviewed her preparations, to make sure she hadn't forgotten anything.

The more Justin saw of Texas, the more ideal it seemed for raising cattle. Large swaths of open range ran from horizon to horizon and needed little clearing. Endless tracts of the land were uninhabited. Water was much scarcer than in Tennessee, but lakes and streams were clearly marked by cottonwood trees and other vegetation. Most everywhere else was an endless sea of grass. On top of that, the weather was quite pleasant for so early in the year, and Justin was beginning to like the idea of being a Texican.

Every few days the small band of men stopped in a small village, where the low, single-story buildings were made from bricks of adobe mud, and the local food was simple but plentiful. Justin had been warned about Mexican spices, and he feared he might not grow accustomed to the unusual flavors. But a plate of beans was a plate of beans, and he enjoyed everything he ate, as long as he stayed clear of any small green peppers. The inhabitants of the territory were an equally exotic mix of people. Mexicans were greater in number than whites, but, in addition to other Americans, Justin met trappers from Scotland, ranchers from South America, and a number of freed black men, or runaway slaves.

As Henry Clay had said, there was little sign of Mexican rule over the territory, or any rule at all in many places, other than common courtesy. Most of the land appeared open for the tak-

190

ing by anyone determined enough to work it. Even so, Joseph Bayliss warned, there might be a fight if the Mexicans resisted the influx of settlers from the States.

With every odd new food Justin ate, and with every new vista over which his gaze lingered, he wondered what Abby would think of it all. Then he would chastise himself and redouble his effort to put any thought of her out of his mind. She could have been married to Toby by then, and already started her new life, and the sooner he forgot her, the better. Of course the harder he tried, the more his heart ached. His inability to banish Abby from his mind drove him on each day, more determined than ever to find some new adventure or some new purpose in life that would fill the gaping hole in his heart that had opened up in Abby's absence.

Eventually, Bayliss led the group to a town called Villa de San Fernando de Béxar, which lay next to the San Antonio River. From the name, it sounded to Justin like Béxar must be a bustling city, at least as big as Lexington. But Bayliss assured him it was only slightly larger than the trifling settlements they'd already seen. If they couldn't find lodging in Béxar itself, they surely could at a nearby mission, just outside the town.

Béxar was said to be a seat of the local Mexican government. Bayliss and his friends had no desire to pick a fight with the Mexicans. Nor did Justin, who remembered his father's admonition that war wasn't always the answer to a country's problems. The men intended to consult with government officials in Béxar to see what requirements there were, if any, for newcomers who wished to settle in the territory. Justin belonged to no country now. He might as well be a Mexican as an American. The dark-eyed, almond-skinned Mexican women he'd encountered were an exotic and stark contrast to the fair-haired Abigail Whitfield. Eventually, perhaps, a Mexican beauty would help him forget the love he left behind.

When the men arrived in Béxar, they were told that Mexican officials had abandoned the town. The mission had been abandoned, too, except that a group of Americans had turned the compound into a makeshift fort. Because of this, the local residents expected trouble. There had already been one battle elsewhere in Texas between Mexican soldiers and American colonists in October of the year before, and there were rumors of another.

Local residents advised the Americans to move on, if they wanted to avoid the growing troubles. But the men had ridden too far, and they had no other destination in mind. To learn more about the conflict and what they should do, they rode out to the mission. It had indeed been converted into a fort, complete with a wooden stockade, which enclosed those portions of the compound that had previously been open. They were briefly challenged by an armed guard on top of a wall, then a gate was opened and they were greeted warmly by the men inside.

A man in military uniform stepped forward and introduced himself, shaking each man's hand in turn as they dismounted.

"Welcome to Alamo Mission," he said. "My name is Travis. Colonel William Travis. I'm in command here. Well, I'm in co-command. The other commander is Mr. James Bowie, but he's taken ill and is indisposed."

"We're late of Tennessee," Bayliss said. "Come to Texas to try some farming. Maybe raise a few cattle."

"Tennessee? We have others here from that great state." He put a hand on the shoulder of the tall man standing next to him, dressed in leathers and wearing a soft fur hat that looked to be made from the skin of a raccoon. "This here's David Crockett. You may have heard of him."

"Congressman David Crockett?" Justin thought the man looked vaguely familiar. "From Tennessee?"

"The one and only." Crockett stepped forward, shaking Justin's hand first. "It's always nice to meet a constituent."

"Well if that don't set all the pigs to dancing," Bayliss said. "Imagine coming all the way to Texas to meet you." He pushed his hat back on his head. "What's my congressman doing way out here?"

"I'm an ex-congressman now, due to the fickle nature of Tennessee voters. And I'm here the same as you, I guess. To find a new life."

Bayliss gestured at his men. "We're looking to settle near some sweet grass and fresh water, if it's possible."

"You're all welcome by us," Travis said. "But the Mexicans will not be as pleased."

"We heard in Béxar that fighting's already started," Justin said.

"It has. And it may come here soon." Travis grimaced. "I'm surprised you got this far into Texas without coming across a Mexican army."

"I guess we were lucky, at that," Bayliss said.

"We'll be ready for them if they get here," Crockett said. "But we could use a few extra muskets, if you men are willing to stay with us."

Bayliss looked at Justin and his friends. "We've got nowhere else to go at the moment, and we'd be in fine company if we stayed."

The men nodded their agreement. Justin nodded, too, but he was indifferent. Travis and Crockett were impressive men, but Justin didn't feel the same need to fight for Texican independence as they. Even so, a war with Mexico might be enough to take his mind off Abigail Whitfield, and, if trouble was coming, what better place to be than in a fort?

Travis's slave, a black man named Joe, led the men and their horses to the stables as the gates of the Alamo Mission closed behind them.

CHAPTER TWENTY-FOUR

Somewhere in Arkansas, Mid-February 1836

Out of an abundance of caution, Abigail kept to the main road leading west. Bandits would consider two women riding alone easy prey, but she hoped any outlaws would do their business on less traveled highways. She also kept to the main road because she knew her father and Toby would follow it as far as they could, it being the quickest route west. That appeared to have been a good choice at first, since a few of the people they encountered remembered seeing her father and Toby. They seemed to be just ahead, almost within reach. That had been yesterday. Today no traveler they met said they'd seen two men fitting the description. If they had turned off the main road, Abigail wasn't sure in which direction they'd have gone.

Abigail was tired, sore, and losing hope.

Now, as the sun dipped low over the tree-filled hills, she was beginning to question her judgment. When they came to a crossroads, she reined her mount to a stop to consider their options. Elly halted her horse next to her.

"Miss Abby, do you think we're still goin' in the right direction? Seems like we've been riding for days. Shouldn't we have caught them by now?"

"I had hoped so," she admitted. "I know they came this way, at least at first."

"How much longer do we need to ride?"

Abigail wiped at the road dust on her forehead with a

kerchief. "Do you mean today, or at all?"

"Either one. My hind end wants to know real bad."

Abigail laughed. "I'm sorry I got you into this, Elly. It looks like it was all for nothing."

"No, Miss Abby. It cain't be for nothing if we're doing this for Justin."

"You're right, Elly." Abigail smiled. "You keep telling me that."

"Are we going to camp in the tent again tonight? I could use a real bed and a warm bath. And we're fearfully low on coffee."

"We might be sleeping on the ground again unless there's a farmhouse or ferry landing at the end of this side road. I think it goes down to a river."

"Well, at least there'll be water. Maybe we should take a look there before it gets dark."

"I agree. We can decide what to do in the morning." She reined her horse off the main road and walked it down the smaller side road. The overhang of maple trees blocked out more sunlight than on the main road, and the encroaching darkness made it more urgent that they find a place to camp. The road was narrow, but it looked well-traveled, and it started to wind back and forth in a series of switchbacks as it descended to the river. On one hairpin curve, Abigail thought she saw lights below them. On the next turn she was sure. There was a dwelling of some kind. At last they turned into the yard of a small roadhouse with peeling white paint and green trim. It was half grown over by vines that grew along the river.

A small ferry landing platform lay to the right side of the house, next to the river. No one moved about outside, but a handful of horses were tethered to a rail, and candle lanterns shone through the slats of two shuttered windows. A wisp of smoke rose from the chimney.

A weathered sign over the door said "Pendleton Crossing

Inn." A pretentious name for a modest business, Abigail thought. "It doesn't look like much," she said, "but it'll do."

"It looks like a king's palace to me." Elly stood up in her stirrups. "I think I smell a stew cooking."

They dismounted, tied their horses to the rail, and went in through the front door. As she stood at the front of the public room with her eyes adjusting to the light, the first thing Abigail noticed was the cook pot hanging over a bright crackling fire in the hearth, and the smell of stewing meat made her mouth water. A counter bar ran the length of the back of the room and half a dozen men were seated around tables in front of it. All of them looked up at Abigail and Elly.

Among them were her father and Tobias.

"Great Caesar's ghost!" her father stood up and roared. "Abigail! What are you doing here?"

Her father's hand, Douglas, stood up but backed away from Henry. Toby stood up, too, but he seemed less excited to see her.

"I had to come," she said.

Henry glared at Elly, then he pulled Abigail over to their table and lowered his voice, even though every man in the room could clearly hear him.

"This is unbelievable! This time your disobedience has gone too far."

Abigail shook off his hand from her arm and lifted her chin in defiance. "You never forbade me coming, Father."

"Well I forbid you to stay. You must go back immediately."

"I will not. I will not go back without Justin." She looked over at the proprietor, who stood behind the bar in an apron with his mouth agape at the scene. "Two bowls of whatever's cooking on the fire, please, for my companion and me." She gestured at Elly. "And some ale."

Her father's face turned as purple as a Tennessee iris.

"Unbelievable," he said again.

"Unbelievable as it seems, they're here now," Tobias said. "Let us all sit down and discuss what this means."

Reluctantly, Henry took his seat. "Go check on the horses," he said to Douglas.

As Abigail and Toby sat down, Elly walked over to the counter to help the proprietor.

Abigail spoke first, since she'd been thinking for two days about what she'd say to her father when she found him. "Whether you believe or not, Justin Sterling did not steal your cattle."

"We won't know that until we catch him."

She leaned toward her father. "As God is my witness, I know that now. And you will not do anything to that man until he's brought safely back to Ridgetop and you prove your awful allegations. I will not leave your side until that happens."

Her father blanched, which Abigail took as a sign he wasn't as sure about Justin as he sounded.

"Your loyalty to our friend is admirable," Tobias said. "But whether Justin is a thief is not your business, Abby."

"It's more my business than you think," she said. "I am carrying his child."

Speechless, Toby looked stricken. Her father's jaw dropped, but the firestorm Abigail expected from him didn't happen. Instead, he grew unnaturally quiet.

"I suspected something like this might happen." He put his head in his hands. "It's more of your disobedience."

Abigail pulled one of his hands down to the table and covered it with hers.

"No, Father. I love you. I don't wish to disobey you, but I must obey my own heart, too."

He looked at her with sad eyes, as though he saw her for the first time as the woman she was. No longer his wayward child,

198

no longer subject to his guidance, his protection, or his punishment.

"And what of Tobias?" he asked. His voice was hard as steel, but almost a whisper.

She looked at Toby. "I'm sorry, Toby. It happened before this arranged betrothal."

"Thanks," he said, although his eyes seemed to lose focus. "I had hoped you were happy with the arrangement, but I, more than anyone, should have known you love Justin."

Her father took his hand away and straightened his shoulders. "Well, then. We have all the more reason to find Justin Sterling, don't we?"

Abigail nodded, but she wasn't sure she had convinced her father of anything.

"You can come with us," he said through barely clenched teeth. "I suppose I can't stop you. And, while you've managed to come this far on your own, it's not safe for you to travel alone. Elly need not go on with us. She can return to Ridgetop with Mr. Douglas. We may no longer need his assistance."

Elly arrived with the stew and ale, and she and Abigail ate. That seemed to settled things with her father for the moment. But even if she had convinced her father that Justin wasn't a cattle thief, he was now guilty of deflowering Henry's only daughter. What penalty would her father have in mind for that?

CHAPTER TWENTY-FIVE

Ridgetop, Tennessee, February 1836

Henrietta Whitfield sat in a cane rocking chair on the covered porch, next to a charcoal brazier to keep her warm. She stared at the carriage path that ran away from the house, across the front lawn to the county road. Portions of the road were obscured by trees, but from her view on the porch, she could see a distance of some ten miles to where the road met a turnpike. The turnpike stretched west, winding through a rocky gap and out of sight. Where it went from there, she knew not. She had never traveled west of Ridgetop, but her husband and her daughter had gone in that direction, and it was from that direction they would return. If they returned. She wanted to be there to greet them if they did.

She had barely touched her lunch. The silver tray of sandwiches and a cup of cold tea sat on a small table next to her chair. The envelope Abigail left for her lay in her lap, unopened. She hadn't read the letter yet. She didn't need to. It came from Archibald Browning, and she knew in her heart what it would say. Every word. Just feeling the thick sheets of paper within the envelope felt like a betrayal of Henry, and she wasn't ready to do that, much less rekindle all those long-lost emotions.

Henrietta had been no more than a girl when she met Archie, but she knew she would never experience that intense kind of love again. When his work took him west, he vowed on his knees to return, and she knew in her heart that he meant every word. She'd insisted on waiting for him, demanded to wait for him, and fought her family hammer and tongs to stay true. In the end they convinced her Archie wasn't coming back, and the rest was Whitfield family history.

Now, with Henry and Abigail gone, she'd never felt more alone, or so fearful that she'd never see them again. That Archie Browning had finally reached out to her only added to her fear and confusion. What was she to make of it? When she wasn't worried about Henry, she imagined what she'd say to Archie, if she had the chance. Over and over, she played out different versions of an imaginary conversation with him in her mind. In one version she was the spurned lover, throwing Archie off the porch, telling him never to speak to her again. In just as many other versions, she welcomed him with open arms and gave him a longing kiss, heedless of what Henry might think, shamelessly eager to begin life again, as she was meant to all those years ago. That version made her blush. Caused her to shake her head in disbelief that she could still have such feelings after all these years.

She wasn't a young girl anymore. Coming to Tennessee with Henry was the best thing she could have done, given the circumstances. It was as much to spare the family her shame as for her own good, but Henry had been a saint to help her as he did. With no news from Archie, she had to go on living. It had been easier to assume Archie had died somewhere on the frontier, full of dismay that he'd never see her again, whispering her name with his last breath. How romantic. But just as often she'd believed that, with too much time apart, Archie had fallen out of love with her and wasn't interested in coming back. Some part of her still resented losing the life she'd been denied. At what point, if ever, had Archie learned she was with child? That could have made all the difference. All these questions raised memories that Henrietta had almost forgotten. Surely they had no bearing on her life now.

But the letter lay in her lap, and she felt the weight of it.

In the distance, at the juncture of the county road and the turnpike, she spied a single man on horseback coming in the direction of the farm. He was much too far away for Henrietta to recognize him, but behind him he pulled a second horse, this one carrying a number of bags. She had a momentary fear that Henry was returning without Abigail, and without Tobias or Justin.

But no. The man seemed familiar, but he didn't sit the saddle in the rigidly upright way Henry did. This was a working man, probably someone from a nearby farm. With no one else moving on the roads, she watched the man's progress. He seemed to be in no hurry and, indeed, stopped occasionally as if to get his bearings. The longer she watched, the closer the man came to the farm. To her surprise, the man eventually turned his horses into the Whitfield gate and paused.

The broad brim of his hat shaded his eyes, and Henrietta couldn't tell whether she knew the man or not. She considered calling for one of the farmhands, just in case the man had less-than-friendly intentions, but she didn't. A man traveling with that much baggage was too burdened and slow to be a highwayman. He was probably a lost haberdasher who needed directions, and he intended to get them from her. She stood up to let herself be seen and brushed a few wrinkles from her dress. She was receiving a guest, albeit an uninvited one. Perhaps he brought news from Henry.

She waited patiently with her hands clasped in front of her, but the man stayed at the gate long enough that Henrietta thought he might go away. Then, having made up his mind, the man gave his horse the slightest heel and slowly came forward at a walk. She tried not to stare when he pulled his horse to a stop at the foot of the stairs, but his face was still obscured by the brim of his hat.

"Good afternoon, sir," she said. "How may I help you?"

"Good afternoon, Henrietta."

The sound of the stranger, speaking her name, prickled the skin of her neck, as if she'd just heard one of Margaret Anne's ghost stories.

"You have me at a disadvantage, sir." She glanced at the bell resting on the table next to her chair and considered again ringing for one of the servants.

"I know many years have passed, dear heart, but do you not recognize me?" The man reached up and removed his broad-brimmed hat, revealing shoulder-length graying red hair and beard. "I'm Archie Browning."

Henrietta felt the blood drain from her face. Her knees went weak and she struggled to keep herself upright. A jumble of once-faded memories rushed through her, each one fighting to be heard. Archie's voice seemed to transport her back to Virginia, where a strapping young man courted her madly, and they were unable to leave each other's sight even for the briefest moment. That had been so long ago.

Archie's reappearance had also dropped her into the middle of one of the many conversations she'd imagined having with the man, if she ever met him again. But which version? She'd never decided on any particular one. Knowing the likelihood of seeing him again was slight, she had entertained them all.

She clutched the buttons at the neck of her wool coat and opened her mouth to speak, but nothing came out. She considered cursing the man, dismissing him at once and sending him away. That would have been prudent. That's what Henry would have her do. But Henry was . . . away. Perhaps Henry's absence had allowed this to happen, but a flickering, almost forgotten ember rekindled inside, flickering just enough to make itself felt once again. It wasn't quite the urge to run into Archie Browning's arms. No. And it wasn't quite a desire to feel the man's lips on hers, as she had ached for so many times. No, not yet. It was a single, faintly glowing ember she had protected from the winds of time and harbored in the depths of her soul for so long, she simply couldn't deny it now. Not now. But what to do? She had to say something.

She coughed lightly into her hand. "Yes, it's been many years since I've seen you, Archie. How odd that I should be waiting on the porch when you arrived. Would you like to come inside for a cup of tea?"

CHAPTER TWENTY-SIX

Alamo Mission, San Antonio, Texas, February 23, 1836
Justin was sitting on a wooden bench near the barracks cleaning his musket, when a guard on the wall at the south gate called out. Someone wanted in. Justin hoped more men had arrived to help defend the mission, but when the gates opened, he dropped his cleaning rod in the dirt in surprise. Henry Whitfield rode into the compound next to Toby Johnson. That was odd enough, but behind them rode Abigail, leading a packhorse.

His heart jumped when he saw Abby, even though she was with her father and Toby, but he shook his head briefly when he realized what their presence meant. Abby was in danger. They were all in danger. Why in the world had they come to Texas? They must have followed him. But why?

He set down his musket, caught Henry's eye, and waved. He was sure Henry saw him, but the older man gave him no more than a stern glance and dismounted. He turned away from Justin and spoke to the men inside the gate. They called out for Colonel Travis, who was already coming out of the armory to see who had arrived. Travis greeted the arriving party, but Justin couldn't hear the conversation. He had a bad feeling about Henry's arrival. Surely the old man hadn't decided to start a new life in Texas.

He stood up and walked toward the gate, keeping his eyes on Abigail, taking in every detail of her. Her long, red hair was tied into a tail with a blue ribbon. Her straight, firm back and the swell of her breasts beneath the riding cloak told him she was well. She needed no assistance dismounting her horse, and she looked around at the fortified compound, probably wondering what they'd gotten themselves into. Plenty, Justin knew. As much as he enjoyed seeing his former lover, they all had to leave the Alamo as soon as possible.

"Justin!" Abigail dropped her reins and started to run to him, but Henry grasped her arm and held her back. Justin reached for her but Henry stood in his way.

"Colonel, this is the man." Henry pointed at Justin with one gloved hand. "I want him arrested immediately."

Travis put his hand on the hilt of his sword and eyed Justin. "What do you say, Mr. Sterling? Cattle thievery is a serious charge."

His jaw stiffened. "Cattle theft? Henry, what are you talking about?"

"Twenty-six head of my best livestock are missing, and you're the only one who could have taken them."

"Hardly," he said. "Henry, you've known me all my life. How could you make such an accusation?"

"It's plain to see. You opposed Abigail's marriage to Tobias. And the cattle disappeared the same day you left Ridgetop."

With a chill, he remembered the day he took his leave from Ridgetop. He looked at Toby. "Someone was herding cattle that day, but it wasn't me."

"You were jealous," Toby said. "You hated that I would marry Abby, and you wanted any revenge you could get."

"I wasn't pleased, that's true." He looked at Abigail. "But that was beyond my control, and I wished you nothing but happiness."

"What did you do with them?" Henry demanded. He looked around. "Are they here?"

"Colonel Travis," he said. "You know I had no cattle with me when I arrived."

"I wish you had," Travis said. "We could use the meat."

"You can ask Joseph Bayliss and the other men I came here with. I had no cattle, and no one mentioned cattle when I met up with them in Arkansas Territory."

"You had plenty of time to dispose of them before reaching Arkansas," Toby said.

Justin almost laughed. "And that's why I carry around a sack of gold eagles everywhere I go."

"It's not funny," Tobias said.

"Toby, you should examine your own sins. I've committed none against Henry Whitfield."

"What do you mean, Justin?" Abigail asked. She looked at Toby. "Do you know something you're not saying?"

"Only that Justin Sterling is a bitter man." Tobias turned away and spat in the dust.

Her eyes grew wide. "I know you couldn't have committed this offense, Justin. It's my father who's bitter. I've tasted bitterness myself over recent events."

Tobias gave her a spiteful look. "In this matter, you should keep your opinions to yourself."

Colonel Travis held up both hands. "That's enough, for now. Mr. Whitfield, we have fortified this mission to protect our claim on this part of Texas, which Mexico has never seen fit to fully rule. But even now an army under General Santa Anna is marching in our direction. They are but a day or two away. The charges you level against Mr. Sterling are serious, but I haven't heard or seen any solid evidence that he's committed a crime."

"I'll make him confess." Henry said.

"For the moment, at least, I am the legal authority here," Travis said. "Any criminal proceedings against Mr. Sterling will have to wait. Right now I need every man and every musket I have to defend this mission against an impending attack. When that business is finished, then we may address your charges against Mr. Sterling. Until then, please take advantage of whatever comfort here we can offer you."

"Thank you, Colonel." Henry glared at Justin. "I'm not through with you. And you will stay away from my daughter if you know what's good for you."

The weary horses were led to the stables, and the weary party of new arrivals was shown to the kitchen for food and drink. Abigail looked over her shoulder at Justin as Henry led her away. The remainder of the morning, her father kept Abby within arm's reach to enforce his edict against her communicating with Justin.

Justin spent much of his time stalking back and forth on the wall, pretending guard duty. He muttered to himself about things, real or imagined, that Henry Whitfield had done to thwart everything he'd tried to accomplish in life. As he paced the wall, he kept his eyes as much on the kitchen door as on the field over which the Mexicans were supposed to attack.

So distracted was he by his thoughts that he didn't see Abby come up onto the wall and stand directly behind him until turned around to walk in the other direction.

"Oh!" He almost stumbled into her.

"Good day, Justin."

They stood looking at each other, not knowing what else to say. He had barely leaned his musket against the wall, when they took each other into their arms and kissed. Long, searching, urgent kisses of two new lovers who hadn't held each other since their first embrace and didn't know if they ever would again.

Finally Justin held her tight to his chest, cheek to cheek. Her hair smelled wonderful. Seasoned as it was by campfires and days of travel, it still reminded him of home.

"How did you get away from your father?"

"I told him I was going to the latrine."

"He'll expect you right back."

"Not so soon. Men aren't well-versed in the workings of the female body. He'll give me some time before he comes looking."

He laughed. Abby pulled away and looked him in the eye with concern.

"You didn't steal my father's cattle, did you?"

"Good Lord, no. But I think I know who might have."

"Who?"

"Do you remember those two men who came to visit Toby when he was injured in the race at the county fair?"

"Of course. Who could forget such a disreputable pair?"

"I had seen them earlier at the fairgrounds, talking to Toby before the race."

"Whatever for? I don't remember any business he had with those two."

"I'm not sure, either, but I've known Toby long enough to learn some of his weaknesses."

"What are you saying?"

"I think he made a few wagers with Bailey and Smith about the race."

"Gambling?"

"Yes, and since Toby didn't finish the race, I suspect he lost whatever bets he'd made. That's why Bailey came to the house. To collect."

"How awful. But how does that concern my father's cattle—Oh! You think Toby stole the cattle to pay off his debts? That's a very tenuous supposition."

"It would be, if I hadn't seen Toby doing it. He didn't see me, but he was herding some of Henry's cattle the day I left Ridgetop."

"Odd, to be sure, but not that odd, given my father's fondness for the Johnsons."

"But odder still since it was barely sunrise and raining that day. Tobias isn't one to work in bad weather without a compelling reason. And, shortly after seeing Toby, I passed Bailey and Smith riding hell-bent for Sunday toward Ridgetop in a buckboard." He looked at the sky. "Of course, I don't really know what business Toby had with Henry's cattle, or if it had anything to do with Bailey and Smith, but any business they were mixed up in can't be aboveboard."

Abigail shivered and held her arms around her shoulders. "You make a compelling case, since Toby wasn't anxious to come with my father, except to see that you receive justice."

"I'm sorry to tell you these things, Abby. Sorrier still that you've come all this way and you're now in danger."

She shook her head. "To think I almost married Tobias."

"Almost?" Justin grasped her by the arms. "You haven't married?"

"No." She looked up into his eyes. "I couldn't marry Toby. Not after what we . . ."

He held her to his chest again and then let go. "That's wonderful! But how did you and Toby not marry?"

"I wanted to talk to you before you left, to tell you I would face my father's wrath before I'd agreed to his plan. I was waiting for the right moment and trying to find the courage, but you left before I could act."

"I couldn't live in Ridgetop without you. Can you imagine me watching you marry and raise someone else's children? I'm ashamed to admit I came to Texas thinking I might die and end my suffering. Now, seeing you again, has made me a happy man, even if Henry has me hanged. I'm glad you traveled all this way, but why? You're in danger here."

"I came because I had to. I couldn't believe you were a cattle thief." She touched his arm lightly. "And I have news for you."

"News? What news? Is my family all right?"

"Your family is worried about you, to be sure, but they're all well enough. Your parents don't know this, nor does my mother yet, but your family is about to grow a little larger." She placed his hand on her stomach.

"Jesus, Mary, and Joseph!" Justin's eyes grew wide with wonder. "You're with child?"

She nodded.

"And it's mine?"

She nodded.

He saw tears spring to her eyes and held her tenderly, but he was grinning from ear to ear. "My love, my love, my love. I have never received better news."

She sobbed into his shoulder. "I'm so happy to finally tell you."

He released her but still held her by the arms. "You're in danger. You have to leave here at once. All of you."

"No. I will not." She shook her head slowly. "I will never leave you again. Not as long as I have any say in the matter."

"But—"

"Abigail!" Henry's voice boomed. He stood at the base of the wall, hands on his hips. "Get down here this instant!"

Justin rolled his eyes. "Not again, Henry. Never again." He'd had enough of Henry Whitfield. He looked down at the older man without letting go of Abby. "Hold your tongue, Mr. Whitfield. I won't let you talk to Abigail in that manner. Not anymore. She's to be the mother of my child, and if you try to keep us apart any longer, I will thrash you within an inch of your life. Do you understand?"

"What?" Henry dropped his arms to his sides. "How can—I won't—you can't—"

"Not another word, man! Listen to me. Your only duty now is to see that Abigail is safely away from this place, as soon as you can mount your horses. Do you understand?"

Henry ripped his hat off and bowed his head, a defeated man.

At that moment a small fragment of the adobe wall near Justin splintered, followed by the crack of a musket shot. Other shots sounded. Justin looked over the wall and saw a small contingent of Mexican troops arrayed in the field, not more than two hundred yards away.

"Mexicans!" he shouted. "We're under attack!" One of the mission's cannons boomed, breaking up the Mexicans' tentative advance. More muskets fired as the defenders rushed to the wall and stockade. Justin pulled Abby toward him and helped her down a set of wooden steps to the ground.

"Go to the chapel," he said, pointing at the rounded façade of the mission. "It's the safest place. Look for Susannah Dickenson. She'll help you."

Abigail nodded. "I love you. Be careful." She kissed him on the lips. She kissed her father on the cheek, then she turned and ran across the compound toward the chapel. Justin and Henry watched her go, then rushed back up the steps, side-by-side.

"Lord help me, I'm a father," Justin muttered. "I'm a father, I'm in love, and I'm in the middle of a war."

The Mexicans had attacked with only a small advanced guard, to test the American's defenses. For the next few days, similar attacks occurred, but they were easily driven off with few serious injuries to anyone inside the Alamo. The main body of the Mexican army had not yet arrived, and it was still possible for someone to escape, but the noose was tightening around the impromptu fort. Colonel Travis sent riders in search of Sam Houston and others, requesting reinforcements, but everyone knew that time was running out. A bigger fight was coming, and the Americans would be significantly outnumbered.

As night fell, Abigail, Justin, Tobias, and Henry finally met as a group to discuss their situation. Abigail saw concern, anger, and confusion flash across her father's face in quick succession. Apparently he didn't know which problem to focus on first: the fact that his daughter was pregnant, that all their lives were in danger, or the idea that his cattle had been stolen either by the man who'd got his daughter pregnant or the man who was supposed to marry her.

"Justin is right," Tobias said. "We must leave at once."

"Yes, but leaving now will be dangerous, too." Justin pushed a cloth-cleaning patch down the barrel of his musket. "You should go at night, when it will be easier to avoid the Mexicans."

His reference to "you" going startled Abigail. "I'm not leaving without you, Justin." She clung to his arm and silently defied her father to object, but he didn't seem to notice.

"Right now we may be safer within the walls," Henry said. "The Mexicans didn't put up much of a fight today."

"They're waiting for reinforcements," Toby said. "It's not our fight, and it's crazy to stay here when we can still escape."

"I'm not anxious to leave," Justin said, "if leaving means I'll be tried for stealing cattle."

"What about your child?" Abigail said.

"Yes, I want my child to be safe. You and Henry should leave now, but I won't be much of a father if I'm hanging from a gallows."

"We can sort that out at a later time," Henry growled.

Her father's grudging statement gave Abigail hope that he wouldn't pursue his claims, but it still angered her that he entertained the slightest notion that Justin was a thief.

"Toby," she said. "Do you know a man named Bailey? Hutchison Bailey?"

"What?" Tobias gave her a startled look. "What do you know about Hutchison Bailey?"

"I've heard of the man," Henry said. "He's a no good. Makes his living gambling, preying on people who should know better."

"Apparently he's acquainted with Toby," Abigail said. "He came to visit you after the county fair horse race, when you were still unconscious."

"I don't know what you're talking about," Tobias said. But Henry gave him an appraising look, one that said his opinion of his almost son-in-law had changed.

"Have you had business with Hutchison Bailey?" Henry asked.

"Cattle business, perhaps?" Abigail added, but Justin put a restraining hand on her arm.

"Of course not," Tobias said. "I've spoken to the man once or twice. That's all."

"I remember you spoke to him just before the county horse race," Justin said.

"Yes, yes, I admit it." Toby wiped his brow with a handkerchief. "But I'd never do business with him."

Henry rolled his eyes and looked at Abigail as if he was sorry he'd ever considered that she marry Tobias. "We can argue about all of this later," he said. "Right now we've more important problems to deal with."

"That's right," Tobias said. "I'm in favor of leaving."

"I gave my word to Colonel Travis and the other men that I'd help them." Justin examined the cloth patch he'd pulled from the musket barrel for soot. "I think you should leave at once. Tonight, if possible. But I'd be considered a coward if I backed out now."

"Nobody would think you were a coward under the circumstances." Abigail placed a hand on her stomach.

"Perhaps not."

"Well, the rest of us haven't made any promise to fight,"

Tobias said.

Henry took off his hat. "This is all too much for an old man to contemplate. Let's get some sleep. We can reconsider our situation in the morning."

They all agreed.

Her father suggested that Abigail bunk with Major Dickenson's wife, Susannah, but Abigail would have none of it. Besides, Susannah and her infant daughter, Angelina, were quartered with the major. So Abigail stayed with Justin in a private corner of the low barracks, shielded by a blanket she strung on a rope. Seeing Abigail's determination to remain with Justin, Henry was finally beyond objecting.

Sometime during the night, Abigail awoke to the sound of half-a-dozen distant gunshots coming from somewhere outside the fort. Then silence.

"It's nothing," Justin said. "The Mexicans are probably shooting rats." He put a comforting arm around her shoulders and they went back to sleep. In the morning they found Toby's bed empty. It was reported that he had gone over the wall during the night with one or two other men.

He did not come back to the fort.

CHAPTER TWENTY-SEVEN

Ridgetop, Tennessee, March 5, 1836

It had been a week since Browning arrived at the Whitfield farm. Henrietta had explained the circumstances of Henry's absence to him, and that she was glad not to wait alone for his return, but Browning still felt uncomfortable. What would Henry think when he arrived and found Archie camped out in his own house, alone with his wife? Not alone, exactly. There were plenty of servants and farmhands around. And not in the same bedroom. Henrietta had set him up finely in a small guesthouse.

Still, Archie could imagine Henry's frame of mind, having just tracked down a cattle thief. He might demand a duel. Swords or pistols? Neither appealed to Browning. He could have taken his leave after that first cup of tea, but he wasn't able. Not after finding Henrietta. If Henry wanted a duel, so be it. That would at least settle things once and for all, one way or the other.

Henrietta appeared to be happy for his company. It was as if she'd been deprived of good conversation for heaven knew how long. She beamed as she recounted for him almost every minute that had passed since they were separated. If he had listened to any other woman's history, he'd have been bored to tears after the first ten minutes. But every moment of Henrietta's life, and Abigail's, fascinated him. It was much as he imagined it would be, with her living in comfort at the Whitfield farm, raising their

216

daughter. Their daughter. Sweet Abigail. It was the life Browning had hoped to provide Henrietta himself. He couldn't have done it as well as Henry, but in a sense, by his absence, he had.

When she tired of telling about her life, he stepped in and told her about his. When he spoke, he merely hinted at the crushing heartbreak and longing he'd suffered for so long. After all, his purpose in coming was to make amends, not to steal Henrietta away. He doubted that was even possible after so much time. But he was happy finally to be able to explain himself to his long-lost love, not to rekindle that love in her heart.

One day, Henrietta unexpectedly reached across the small table at which they sat and clasped his hand. Feeling her hand on his, he dared not move.

"I'm so glad you found me," she said. "But I've unburdened my heart to you, and that I never intended to do. You must forgive me."

"I must forgive you?" Browning was astounded at the kindness of the woman. "It's you, Henrietta, who must somehow find it in your heart to forgive me."

"We both did what we had to do, I suppose."

"And you've done well with Henry," he said.

"I could not have asked for a more comfortable life." Her gaze went out the window, as if she anticipated Henry's return, and the end of their unfettered conversation.

Before that happened, he wanted to talk about a less personal subject. "I am curious about some of the other families in the valley," he said. "From a professional viewpoint."

"Oh, which families would those be?"

"Specifically the Johnsons," he said. "And the Sterlings."

"Do you know them?"

"No, not personally, but I learned about them from my father, who was also a surveyor. His work brought him here in an earlier day, when the families were first settling the valley. Henry's father among them."

"How interesting that you have such a connection to us," Henrietta said. "But what of the Johnsons and the Sterlings?"

"My father told me an odd story about the families. In part, it's what sparked my interest in surveying. It's a profession that demands as much precision as possible, to prevent any disputes over property that might arise."

"Disputes? Were there many disputes among our families? I thought Henry's father kept a certain peace with the other landowners."

"There are no disputes I can see from the official records, but it's what may not be in the record that concerns me. My work has revealed some inconsistencies. Not in the record as it is kept by law, but in the story I was told by my father. I wonder if you could confirm or dismiss the details for me, if you know them."

"I can try. I've heard many stories from the days of the first settlers here, but I am not aware of any that call into dispute our property boundaries."

"And yet those very boundaries are at the heart of my story."

"Truly? You must tell me this story. Henry will be interested, too, if it concerns Whitfield property."

"Very well. Pour me another cup of tea, and I will tell you what I know."

Justin accepted a plate of corn pone and beans from the garrison's cook and sat at a long table in the kitchen. He'd just come off guard duty and he warmed his hands over the hot bowl before taking up the spoon. He'd taken his first bite when someone sat across from him at the table. Henry Whitfield.

"Good morning, Henry. If it's all the same to you, I'd rather I finished my breakfast before we come to blows."

"I'm not here to confront you. I'm here to make amends, if I can."

Justin looked at Henry, then he swallowed. "You're always welcome to have your say."

"I realize Abigail had a hand in, well, certain events that led to her being with child."

"It does take two, as you know."

Henry started to slap the table but stopped himself and lay his hand softly in front of him, palm down. "You're not making this easy, boy."

"I'm sorry, Henry. It's just that I've been in love with your daughter all my life, from the first moment I ever set eyes on her. And many's the time I thought you'd dedicated your own life to keeping me away from her."

"I did, at that." Henry grinned. "Don't get me wrong about the Sterlings. I've always admired your father. Walter's taken the worst land in Ridgetop County and turned it into a fine farm. He's a good man. And, in truth, so are you."

"Thank you. Even though it's late in coming, that's good news to my ears." Justin offered the plate of bread and beans to Henry, but the older man waved it off.

"I know my Abigail's had her eye on you, too, ever since we moved to Tennessee. Why else would I have done what I did? But she's no slouch when it comes to sizing up a man. Lord knows I've given her plenty of practice with other young men."

"And you did a fine job of it, up to a point."

Henry clenched his fist, then relaxed and reached for a biscuit from a wooden bowl on the table. "It's all for naught, since everything's changed. Look, Justin. We're in a proper fix here, you know that." He bit into the biscuit. "The Mexicans have got us fairly surrounded."

"It would only have been me in this fix, if I'd had my way. Not you and Abby."

"Yes, and I'm to blame for that, too. That's why I'm talking to you, Justin."

Justin dropped a half eaten piece of bread on the plate and pushed it aside. "What is it you want from me, Henry? I haven't stolen your cattle, and I will not apologize for loving Abby. I wish to the stars above that we'd had your blessing long ago, but I love her and I won't apologize for fathering her child."

"None of that. I'm the one who's apologizing, if you'll give me the chance. Let's look at the cards we have on the table. One or both of us may not survive this little encounter with the Mexicans, and I don't want to die without making amends."

Justin lowered his head, considering his options. For all the trouble Henry had caused him in his life, he might rightfully reject the old man's overtures, but he would take the high road for Abby, if not for himself. He looked Whitfield in the eye. "I forgive you, Henry. I do. I only wish it had never come to this."

"As do I, son. But let me be clear. I've always wanted the best for Abigail. That's why I've done what I've done. You know that."

"Aye." Justin nodded.

"As fine a man as you are, Justin Sterling, I never wanted my daughter to . . . well, have to struggle in this hard life, or to live below her means."

"I know, I know. I'd have felt the same as you, if she were my daughter. What little I've accomplished in my short life, I've done to impress you as much as Abby."

"And I was a fool not to see it."

"No, not a fool. Simply a loving father."

Henry nodded. The two men sat in mutual silence at the table, watching other defenders come and go through the kitchen, each one armed to the teeth with musket, pistol, and knife.

"What are we going to do for Abby now?" Justin finally asked.

"Prayer would be in order for all of us. But whatever happens, I do not believe the Mexicans will deliberately harm the women. They'll fight to the end, but they're a proud people, and murdering innocent women and children is beyond their ken."

"I hope that's so, but I'll pray that we all live," Justin said. "I have nothing more to desire in this life than to see your grandchild born. If only the women survive our little misadventure, I'll accept that as God's judgment. But know this, Henry Whitfield. If I live, I will never leave Abigail's side again. I will dedicate the rest of my life to her, and to our child."

"I've seen the way my daughter looks at you more often than I can recall, Justin, and I wouldn't want it any other way. I've spent much of my life a fool, but in my bones I've always known what kind of man you were, and I'd be proud to call you my son."

Henry held out his hand and Justin clasped it in both of his.

"Thank you, Henry. Now that we're all on the same side, let's find a way out of this mess."

CHAPTER TWENTY-EIGHT

Alamo Mission, March 5, 1836

Early the next morning Justin, Abigail, and her father sat at a table in the kitchen. The overcast sky outside threatened a cold spring rain, but the confidence of the mission defenders had grown since the first Mexican attack had been driven off so easily. A few men suggested the Mexicans might not attack again, if they knew what was good for them. Abigail's father wasn't so sanguine.

"I've read about this General Santa Anna in the newspapers," he said. "He's got too much pride to let a bunch of Texican farmers beat him at soldiering. He'll be back. He'll send more troops each time to test us, then hit us with everything he's got."

Other men knew about Santa Anna, too, and some had talked about slipping over the wall at night, as Tobias had, to sneak through the Mexican lines and escape, but no one else did. The afternoon of the day before, Colonel Travis gathered the men in the courtyard and explained their circumstances in no uncertain terms. Messengers had been sent to Sam Houston, and Travis hoped enough men were coming to break the siege. But they could not count on anyone else arriving before their battle with the Mexicans was decided.

Their situation was dire. Travis had drawn a line in the sand with his sword and asked every man who intended to stay and fight to cross the line and stand with him. Everyone did, including Justin and Henry. Abigail was proud of them, but she knew they and the others had little choice. They were surrounded, and it was better to fight the Mexicans in the light of day than try to run from them like frightened rabbits in the darkness. The men would fight and win, or face defeat and whatever that meant.

Abigail wouldn't let herself sink into despair. Somehow they would get through this. They had to. She and Justin would return to Ridgetop, start their family, and live to a ripe old age together. She clung to that hope in the face of mounting evidence to the contrary.

She and Justin were finishing a simple stew for breakfast when shouts went up from the men stationed on top of the chapel façade. As the highest point on the garrison and with a view in all directions, it served as the primary observation post. Abigail cocked her head at the sounds. She couldn't quite hear what the men were saying, but the meaning of their shouts was clear. The Mexicans were mustering for another attack. A small cannon mounted atop the chapel fired, and men snatched up their muskets and rushed from every part of the compound to the walls.

A familiar shaft of fear jabbed at Abigail's chest when she looked up at Justin. Somehow she'd hoped the Mexicans would go away, or the conflict could be settled without bloodshed. But it wasn't to be. Today would bring another chance that Justin or her father could be injured or killed. Justin swallowed one more sip of coffee from his tin cup, then pressed his lips to Abigail's.

"I love you like King Midas loved his gold," he said. "Don't worry. I'll be careful."

She gave him a wan smile. "You'd better be, for me and your baby."

Justin placed his hand lightly on her stomach. "I'd fight off a hundred Mexicans all by myself before I missed this child's birth." He kissed her again, then lifted his musket and ammunition bag and ran from the kitchen. Henry Whitfield was already on the wall.

In the last few days, Abigail had heard the skirmishes, had watched the growing army massing outside the walls, the menacing glint of bayonets in the sun as they marched. She knew that Justin fighting a hundred Mexicans all by himself might not be such an exaggeration.

As she had before, when the fighting started, Abigail went to the chapel and helped Susannah Dickenson and a handful of Mexican women at the fort tend to the wounded. A woman named Juana Alsbury, married to one of the men on the wall, showed Abigail where the medical supplies and equipment were kept. The sound of the battle outside threatened to unnerve her almost as much as knowing that Justin and her father were in the midst of it.

It wasn't long before wounded men were brought into the chapel, and she went to work. She steeled herself and tried to ignore any fearful implications, but a new, more threatening sound was heard. The Mexicans had opened fire with newly arrived cannon. They boomed in the distance in their own, strange language, then men and horses screamed as shells exploded on the walls and in the compound, sending up clouds of dust.

A few minutes later, Henry and another man carried Justin's limp body into the chapel.

"No!" Abigail almost screamed when she recognized his bloody face. They laid him down, unconscious, on a pallet in front of her.

"He's still alive," her father said. "Cannon fire hit the stockade near us. Others were not so lucky. It's a head wound, and I can't tell how serious it is."

"I've got him now." She steeled herself one more time.

Her father kissed her on the cheek and ran back to the wall

with the other man. By now Abigail had enough experience treating wounded men that her actions were nearly automatic. She ripped new bandages and cleaned a bleeding gash near Justin's hairline. When she doused his torn flesh with alcohol, Justin didn't react, but she knew he was still alive because the bleeding didn't stop. She wound a thick bandage around his head tightly enough to staunch the flow of blood. Then she checked him from head to toe for other wounds. There weren't any. The gash on Justin's head wasn't life-threatening by itself but until he regained consciousness, if he regained consciousness, she couldn't tell how badly he'd been wounded. At least he was alive, and for the moment he was no longer on the wall in the middle of the fight.

Browning sat back in his chair, uncertain how Henrietta would react to his tale. "By 1780 or thereabouts, all three families had begun to settle the Ridgetop Valley."

Henrietta sipped her tea. "That would include Henry's father, Abraham."

"Yes, as well as Wentworth Johnson and Josiah Sterling. They were all here by then."

"The family history says that Abraham died of smallpox."

"Aye, as did many others. That winter in the valley was hard, and everyone pitched in to survive. As spring approached and the first planting came nigh, neither Abraham nor Wentworth was up to the task. Few in the other families were, either. Many had been laid low by illness. It was Josiah Sterling who did the planting for himself and the Johnsons and Whitfields. Of course, the families' homesteads were somewhat smaller in those days. At least those of the Whitfields and Johnsons. But without Josiah, everything would have been lost."

"I hadn't heard that story, but I'm grateful to Josiah Sterling if it's true. It was very fortunate for us."

"Indeed." Browning took a bite of biscuit and watched Henrietta, gauging her reactions. "The thing about it is, in the beginning, all three families homesteaded more-or-less equal parcels in the valley, or so they thought. Boundaries, such as they were, were the stuff of common knowledge. Often they were described by the location of prominent trees, rocks, or bodies of water. Records were not well kept in those days, at least not in Ridgetop. And when the fever descended, some thought it was the end for everyone. As families lost loved ones, they joined with others in the valley to make do, and those who survived feared they might not be able to carry on. But Josiah persevered, and so grateful were the survivors of the other two families, that all three pledged their profits and land in common. Essentially they had become one, at least for the business of farming."

"How admirable," Henrietta said. "Those times were so hard."

Browning continued, knowing Henrietta still did not fully understand the implications of what he was telling her. "This history isn't reflected in what we now have as an official record of property deeds, but my father told me the families entered into a compact—a contract, if you will—by which their land was to be held and worked in common, for the good of all. The document was signed and dated, but no record-keeping office was available at that time for its safekeeping. Indians were still a threat, of course. Only one copy of the document existed, so who was to keep it? How would they know it was safe?"

"I can't say that I've ever seen such an historic document," Henrietta said. "Who did keep it? Where has it gone?"

"My dear, that is the kind of mystery that plagues a surveyor's heart. The families are said to have buried the document in a small chest, the location to be marked by a stone."

"Like pirate treasure? What fun!"

"Aye, but no one knows if the story is true, or what actually happened. And someone surely would have noticed such an odd stone, even if they weren't aware of its purpose. Unfortunately, Josiah, too, eventually succumbed to the pox. As time passed and the survivors among the families got themselves better secured, knowledge of the location of the agreement, or even of its existence, was eventually forgotten."

"How sad," Henrietta said.

"Hmmm." *Not sad for the Whitfields,* Browning thought. They managed to do better than the Sterlings, and, from the looks of it, even the Johnsons. He gazed out the window at the acres of mowed pasture and carefully tended fields.

"Henry came later to Ridgetop," he said, "and I doubt he knows anything about the history of the valley."

"He's never mentioned such a thing to me," Henrietta said. "Although he's always held the business close to his vest. I'm not sure he'd approve of this land agreement you speak of. Thomas Johnson surely would not."

"At this point it's only speculation. If such an agreement were found, and it proved to be legal, it would take some sorting out. It could change everything for the families."

"I'm glad it's Henry's problem. If something should befall the poor man and he doesn't return, I'm not sure I could carry on with this farm by myself."

Browning put a reassuring hand on her arm. "I have no doubt he will return, Henrietta. A team of oxen couldn't keep him away from you." Browning smiled, but he looked away to keep from revealing his true thoughts on that matter. He hadn't consciously considered the idea that Henry might not come back, and he couldn't bring himself to wish the man ill.

Later that evening, after Browning had excused himself, Henrietta sat on the porch again in the dark to watch for Henry.

Left alone, her sadness returned. Henry's and Abigail's absence, the idea that her family could be in trouble somewhere, and Browning's talk of history, caused her to dwell on her own long life in Ridgetop. She wondered where she'd be that very day if Browning had come back to her in Virginia so long ago. They'd have been married and life might have been very good.

But her life hadn't been so bad in Tennessee with Henry. Watching Abigail grow up and playing with her friends. Seeing her become a fine young—wait. A dim memory of Abigail's childhood intruded on her thoughts, unbidden.

It was a late summer day when the children came into the house after a game of hide-and-seek. Henrietta had been more concerned about the children's muddy feet but, yes, the children had told a fanciful story about an odd stone with carvings on it. They thought it might be a grave, or a marker for buried treasure, but the grownups had dismissed those foolish ideas. What the carvings were she couldn't remember, but they'd had something to do with the families. Could that have been the stone in Archie's story?

She rose from her chair, went out the screen door, and walked down the familiar path in the moonlit darkness to the guest cottage. A candle glowed in one window, indicating that Browning had not yet retired, even though the hour was late. She started toward the door to knock. Then she thought better of it.

Could the candle have been meant for her? Was it an invitation to join Archie in the cottage? Or did she simply wish that were so? Archie hadn't made any personal advances toward her since arriving, but he wasn't the kind of man who would. He would naturally want to know whether Henrietta still had feelings for him first. Then a candle at such a late hour might be his way of letting her take the first step, if she chose.

She hadn't come there for love, although surprisingly, the idea of it warmed her. She sighed and ran her hand through her hair to straighten it, but then she turned around and walked away. She got no more than twenty feet from the cottage before she turned back around to look at the candlelit window. She stood in the dark a full ten minutes, playing visions in her head of what might happen if she knocked on the door, or if Browning came outside and discovered her. The longer she stood there, the more she ached to knock, to see if any of her fantasies came true. No, of course they wouldn't. She'd made her choices long ago and she had to live with them. She sighed again, picked up the hem of her skirt, and walked back to the main house, to her own chilly bedroom.

They could talk about the odd, three-sided stone in the morning.

At breakfast, Henrietta couldn't help but consider Archie Browning in a new light. She watched him butter his toast and sip his coffee. He smiled at her and made small talk, but the ordinary tasks of eating the morning meal gave her no clue as to his deeper thoughts or how he felt about her now. Obviously he still had some feelings for her, although until the previous night she hadn't seriously considered the implications. She didn't need to speculate.

The man still loved her. He wouldn't have come to the farm, much less stayed as long as he had, if that weren't true. But he truly had been a gentleman. He made little mention of their courting days in Virginia, or of the longing he felt for her in all the intervening years. He wanted nothing from her now, or so he said. He simply acted as her steady companion as she waited for Henry and Abigail to return.

She shouldn't have been surprised. They were grownups, after all, and not subject to the barely controllable urges that tortured youngsters in love. Ah, but the urges hadn't disappeared entirely. Her cheeks turned warm as she remembered standing outside the cottage in the dark.

"You seem rather distracted this morning," Browning said, setting down his coffee cup. "I'd give a penny for your thoughts."

"My thoughts?" Henrietta started from her reverie. "They're not worth a penny, I assure you."

"You have a lot on your mind, I know. I'm sure he's fine, but I wish we had some news from Henry to end the mystery of his absence."

"The mystery? Yes!" Henrietta remembered their conversation of the day before. "I don't know about Henry, but I may know something about the stone you spoke of."

"Ah, the stone. Tell me. I need a clue."

"There is a stone, I'm sure of it. Abigail and her friends found it when they were children. We thought they were making up stories. They were quite insistent at the time, but nobody went looking for it."

Browning sat up straight. "Do you remember where they said it was?"

"No, they weren't very specific, if I recall. But they'd been playing near the creek. I remember that."

"That might be good enough. I have the current legal descriptions of the county properties, and I have my equipment. With your permission, I'll do a little snooping near the creek. See what I can find."

"Of course." Henrietta smiled, happy to give Browning something to do besides tend to her needs. Then she wondered what Henry would think.

CHAPTER TWENTY-NINE

March 6, 1836

Just before sunrise, Abigail found her father standing guard, his musket resting between the sharpened points of the wooden stockade, his gaze on the Mexican cooking fires, which were visible in the dim light almost a half mile away.

It struck Abigail that she still thought of him as her father. Even if Archie Browning's story were true, how could she not? She marveled at the changes she'd seen in him over the last few days. He seemed kinder, gentler than she'd ever known him. Had he always been that way and she hadn't realized it, or had her reckless behavior caused him to become a different man? She might never know. What she finally understood is that the stern father she had grown up with loved her with all his heart. As only a father could have.

He must have heard her footsteps on the wooden planking, but he kept his gaze outward, toward the enemy. When she finally stood at his shoulder, he looked down and put an arm around her.

"How's he doing?" he asked.

"I don't know. His wound has stopped bleeding and we've kept it clean, but I'm worried."

"There's not much more you can do."

"His injury doesn't seem so severe, but he hasn't awakened."

"It's a head wound." He put his hand back on the stock of his gun and looked out at the Mexicans' camp. "We know so little about what head wounds do to the human mind. Only time will tell."

"I keep thinking of Tobias's Uncle Abraham."

"The one who fell from the barn loft two years ago?"

"Yes. He slept for more than ten days, and only then passed away."

"I remember. But poor Abraham didn't have you waiting by his bedside."

"I wish there were more we could do for Justin. He calls to me in his sleep."

"I'm not surprised. You're the most important thing in the world to him."

"And he to me. I don't know if I'd want to go on living without him."

"I know," her father said. "More importantly, Justin knows it, too. Right now he's wrestling with God. They're trying to work out between them if it's Justin's time. I'm certain Justin is presenting a very strong argument before the Lord. You should have faith. I know he'll come back to us, but . . ."

"But it may not be in time? Is that what you mean?"

He looked down at his hands, then at her. "Abigail. If you can find it in your heart, please . . . please forgive me for not seeing earlier the feelings you and Justin have for each other."

"Oh, Father." She put her arms around him. "There's no need—"

"No," he said. "That's not right. I did see it. I did. I just thought. I just didn't—"

She hugged him. "You did what you thought was right."

"I was a fool."

"No, Father. You love me. I know that."

"You're a wonderful girl, Abby, and I always wanted the best for you."

Abigail noted his use of the past tense. She, too, looked over the wall at the Mexicans making preparations for the day's battle.

"Is it hopeless?" she asked.

His gazed dropped to his musket. "I can't lie to you. For me, perhaps, and the rest of the men, it may be. You heard the Mexicans' bugle call, earlier?"

"We all heard it. It was a strange thing to hear over a battlefield."

"The Mexicans called it *El Degüello*. They play it when . . . when they want you to know they don't intend to take any prisoners."

"What? How can they do that?"

He chuckled. "They have all the guns, dear. In the end, they'll do pretty much whatever they want."

"But there are women here. And children."

"Aye, and God willing, the Mexicans will spare them since they're not combatants. The men tell me Santa Anna is a crazy fool, but he still has the Spanish sense of dignity."

"Perhaps he's had enough fight. Perhaps he'll decide it's not worth attacking the mission again."

"No, lass. It's precisely because we've bested his men so far that Santa Anna won't quit. That is the Spanish pride. Unfortunately, we no longer have enough men, powder, or shot to stop him."

"Hasn't Colonel Travis sent for reinforcements? They could—"

He put a hand on her arm. "Abigail. When Santa Anna comes again, it will be the end. We may all be with God by the end of the day."

She stood next to him, her mouth open in shock as they looked out over the calm, grassy field that lay between the mission and the Mexican troops.

"Justin," she said. "He doesn't deserve this."

"Nor do you, or any of us, I suppose. But it's the price men pay when they take up arms for a cause."

"Justin is wounded. He can't even fight back."

"I wish there were something I could do," he said.

"Maybe there is. Father, do you have any orange blossoms?"

"Aye. Your mother thought I might have trouble sleeping on the ground. But—"

"Where are they?"

"They're in the saddlebags, next to my bunk." He pointed along the wall to the low barracks at the end of the stockade.

She put both hands on his arm. "May I have them, please, for Justin?"

"Of course, my dear."

"Thank you."

She kissed him on the cheek and hurried to the barracks. She found the soft, deer-leather bag and held it in her hand, gauging the weight of it, trying to determine how many of the orange blossoms she'd need. She took the whole bag and hurried outside, past the stockade where Henry still stood guard. The sky had lightened. Morning had come. She went into the chapel where the wounded lay and found Mrs. Dickenson talking softly to a man with a shoulder wound.

"Everything will be all right," Mrs. Dickenson told the man but, by the look on his face, Abigail could tell he didn't believe it.

"Pardon me, Susannah." She gestured toward the back of the chapel near the altar, where Justin and the more seriously wounded men lay. "Could you help me for a moment?"

"Surely, dear." Susannah patted the wounded man on his good arm, rose to her feet, and followed Abigail.

She found Justin lying in the same position on his pallet as she'd seen him almost an hour earlier, and she feared he might be dead. She paused a moment and watched his chest. When it rose with his next breath, she relaxed and turned to Susannah.

"My father has given me a quantity of orange blossoms. I wish to make a potion for Justin to make him sleep."

Susannah gave Abigail a questioning look. "It's a remedy I have used myself on occasion, but Justin is already asleep."

"My fear is that he will awake and return to the fight, but he's in no condition—"

"And the Mexicans may spare the wounded, especially one who's not conscious." Susannah finished her thought. "That's exactly what Justin would do. It's a good plan."

Susannah helped her prepare the potion, using a measure of brandy, the only liquid other than water available for cleaning wounds. She handed Abigail a full cup. "That should be enough. With your permission, I will use the rest of this, and make some additional mixture to give to the other wounded."

"Of course."

Susannah left. Abigail sat down and cradled Justin's head carefully in her lap. Lifting the cup to his lips, she coaxed him to swallow the potion.

"Drink, my love," she whispered.

"Mmmm?" Justin moaned. His eyes fluttered but didn't open.

"Drink for me and sleep." She stroked his forehead, brushing back his long black hair, careful not to touch the darkly stained bandage around his head. Justin's lips parted and Abigail fed him the slightest bit of the potion that would keep him from choking. He swallowed, started to cough, but then sighed. She gave him some more and continued to feed him until the potion was gone.

"I wish we were home," she whispered. "You and me, lying under an elm tree, next to the cool creek. I would feed you grapes. You would tell me how beautiful my hair is, shining in the sunlight. I would tell you how much I love you."

A tear trailed down her cheek, but she brushed it away before

235

it could fall on Justin's face.

"You must forgive me for what I'm going to do," she said. "I need you to live. Our baby needs you to live."

Gently she laid his head back on the pallet. Then she rose to her feet and looked around the nave. Daylight was beginning to show through the glassless windows. Susannah and the other women were tending the wounded. No one was watching her.

She stepped carefully behind the slightly elevated chapel altar. Hidden from view, she tested the floorboards with her feet, alternately putting her weight on one leg, then releasing it. The flooring here consisted of dry wooden planks almost a foot wide and six feet long. They were as old and badly worn as those in the rest of the chapel, and she quickly found what she was looking for. The end of one wide plank squeaked when she put her weight on it, and one end rose almost half an inch. She got down on her knees and gripped the loose end of the board, pulling at it until the full length of it popped free. She stopped, fearful someone would look behind the altar to find out what had made the odd noise. All she heard were a few moans from the wounded and snoring from some others. She carefully set the board aside and peered into the dark space where the plank had been removed. She couldn't see what was below, so she reached down into the space, hoping her hand wouldn't land on a scurrying rat, or a hairy tarantula. Her fingers found dry dirt nearly an arm's length below the floor. Good. Plenty of room. She worked at a second plank until it, too, came loose, and she had created an opening in the floor six feet long and two feet wide.

She rose to her feet and went back to where Justin lay. His breathing seemed deeper, his sleep more sound, hopefully the result of the orange blossoms. Standing at Justin's head, she bent down and gripped the corners of the blanket on which he lay. Slowly, carefully, she lifted and pulled, using greater effort until at last Justin started to slide toward her. Taking advantage of her momentum, she continued to pull, sliding him and his blanket behind the altar until his head lay at one end of the long opening in the floor. She stopped to catch her breath. Then she stepped into the hole, turned and pulled Justin toward her, holding the blanket up to keep his head and shoulders from falling. When she had pulled him far enough, his bottom dropped. Now he was sitting in the hole, his ankles still resting on floorboards, and his head and shoulders suspended on the blanket she held in her hands. With one last tug, his feet dropped into the hole, and she gently set the rest of his body down.

Justin moaned, but he didn't wake up.

As gently as she could, she wriggled out from under Justin and climbed out of the hole. She made two more trips to the hole, leaving Justin's musket and a few other belongings. Kneeling over the opening, she made sure he lay fully on the blanket, and that his arms and legs were in a comfortable position. Sitting on her knees, she bent down and placed a soft kiss on his lips.

"Goodbye, my love. I'm counting on you to live."

Justin moaned again, but this time it didn't sound like he was in pain.

She stood and took her time replacing the floorboards. She stood on the square metal nails as hard as she could to fix them back in place. When she finished, she heard the first sounds of Mexican cannon fire. Shells exploded in the courtyard, throwing up dirt and dust. Shouting men ran to and fro.

The battle had begun.

Abigail ran toward the front doors of the chapel, but Susannah reached out and clutched her sleeve, stopping her.

"You'll only be in the way," she said.

"My father's out there. I have to go."

Susannah gave her a wan smile and let go of her sleeve. "We'll be here when you come back."

Abigail ran from the chapel and into a mass of confusion, cannon fire, and smoke. Musket shot rattled from all sides. She raced toward the wooden stockade, dodging men carrying powder and shot to the walls and wounded men stumbling back. She made her way to the wall, just beneath where her father stood. As she watched, he fired his musket. When he turned and crouched down to reload, he saw her.

"Get away," he said. "Go to the chapel!"

"Let me help you!" she shouted.

"We have enough to worry about." He reached down and briefly held her outstretched hand. "I need to know you're as safe as you can be."

Half a dozen bullets shattered the wood on the tips of the stockade wall behind him. Splinters tore through Abigail's hair and raked her cheek. Involuntarily she turned her head and let go of her father's hand.

"Go now!" he shouted. "Remember me and tell your mother I think of her. I love you!" He cocked his musket and stood up to fire over the wall.

Tears filled her eyes as she turned away. She could barely find her way back to the chapel, stumbling through a confusion of smoke and dust, and screaming men. Inside the chapel the din outside barely diminished. She found Susannah and the other women tending the newly wounded and went to help them.

She tried not to think about what was happening outside, what could happen to them all.

CHAPTER THIRTY

Whitfield Farm, Ridgetop County, Tennessee, March 7, 1836

Archie Browning stood in a field of tall grass and leaned on his shovel. He was near the edge of the Whitfield property, beyond the fields they regularly planted or grazed. Fifty yards or so in front of him lay what his survey papers called Little Elk Creek. It wasn't hard to make out the path of the creek bed, lined as it was by broad-leafed ferns, black willow trees, and cottonwoods. It formed a natural barrier between the Whitfield property and the neighboring lands. As he scanned the area, he tried to imagine himself a boy, ten or twelve years old, and playing hide-and-go-seek in the field. Where would he run? Where would he hide? A number of small, man-made structures, sheds, windmills, and farm equipment dotted the field, all of them inviting places for a child to hide.

But that wouldn't be where he'd find the stone, if it existed. Nor would the stone be placed in the middle of a field, where it might be struck by a plow or take up valuable planting space. No, the early settlers would have placed it near a prominent natural landmark, where it could be located later. Like the creek.

Studying the survey drawing in his hands, he realized the creek branched almost half a mile upstream from where he stood. The narrowing Y-shaped point of land formed by the intersecting creek beds enclosed the lower portion of the Sterling property, which reached uphill from there. Not the best land for cultivation. But, if the stories about the stone were true, the confluence of the creeks would be a natural location for the stone monument, since it marked the one place were all three families' properties met.

He decided to look there first. He picked up his shovel, tucked his survey papers under his arm, and started walking toward the confluence. His gaze swept back and forth, searching for anything out of the ordinary. Where he saw deer paths worn through the grass, he followed them, since a running child might also follow them to a hiding place, even though he knew the stone wouldn't be in the middle of a path. At the confluence, the banks of both creeks were overgrown with grasses, ferns, willows, and other vegetation. A good hiding place, but it wouldn't afford complete concealment.

Just below the confluence the larger, combined, creek bed turned away from him, toward the Johnson property. He stepped to the edge of the creek and looked over the bank. Below him, water burbled and bounced over rocks. The increased volume and flow had cut away a portion of the near-side bank beneath him. Essentially, he was standing on a ledge. Leaning outward, he could see the dark shadow of the empty space below. It would have been an excellent hiding place, especially at a time of low flow, as in late summer when the water wouldn't rise high enough in the creek to fill the undercut space.

But the creek bed on that day would not be the same as it had been ten or fifteen years earlier. With the force of rushing water, the bend would have moved downhill and downstream over time. If such an undercut bank existed earlier, it would have been upstream from where he now stood, but probably not far away.

He turned north, toward the Sterling property, and made his way with some difficulty along the creek. Here there had not been many cattle, at least recently, and there were few worn pathways. His pant legs swooshed through thigh-high grass and he had to bend low to pass under willows. He saw nothing unusual, nothing that looked like a stone monument.

Finally he stopped and set down the shovel. He pulled off his broad-brimmed hat and wiped his brow with a handkerchief. What kind of foolishness was this, anyway? Here he was, tramping around in an overgrown field, looking for a stone that no one living could remember, and which could have been nothing more than a children's story. He was lucky he hadn't stepped on a cottonmouth or a copperhead. No, without more information, he might as well be searching for the proverbial needle in a haystack.

He wasn't sure how Henrietta would feel if he found the monument, anyway. If there was a contract among the families, it would only serve to dilute the Whitfields' interest in what they'd considered their land for at least three generations. Of course, the contract also would have provided them with an interest in tracts of land well beyond their own holdings, but that interest would be shared by the other families. Perhaps it was better that he never found the mythical stone.

He plopped his hat back on his head, scooped up his shovel, and started walking away from the stream. He shielded his eyes with one hand and looked to the far side of the field for the quickest route back to the Whitfield house without retracing his steps.

"Ouch!" His foot hit something solid and he barked his shin. He pitched forward and his hat flew off as he let go of the shovel and survey maps. He landed facedown in the thick, damp grass. Lying on his stomach, he propped himself on his elbows and whispered a curse through the tall blades of grass that pressed against his face and tickled his cheeks. He could tell without looking that he'd torn his pants and that his leg was bleeding. Not badly, but the injury smarted. The injury to his pride was worse. Surveyors were supposed to know where things were, not trip over them.

He crawled to his feet and went to examine what he'd stumbled over. A stone. He almost kicked it, but then saw that it had three smooth sides and was capped in a pyramid. Moss and lichens had grown over most of the stone's three faces, but he could still see where writing had been chiseled into each flat surface, like a gravestone.

"Lord a'mighty," he said. "It's true after all."

He looked around for his shovel.

The Alamo Mission

Early in the battle, the flow of wounded men brought into the chapel on stretchers seemed unending, but now it began to slow. To Abigail, this was an ominous sign. There might not be enough men left outside to carry on the fight and help the wounded at the same time. Thankfully, so far none of the wounded men was her father. He would either be killed outright or taken prisoner, if any prisoners were taken. He'd said their situation was hopeless, that the Mexicans were sure to win. But what that meant for any surviving defenders she didn't know. If the Mexicans won, they would come to the chapel sooner or later. She would face that when it happened.

The noise of the battle outside gradually rose to a crescendo, then the cannon and musket fire diminished, replaced by the clash of steel and shouts of men. The enemy was within the walls. The men were fighting hand-to-hand now, with no time to reload. As a precaution, Abigail took the small pistol from her purse, checked the load, and put the gun in her apron pocket. What good it would be against the entire Mexican army, she had no idea, but having it with her gave her some comfort.

She returned her attention to the wounds of the men lying in front of her. She stripped bandages from sheets of cotton, cleansing and dressing wounds as quickly as she could. Every few minutes she would glance in the direction of the chapel altar, half expecting Justin to stumble forth and demand to get back into the fight. She prayed he would sleep long enough for the battle to be over.

In the middle of helping Susannah dress a man's torn leg, she realized she no longer heard the relentless din of fighting. On the other side of the wounded man, Susannah's hands stilled. Abigail looked up. More than a dozen uniformed Mexican soldiers crouched in the doorway of the chapel. Their bayonets were leveled, ready to attack, but they waited, seemingly uncertain what to do with women and the wounded.

Susannah stood up and faced the soldiers, wiping her bloodied hands on a rag.

"*Espere.*" She gestured at the men lying on cots around her. "*Sólo tenemos aquí los hombres heridos.*"

Abigail hoped they got the gist of what she'd said. There would be no resistance. There were only wounded men left in the chapel.

One Mexican soldier pushed through the group. From the gold braid on his uniform and his sword, Abigail assumed he was an officer. He glanced around at the many wounded men lying on pallets and low cots. Then, looking at the women, he pointed his sword back at the chapel entrance.

"*Todas las mujeres tienen que salirse . . . Ahora!*"

The Mexican women nodded and gathered up their skirts. Juana Alsbury looked at Abigail. "They want us to leave, go outside."

"*Vamonos!*" the officer shouted.

"I think we should obey." Susannah picked up Angelina.

Abigail set down her bandages and walked with Susannah, Juana, and the other Mexican women toward the chapel entrance. The soldiers kept their bayonets leveled at them as if they expected the women to attack them as fiercely as their men

243

had. But they gradually moved aside so the women could pass.

In the yard in front of the chapel, the light of the midmorning sun was shrouded by dust and smoke, which lay like a pall over a scene of complete destruction. At the smell of it, Abigail took a bandage from her sash and held it over her nose and mouth. The wooden stockade where her father and Justin had fought was breached in several places and lay in ruins. Parts of it were smoldering and on fire. The bodies of soldiers, Mexican and American, lay everywhere, some still in each other's grasp, where they'd fought to the very the moment they died. Muskets, swords, and all manner of equipment lay broken and scattered. Even the branches of the apple trees in the courtyard had been shredded by gunfire.

Abigail scanned the ruined stockade with every step she took. She wanted to run to the wall and look for her father, but her feet were leaden, and she and the others were hemmed in by soldiers. Any Americans or Texicans she saw appeared to be dead. The only men left standing were Mexican soldiers and the black man, Joe, whose hands were bound as a prisoner.

She and Joe caught each other's eye, and she felt the despair written on his face. Joe had fought alongside Colonel Travis, but the Mexicans must have spared his life for some reason. Perhaps they thought Joe, a slave, had been forced to fight. Perhaps they were saving him for some special execution.

Her father might have been taken away, too, but he'd said the Mexicans wouldn't take any prisoners. Other than Joe and the women and children, it didn't look as if they had. She thought she'd seen enough fighting and death to have become accustomed to it, but the idea that her father and all the other men she'd talked to that morning were gone threatened to overwhelm her. She no longer wanted to see her father in death, especially if his wounds were severe. Now she only feared for Justin. She prayed he remained hidden, at least until the fever

244

of battle subsided, if not his own fever. With the conflict over and won, perhaps the Mexicans wouldn't execute him on sight.

Abigail and the others were herded toward the south gate, which had been thrown open. Since they were mere women, the Mexicans might have considered them harmless. In any case, they were not searched. She could feel the weight of the small pistol bumping against her thigh as she walked. The women were brought to a halt in front of a group of officers, deep in discussions, who paid them no attention. One man noticed them, then the others. One officer came forward. He was shorter than most of the others, but with a more impressive uniform and braiding. He removed his bicorn hat and nodded courteously. When he spoke, his English was excellent.

"I am Generalissimo Antonio López de Santa Anna," he said. "And you are my prisoners."

CHAPTER THIRTY-ONE

March 8, 1836

The distant noise concerned Justin, demanded his attention, but he wasn't sure of its source or why it was so important. His eyes fluttered, not fully opening, but he saw nothing but darkness. He felt his coat covering him like a blanket. His head throbbed too much for him to want to open his eyes. His shoulders and hips ached, and his stomach rumbled with hunger. Through his pain he remembered that he'd injured his head somehow. At that moment the "how" didn't matter as much as the hurt. He knew Abby would be concerned about him, but the idea that she was somewhere nearby comforted him. Not wanting to worry her, he let himself slip back into unconsciousness.

In his dream, Justin was back in the Ridgetop fields near his home, near the creek where he once played hide-and-seek with Abby and Tobias. The sun was shining, he was a child again, and he was happy. Not a care in the world. Barefoot, he lay on his back under the shade of an elm tree with a long piece of sweetgrass in his teeth. Abby stood over him, trying to get his attention. He had a dopey grin on his face as he admired her every moment. But Abby wasn't smiling. She reached down and shook his shoulders.

He looked in the direction she pointed and saw row after row of uniformed Mexican soldiers marching slowly, mechanically toward them. Their faces were blank, expressionless. Their ranks stretched to the horizon on either side, an endless army of identical soldiers, each one wearing a tall uniform hat, with bayonet leveled and coming steadily toward them. Then he was running, pulling Abby away with one hand, while he tried to load his musket with the other. Fumbling, he managed to get off one shot at nearly point blank range, but hit nothing. The Mexicans continued their lock-step advance, and no matter how fast he ran or how much he pulled Abby, he couldn't put any distance between them and the slow marching enemy. Abby screamed and he awoke.

He saw nothing but blackness, and his eyes couldn't quite focus. He tried to raise his head and quickly hit his forehead on a wooden plank. That hurt. He lay back down to let the pain subside while he tried to make sense of his surroundings. At the corners of his vision he saw dust particles dancing in the air. They shone along narrow bands of sunlight that streamed through slits, which ran from head to toe on either side of him. The slits were about a foot apart. He felt like he was lying down with his coat over him, but he was facing a wall of wooden boards. How could that be?

For a moment he almost panicked, thinking he was in a coffin, mistaken for dead and prematurely buried. But the sunlight streaming through the slits reassured him. If he was in a coffin, it was one of sloppy construction, and he wasn't underground. Not yet, at least. He turned his head slowly against the pain and looked to either side. More boards formed walls on both sides of him, a few inches away. They didn't quite touch his shoulders and, as far as he could tell, the distance between them didn't narrow toward his feet, as they would in a coffin. Then he recognized the construction. The boards on either side of him were joists. He was lying on a blanket underneath a wooden floor. Who had put him there? Why?

He almost called out for help, but something stopped him.

The last thing he remembered, he was at the Alamo Mission and facing an overwhelming army of Mexicans. But he heard nothing overhead. No sounds of battle. No footsteps. Not even conversation. The silence from the other side of the boards wasn't natural and he remained cautious. Besides, whoever had put him where he was must have had a good reason.

He judged the distance between his nose and the surface in front of his face at no more than five to six inches. Not much, but enough room to move his arms up to his sides to get some leverage against the boards. He listened again but still heard nothing. He pushed aside his coat, pressed his hands flat against the boards, and increased the pressure. The nails squeaked, but they moved easily. He stopped and listened. Still no sound. Finally he pushed the boards away from his face and let them drop to the side. Staring up at the distant ceiling, it took him a few seconds to realize he was lying in the chapel. The stale, acrid smell of burned wood, gunpowder, and, yes, flesh filled his nose and he almost gagged. With some effort he sat up and rested his elbows on the floor next to the hole. From that angle he saw his saddlebag lying at his feet, along with a length of rope. His musket lay under the floorboards too.

"Interesting," he muttered. "I've been buried like an Egyptian pharaoh, with all of my belongings." He touched the bandage around his head and winced. "I'm not dead, but I might feel better if I were."

He threw his coat aside, lifted himself up and out of the opening, and rolled over until he lay on the floor. His mind raced at the implications of what had happened to him and the lack of any significant sounds. Only a steady spring breeze gusted through the gaping chapel windows. A thousand questions ran through his mind. Where had everyone gone? Had the battle ended? Was Abby still alive? If so, where was she? Was it she who'd put him under the floor? Why? He had to get outside and find someone for answers.

Moving his limbs took away a bit of their ache and stiffness. Feeling better, he got to his knees, then stood up. His head spun for a moment, but he steadied himself against the wooden altar, which was taller than he by four feet. He knelt back down and reached into the opening to retrieve his musket, bag, and rope.

He also found a small leather pouch. It wasn't his, and it must have lain under the floor much longer than he had. It was so covered with dust that it was almost indistinguishable from the dirt. He picked it up and blew at the dust. Inside the faded, cracked leather he felt what must have been metal coins.

"My lucky day," he said. "In more ways than one." He put the pouch in his coat pocket.

He coiled the rope and put it over his head and one shoulder. Then he looked at the bag and remembered that he had carried a portion of jerked beef. He flipped the bag open, found the beef, and tore off a chunk with his teeth, letting it dissolve slowly in his mouth. The salty taste of it almost overwhelmed him, but he refused to chew until the beef had softened, since chewing hurt his head. After swallowing the beef, he looked into the bag again and realized whoever had placed him under the floor included a small leather water flask and some hardtack. He popped the cork stopper from the flask and swallowed a mouthful of water. His strength was slowly returning. He replaced the cork, put the water flask in his saddlebag, and hoisted the bag onto his shoulder.

Taking up his musket, he stepped around the weathered chapel altar. What he saw of the open nave concerned him greatly. There were no bodies, but the floor was strewn with pallets, stretchers, blankets, bandages, and other materials necessary for tending the wounded. There must have been a lot of wounded. Dark pools of blood ran over on the floor and stained most of the bedding materials. No one had bothered to clean the room, which didn't bode well for the outcome of the battle. Then to his left, he saw two elderly Hispanic women. They had been kneeling in silent prayer, but they looked up at him in disbelief. His sudden appearance from behind the altar must have startled them. They crossed themselves repeatedly and stared at him.

"Buenos días," he said, using some of the Spanish he'd picked up during his time in Texas. *"Por favor. Donde estan los hombres Americanos?"*

"Ah," one of the women said. *"Muerte."* She crossed herself again. *"Todos son muerte. Lo siento, mucho, señor."*

Muerte was a word he understood. Dead. Everyone? Could that be? He refused to believe everyone had died. Not Abigail. Not his child. He couldn't face that, and he wouldn't believe it until he saw the proof with his own eyes.

"Y los soldados Mexicanos?" he asked carefully. He wasn't sure where the old women's sympathies lay.

"Ido. Todo se ha ido."

Justin didn't understand the words, but the woman waved her hand in the air, indicating that everyone had gone away.

"Gracias."

The woman talked rapidly to each other in Spanish while Justin stumbled toward the chapel entrance, fearful of what he'd see. Outside, squinting in the sunlight, he could tell the destroyed compound had been the scene of a fierce battle. Once again, there were no bodies, but bloodstained sand and ruined equipment lay everywhere. Whiffs of smoke still rose from the smoldering wood of the stockade, and from the interior of the low barracks. He didn't want to look inside, but he made himself. He didn't find anyone alive or dead within the wreckage of the rooms. That might have been a good sign had it not been for the foul smell of burned flesh, hints of which wafted through the air.

The main gate of the compound lay open and, outside the walls, Justin immediately came upon a large disturbed area of scorched earth. Apparently the bodies of the dead had been burned, and then hastily buried in the Texas soil. He did not look too closely, but a piece of scorched buckskin and a twisted, melted pair of spectacles told him the men buried here had been defenders, not the Mexican dead. He wouldn't know whether Henry, Abigail, and his child had met their fate in this funeral pyre, but many of the men he'd known surely had. Undoubtedly he'd been hidden under the chapel floor while he was unconscious to escape this fate. They must have known the fight was hopeless. Tears sprang to his eyes. He dropped to his knees and wept, his fingers clawing at the charred earth.

After a few moments he set his jaw and wiped his eyes. He refused to believe God was cruel enough to make him a father and take away the mother and his child so quickly. He would seek news elsewhere and find out if any of the Americans had walked away. If no one survived, truly he had nothing to live for. He would find other Texicans, men who continued the fight, and he would avenge the loss of his family.

He heard a nickering sound. When he looked up he saw a brown and white pinto mare. It had no saddle, and it was grazing quietly on the spring grass just outside the wall, a mere thirty yards away.

"Hello there, girl." He made some quiet kissing sounds. The horse raised its head and looked at him briefly, then it went back to eating. More importantly, it didn't run away. It probably wasn't wild. Justin dropped his musket and saddlebag and fashioned a loop in the end of the rope. Then he pulled up a few sprigs of nearby alfalfa. With the rope behind his back, he rose to his feet. Holding the alfalfa snack out in front of him, he slowly made his way toward the grazing animal.

Susannah Dickenson, a soldier's wife, seemed to know what was expected of prisoners of the Mexican army. Abigail stayed close to Susannah and helped her with Angelina whenever she could. They were fed as well as could be expected by an army on the march, often dining with General Santa Anna in his personal tent, but Abigail had little appetite. Occasionally she thought about the pistol still hidden among her meager belongings. Using it on General Santa Anna would have been appropriate revenge for her father's death, but such an act would certainly mean her own death, too.

As much as she might want revenge, she wouldn't do anything. She was with child and her life was no longer her own. Justin might still be alive, somewhere, and that let her cling to the dim, flickering hope that someday they'd be reunited. That they could go back to the life they'd once known, only now as man and wife. Those thoughts, foolish as they might have been, sustained her and kept her going with each passing day.

The general seemed particularly taken with Susannah and Abigail. He did everything he could to make Abigail comfortable, too, after learning she was pregnant. He expressed sincere regret that Susannah's husband had been among the casualties. Such was his concern that he offered to send Angelina to a school in Mexico City and raise the girl as his own daughter. Under the circumstances, Susannah expressed gratitude for the general's concern and politely declined his offers of help. Fearing to press the matter, the women had no idea when or if they would ever be freed to return to the United States. They were allowed to ride in a supply wagon when the army marched away from the ruined mission, looking for other rebellious Americans who claimed territory belonging to Mexico.

Abigail was numb to the buzzing activity around her. She couldn't quite grasp that her father had been killed, along with all of the other men who'd defended the Alamo, except Joe. She hadn't seen her father's body, but the Mexicans insisted there hadn't been any other survivors. She wept at night when she was alone in the women's tent, but she had to accept the awful truth. Her father was gone.

No one ever mentioned a man hiding under the floorboards of the chapel, but Abigail understood little of the many conversations in Spanish she overheard. If Justin survived his wound and found his way out of the Alamo, he'd probably assume Abigail had died along with everyone else. He'd go back to Tennessee and give the grim news to her mother. She had no idea what he'd do then, but at least he'd be alive. She took some comfort in that thought. She could only imagine how her mother would receive the news of Abigail and her father's death. All alone at home, the poor woman would be beside herself with grief. If only Abigail could send word to Tennessee. For the time being, however, they were in a strange and hostile land, and at the mercy of the Mexican army.

The woman talked over their situation one night after a meager but filling supper of Mexican beans and tortillas.

"I think the army is heading toward San Jacinto," Susannah said.

"Is that north or south?" Abigail asked. She wanted to be as close to home as possible if they had any chance of being released.

"It's east of here."

"Even better," Abigail said.

"Look, Abby, I have some bad news."

"What news?" A shaft of fear iced her chest, but she couldn't imagine any worse news than she'd already been given unless

Justin, too, had died.

"The Mexicans are letting me go, along with Angelina and Joe. They're taking us back to Béxar."

"That's good news. But—"

Susannah shook her head again. "Santa Anna isn't releasing you or the Mexican women. Not yet at least. He wants Joe and me to tell the Americans about his glorious victories. They want to demoralize any more settlers who might be coming from the States. They've freed Joe, hoping other slaves will escape and come to Texas."

Abigail reached out and took Susannah's hands in hers.

"That really is good news. I'm happy for you. And for Joe."

Susannah shook her head. "I wish you could come with us. I don't know what Santa Anna wants with you or the other women, but I can imagine."

"Don't worry. I'll find a way to make him let me go, I promise you that." Abigail held her chin up, but she didn't feel her own bravado.

Susannah gave her a wan smile.

"I should stay here. I can protect you."

"No." Abigail squeezed Susannah's hands. "I need you to go. I need you to tell the world that I'm here. If you do that, Justin might find out I'm still alive."

Susannah looked perplexed. "Abby. There were no other survivors. You know that."

"That's what everyone says, but it may not be true. There's something I haven't told you. Justin still wasn't awake by the time the Mexicans began their final assault."

"I know, Abby, and I'm so sorry."

"No, you don't understand. Just before the attack, I hid Justin under the floor in the chapel. Behind the altar."

"What?" Susannah grinned. "Clever girl."

"I don't think the Mexicans ever found him. I haven't told

anyone this. I was afraid we might be tortured or something, and I wanted to keep him safe."

"I understand. He may have awakened and escaped. I will go back to the mission to find out. If he's . . . if he's still alive, I will try to find him. I'll tell him you're alive and where you are."

"Thank you. I would also like you to send a letter to my mother when you can, to tell her what's happened."

"I can do that, too."

"I don't know what's going to happen, but if I must stay with the Mexicans I will, until I can find a way to escape or convince Santa Anna to let me go."

Susannah touched a hand to Abigail's cheek. "Do what you must to stay alive, but don't take any foolish chances."

They found a few sheets of paper and a pencil among Major Dickenson's belongings, and Abigail sat near a candle to write a letter to her mother.

CHAPTER THIRTY-TWO

Ridgetop, Tennessee, April 8, 1836

As usual, Henrietta sat in her wicker rocking chair on the porch, sipping tea and waiting for Henry and Abigail to return. It had been almost three months since their departure, and she hadn't received any word of their whereabouts. Neither had the Johnsons or Sterlings. Henrietta had passed the breaking point. She was gradually steeling herself against the worst possible news. She had begged Archie to stay with her until Henry returned, and he not-so-reluctantly agreed, even though they both knew how such an arrangement would look to her husband.

Then the postal service delivered Abby's letter. She was a prisoner but alive, and Henry had been killed in a battle in Texas, of all places. The letter didn't explain how or why they'd gone to the Alamo, but they must have followed Justin. Now he was missing, too, but there was hope he was still alive. Archie had stood next to her as she read the letter, and when realization of what had happened sank in, she buried her face in his chest and sobbed. Then, after begging Archie once again not to leave, she locked herself in her bedroom and mourned Henry for six days. Archie left meals on trays outsider her door. Then he would stand for a while on the other side of the wooden barrier, giving her news of the weather, the farming operations, and sympathies passed on from neighbors. He never insisted that she respond in any way, other than to assure him she was all right. As all right as could be expected.

Walter Sterling came to call, but there was little he could do for Henrietta and nothing more he could learn about Justin. Other neighbors left hot casseroles and cold fruit pies, little of which Henrietta touched; until, on the sixth day, she emerged from her bedroom. She had bathed and fixed her hair, and wore one of her finer charcoal, not-quite-black, dresses. A string of brilliant white pearls adorned her neck.

She appeared in the doorway of the library, where Archie sat in a stuffed chair, leafing through Parson Weems's biography of George Washington.

"It was his fault," she said.

Browning looked up, startled as much by the care Henrietta had taken with her appearance as the fact that she had finally come out of her room.

"Henrietta! Who's fault?"

"George Washington. He's to blame."

"How's that?" Browning cocked an eyebrow and wondered if the long, isolated mourning had crazed the woman.

"Don't you remember, Archie? We met at George Washington's funeral."

He chuckled "Of course I remember. How could I forget the happiest day of my life?"

She smiled, but he wouldn't dwell on his happiness or those bygone days, not with Henry so recently departed. "I think Henry would want you to have that," she said, pointing at the book. "It's a gift that would fit his sense of humor."

"He was a kind man," was all Browning could say. "Is there anything I can do for you, my dear?"

"You can fetch me some of the neighbors' cooking you told me so much about from the other side of my bedroom door. I am famished."

Browning set the book aside and leapt to his feet. "I'm told there is a fine squash pie in the kitchen."

"That sounds marvelous."

He rubbed his hands together. "And may I suggest a brandy, to accompany your repast?"

"I believe you're going to spoil me, Archie."

"In any way I can, my dear. In any way I can."

He held out his arm. She took his elbow, and he led her to the dining room.

April 17, 1836, somewhere in Texas

As near as she could tell, Abigail figured it was mid-April. The actual date didn't matter. The days had worn on, one much the same as the next, and she slowly descended into a steady, unshakeable sense of despair. At night she wept for her father. During the day she scanned the horizon, hoping to see Justin, astride a horse and watching from the top of a distant hill, ready to rescue her. She knew that wasn't likely. At last she decided to resist her sense of hopelessness and make the best of her situation. Santa Anna still treated her with respect, but she had no better idea what he intended to do with her. Was she now his slave? Did the Mexicans even keep slaves? Perhaps he wanted her child, as he had hinted he wanted Angelina. That thought chilled her, but what could she do? The Mexicans appeared to accept her, but in what capacity, she didn't know.

To keep herself busy, she helped Juana and the other women who'd been with her at the Alamo. They all pitched in to assist the many families of the soldiers who followed the army wherever it went. These women's husbands had been killed, too, but they had nowhere else to go. Usually, she found herself washing dishes or cooking beans or jackrabbit stew, which bubbled in giant pots over open campfires. It was a far cry from the kitchen in her family's Ridgetop home, and she learned a greater appreciation for the talent of the Whitfields' cook, Margaret Anne. Abigail didn't feel like a prisoner, exactly, although clearly she was. She knew Santa Anna had an interest in her, but that hadn't given her too many privileges except, perhaps, that his interest kept other men away.

A few of her captors spoke English, but Abigail's rudimentary knowledge of Spanish was improving, and she could communicate a basic understanding of her needs. When she couldn't make herself understood, Juana translated for her. Abigail's minimal language skills simply emphasized that she had very little chance of escape. Among the hundreds of men and women who moved as one with the army, she alone stood out like a signal beacon with her fair skin and long, red hair. Everyone in camp knew where she was at any given moment, and the soldiers were not shy about looking.

Mostly she grew numb to her new existence. She didn't know whether the army had a home base or if it would ever settle in one place. To some extent it didn't matter. So long as they kept moving, there needn't be any final disposition of her status as a prisoner. The constant travel and the strenuous work wearied her, and each night she slept soundly in a tent with Juana and the three other women, all of whom were sympathetic to her plight. Abigail never had a chance to take a proper bath, but when the army camped near a creek or river, the Mexican women showed her how to bathe wearing a serape, discretely exposing and washing separate parts of her body, one at a time, while leaving the rest of her body covered.

On the night of the twentieth of April, the army camped near a place called San Jacinto, and Abigail helped cook tortillas for a hundred Mexican soldiers. The men toasted each other with their favorite drink, tequila, which was distilled from the local agave cactus. They said they were honoring Santa Quitéria, but the Mexican women assured Abigail that was just an excuse. Santa Quitéria's feast day wasn't until May. Abigail suspected

they were celebrating a victory by another part of the army at
Goliad.

Such news only damped any thoughts she had of escaping.
She accepted a small cup of the tequila liquor when she was offered one, but she took only a modest sip, to keep from giving
offense. She found the taste foreign to her tongue but pleasant
enough. She refused any more by patting her stomach and saying, *embarazada*. It sounded to her like she was apologizing for
being embarrassed, but the Mexicans understood. She was
pregnant and didn't want to drink too much alcohol.

Feeling fuzzy with a hint of inebriation, she made her way to
the women's tent to lie down. The party lasted well into the
evening but she slept soundly, undisturbed.

And as she slept, she dreamed again of Justin, and of home.

CHAPTER THIRTY-THREE

San Jacinto, Texas, April 21, 1836

Abigail awoke to the sound of gunshots. Horses and men were screaming. She and the women in her tent scrambled out of their bedding, pushed their way outside, and stopped. The Mexican army was in chaos. Many of the men were just waking up and hadn't had time to put on their boots. Officers shouted orders; men reached for their weapons and ran in every direction. Gunshots were coming from the edge of the camp.

"Los gringos!" one of the Mexican women said. *"Siendo atacados!"* The Americans were attacking. In the distance she heard men shouting in English. "Remember Goliad! Remember the Alamo!" Abigail was thrilled that she might be rescued, and her first instinct was to run toward the Americans. But one of the Mexican women clutched her coat and started pulling her toward the creek bank.

"Espera!" Juana said. "Wait!" A musket ball whistled past Abigail's ear, pulling a strand of hair over her eyes, and she understood. They had to take cover. Even so, Abigail scanned the outskirts of the camp, looking for her father or Justin, even though she knew they couldn't be there. The women crouched low and hurried down a creek embankment to the water. They huddled together behind the protection of the creek bank while the world above them exploded with gunshots, shouting men, and the scrape and clash of steel. A soldier staggered past them, clutching his chest, and collapsed facedown in the creek. One of

the Mexican women started to rise to help him but the others held her back.

"*Muerto*," they said. The man was dead, and the woman sat back down. The trunk of a tree overhead splintered from cannon shot, and fragments of wood rained down on their heads. Abigail thought she had become used to the sounds of battle, but the noise, the smoke, and the presence of the Americans brought back all the fears she had known at the Alamo. Would she survive this battle, too? If the Americans were defeated again, her despair might overwhelm her. She realized with certainty that she couldn't cower next to the creek any longer. Win or lose, live or die, she had to go to the Americans. She pulled her coat around her and looked at the other women.

"*Gracias por todo*," she said to Juana. "*Necessito ir.*" I need to go. She hooked her thumb over her head at the battle, in the direction from which the Americans were attacking.

"*Buena suerte*," Juana said. "Good luck." The other women nodded. They understood. Abigail started to rise, but the noise of fighting ended, and the sudden quiet stopped her. As quickly as it had started, the battle sounded like it was over. Men were still shouting, but the shooting had stopped and the cannons were silent. She started to scramble to her feet again when she heard a familiar voice.

"Can I help you?" Justin was on one knee at the edge of the creek bank, musket in one hand and reaching his other hand down to help her up. He wore a clean bandage around his forehead. "You always did like to hide by the creek."

"Justin!" She needed no help jumping to her feet and scrambling up the creek bank. She ran to him, almost knocking him backward. She threw her arms around his neck and planted kisses on his lips, his cheek, and his neck.

"Slow down," he said. "The battle's over now. We've got the rest of our lives."

"That may not be long enough," she whispered. Tears sprang to her eyes, even as he pressed his lips to hers.

Abigail savored every moment of their journey home. They fell in with a small company of men and women who traded beaver skins in Texas for knives and cook pots from the east. They were traveling to New Orleans and willingly shared their food and other supplies, thinking themselves more than compensated by the stories Abigail and Justin told them about their adventures each night around the campfire. Justin's injury was healing and, although Abigail kept a close eye on him, there didn't appear to be any long-term effect from the wound.

Once in New Orleans, they were hired to work on a riverboat; Abigail in the galley, while Justin helped feed fuel into the steam boilers. Before they left on their working river cruise, Justin insisted that they see some of the city.

"We may never have this chance again," he said.

Abigail couldn't resist. They found a lively but not-too-disreputable saloon and spent an evening savoring Creole cuisine and listening to quick fiddle tunes, slow-moving ballads, and the keening voices of Cajun musicians. So exhilarated was Abigail to be free from the conflict in Texas and safe in Justin's arms that she grabbed him by the hand to pull him onto the dance floor.

"Wait!" Justin said. He had always been a reluctant dancer.

"No," she said. "We're never waiting for anything ever again."

To the amusement of the locals, it took them a few minutes to adapt to the quick, two-step rhythm of the Cajun fiddle. Abigail thought Justin's halting steps were charming, hampered as he was by her growing stomach as they shuffled around the floor, trying not to bump into other dancers. Eventually they found their rhythm and moved in a way that satisfied them both. They shut out the rest of the world and danced through slow tunes and fast as though the musicians played only for them. In the wee hours of the morning, when the final tune had finished, the musicians and other dancers applauded them as they left the floor. Justin bowed and held her hand as she curtsied as delicately as she could.

In the morning, Justin insisted they make one more stop. He wouldn't tell Abigail where, but he took her hand and walked her through the *Vieux Carré* to one of the more exclusive dress shops.

"Why don't we go in here?" he said. "I saw shops like this in Lexington."

She stared at the silken dresses in the display window, most of which, by the looks of them, had come from Paris, London, or elsewhere in Europe.

"Oh, Justin." She felt her mouth water, but she shook her head. "I appreciate the thought, but we can't afford any of these."

"I never thought I'd hear a Whitfield say such a thing. Let's take a look anyway, to see if there's anything you like."

"You mean something you'd like to see me wear?"

Justin winked. "You've caught me out. You'd look splendid as a queen in a flour sack, but I was thinking of something suitable for a wedding."

She stepped between him and the shop, took his two hands in hers and looked him in the eye. "Justin. You know I'm yours. Come rain or come shine, I'm yours forever. As much as I appreciate it, you don't need to do this for me."

"Perhaps not, but I don't think I've properly thanked you for saving my life."

"Saving your life? That isn't why I did it. I wasn't going to let you escape your parental duties by getting yourself killed." He laughed and she punched his shoulder. Then she gestured at the display window. "This is an extravagance. I may be a Whit-field—"

"Soon to be a Sterling," he admonished her.

"So how do you, a poor Sterling, expect to pay for anything in this shop but the plainest sash or the meanest hair comb?"

"Ah, I have a secret. Some amazing things can be found beneath the floorboards of an old Spanish mission, besides the occasional wounded warrior."

"What do you mean?"

"If you had looked more closely in the space where you dumped me in, you might have seen it."

"Seen what?"

He reached into his coat pocket and pulled out a small leather bag. It jingled with coins.

"Justin, have you robbed a church?"

"It wasn't a church when I was there. Besides, whoever left these was long gone. I've been waiting for the right moment to use them. They're Spanish colonials, pure gold. New Orleans was a Spanish town, once, so I assume these will still pass for currency. If not, everyone loves gold."

She put her hands on her hips. "Why didn't we use these to pay our boat passage?"

Justin cocked his head, as if he'd given the matter some thought. "I admit it. I wanted to watch Abigail Whitfield work as a common laborer, if only for a little while." He squeezed her arm. "I needed to make sure you're sturdy enough to survive as a poor farmer's wife."

"After all I've been through?" She started to swing a punch at his chest, but he caught her arm, drew her face close to his, and gave her a quick kiss.

"Careful, dear. We don't want the shop ladies to think I'm here to dress up a plow horse for the Easter parade."

She pushed away from him with a huff.

"Shall we go shopping?" he asked.

"Of course." She started pulling him into the store by the sleeve. "I can't wait to see how much you think your life was worth."

For Abigail, the journey upriver to Nashville was quiet and mercifully uneventful. In their free time she and Justin ignored the gambling and other entertainment in the main cabin. Instead, they sat next to each other on deck chairs and held hands. They were content to watch the scenery go by, or the moon and stars when their free time fell in the evening.

"I think it's only fair to warn you," she told Justin one evening. "I am more than happy to raise your children, but I still want to raise some horses."

"I never doubted it. When I was in Kentucky, I considered buying a few tired old nags for you and Toby."

"You wouldn't have!" She tossed his hand away and bent forward to look at him in the evening light. "I knew you were jealous, but I didn't know you could be vindictive."

"Jealous enough to sabotage your business. I admit it. But then I figured I wasn't finished trying to win your hand. And I was sure enough that I would succeed, eventually, that, when you were finally mine, I didn't want to inherit any of your worthless stock as part of a dowry."

She laughed and lay back on her deck chair. "That's my Justin. Always thinking about himself."

"About us, dear. Always about us."

They sat in silence for a few minutes, and Abigail's thoughts wandered back to her martyred father and the battles she and Justin survived. The memories were burned into her mind, never to leave, and she wasn't sure she'd want them to.

"What do you think happened to Toby?" she asked.

"I don't know. I hope he's waiting to greet us in Ridgetop

266

with a whiskey in each hand. I'd like to see the look on his face when he finds out about . . . us."

She reached out and slapped his shoulder with the back of her hand. "You really were jealous."

He turned toward her and took her hand again. "Abigail. When I look back on my life, I'm certain I fell in love with you before you even knew I existed."

"That would have been a long time ago." She said this so quietly, she might have only thought it.

"So now you know how long I've struggled to capture your attention, if not your heart, to overcome Henry's objections, and to worry about every other young gentleman like Toby who buzzed around your front door like bees on a pea vine."

"Oh, dear. I hope that didn't wear you out."

He laughed. "Not by a long shot." Then he drew quiet. "But I fear that Toby may no longer be a problem."

She sighed. "It would have taken a miracle for anyone to get through the Mexican lines, I suppose."

"Maybe not a miracle, but . . ."

She squeezed his hand. "So many losses."

From Nashville they hired a coach to take them the rest of the way to Ridgetop. In midafternoon, as they drew near the Whitfield farm, Abigail knew her mother might notice their approach, given her penchant for taking tea on the veranda. Sure enough, when she looked out the coach window, Abigail spied her mother waiting at the bottom of the front steps.

At first she didn't recognize the man standing next to her. Then she knew. It was Archibald Browning, the man who claimed to be her father. Somehow he'd managed to come to the house. And he was holding Henrietta's hand. Abigail assumed this meant her mother had received the letter she'd given to Susannah to mail, and that everyone knew her father, or Henry, was dead. What this meant for their future, she couldn't guess. And how would she explain Archie to Justin? She wouldn't need to, she knew, and Justin wouldn't be troubled in any case. She was truly home.

"Mother!" She stepped out of the carriage and ran into her mother's arms.

"Abby." Her mother hugged her harder than she ever had. Browning stood at a respectful distance and introduced himself to Justin without saying anything else.

"I'm sorry about Father," Abigail whispered.

"I am too." Her mother let go of her. "He was a good man, but Henry was stubborn as a Missouri mule." Her eyes glistened with tears.

Abigail glanced at Archie. "I see you've met Mr. Browning."

Her mother put her hand to her mouth. "Oh, Abby. I have so much explaining to do."

"It's not explaining, Mother. You just have family stories. So do I, now, and your grandchildren will be fascinated by them all." She placed both hands on her stomach to draw attention to her condition.

"Oh, my!" Her mother clapped her hands.

CHAPTER THIRTY-FOUR

Ridgetop, Tennessee, May 24, 1836

The warm spring morning dawned without any threat of rain, and Abigail decided to walk to the Johnson farm, to learn if anyone had news of Toby. The distance was more than two miles, and she could have ridden a horse, but she wanted to see the land, the home she had missed so much. She walked through the fields, brushed the tops of the tall grass with her hands, and listened to the birds sing. At the creek, she carefully tiptoed over the flat gray rocks as she had so many times in her life, and crossed over onto the Johnson farm.

As she approached the house, she saw two men standing near the front porch with Thomas Johnson. One wore a top hat, the other an old tricorn. When she drew closer, she realized the two men were Bailey and Smith, the men who'd come to see Toby when he lay unconscious after the county horse race. Thomas faced them with his feet apart, his arms folded across his chest.

"I don't know what you're talking about," he said. He clenched his fists, and his cheeks flushed red. He glanced at Abigail and briefly raised one hand as if to warn her away.

"It's very simple," the man in the top hat said. "Master Tobias owes us a sum certain, and we have come to collect it."

"I would know about my son's debts, if he had any," Thomas said. "And this is the first I've heard of any debt to you."

"Master Tobias may not have confided in you, true, but that is not our concern," Bailey said.

Abigail saw a long knife on Smith's belt, and both men were of such questionable character that they likely carried pistols under their coats. They were up to no good, she was sure. She wished Justin were there.

"What kind of debt are you talking about?" Thomas demanded.

"Let's just say it was a lending arrangement. We often provided Tobias with funds, and he always paid us back. Until now."

"He paid you? How?"

"Sometimes in money, sometimes in livestock. I calculate he now owes us thirty head of cattle."

"Thirty head? What kind of usurious lending are you about, Bailey?"

"My client's, that is to say, Tobias's, business is his own concern. We merely fronted him the capital."

"I don't believe you."

"Perhaps you should call for Master Tobias and let him explain it to you."

"He isn't here." Thomas glanced at Abigail, as if she might know where Toby was. "Have you got this supposed lending arrangement in writing?"

"No, but I was told the word of a Johnson is as good as any writing, if not gold."

"You're not going to get away with this, Bailey. I'll give you nothing. That's all I have to say. Now go away. I never want to see your face again."

"I urge you to reconsider," Bailey said, glancing conspicuously at Mr. Smith. "Where I come from, it's considered very bad luck not to repay one's debts."

"Don't you threaten me. Get off my land. Now, before I send for the sheriff."

270

Bailey started to protest, then looked at Abigail and thought better of it.

"We can't wait much longer," Bailey said. "It's a matter of considerable urgency for Mr. Smith and myself. But we are willing to give you, say, another brief period of time in which to reconsider. But not long."

"Go!" Thomas bellowed.

Bailey and Smith barely reacted. They gave each other a knowing look, then turned and walked down the drive toward the county road. Thomas started to go into the house, but he stopped and pointed a finger at Abigail.

"You tell that boy of yours if he tries anything, I'll say the same thing to him, too."

"I beg your pardon?" What was he talking about?

"It's my land," Thomas growled. "And I intend to keep it." With that he strode heavily across the porch, went inside, and slammed the front door hard enough to rattle its leaded glass.

Abigail stood for a moment and stared at the front of the house, thinking Thomas might calm down and come back outside. He didn't, but she had learned what she'd come to find out. Toby wasn't home. She might also have confirmed what had happened to her father's missing cattle. She never believed Justin was a cattle thief, but she never really believed it of Toby, either. Now it seemed that Toby had been paying off his gambling debts by stealing cattle.

She lowered her head, turned around, and began walking slowly back toward home. How tragic, how ironic, life was. If Toby had simply confessed his gambling debts and sought help, rather than accuse Justin of stealing cattle, he might still be alive. Not to mention Henry. She wondered if Toby's body was lying in a Texas field near San Antonio. She wondered if he had died alone.

When she came to the creek, she turned right instead of

crossing over onto the Whitfield farm. She walked north, along a deer path, in the direction of the Sterling house. She wanted to tell Justin what had just happened. She and Justin had not yet settled on where they would live, and they decided to keep to their respective homes for the first few days since their return, to give their families time to adjust to their new status as a couple. Her mother had no trouble at all, and she was at that moment busily planning a wedding. Walter and Anne Sterling were not surprised either. They just wondered what had taken so long. She smiled. Some part of her, too, had always known that she and Justin were destined for each other. And there would be no Whitfield family shame this time. No one would escape to the west to avoid the scandal of a pregnancy out of wedlock. Her pregnancy was as natural and timely as the spring rain. A wedding would be great fun, to be sure, but it would only be a formality.

She found Justin and Walter in their kitchen, leaning over some drawings and papers that were spread out over a work table.

"Hello, young mother," Walter said. He gave her a light hug. "How are we feeling today?" He took the liberty of patting her ever-growing stomach.

"He's kicking. He wants to come out and see his grand-father."

"That's my boy." Walter beamed.

Justin gave her a kiss on the cheek.

"You'll never guess who I just saw at the Johnson farm," she said.

"What? Who?" Justin and his father gave each other cautious looks.

"Do you remember those two men who came to see Toby after the race? After he was hurt?"

"Who could forget them? They were gamblers and cutthroats," Justin said to Walter.

"They were at the Johnsons' again today, demanding payment for one of Toby's debts."

"I'm sure that pleased Thomas." Justin put his hands on his hips.

"As much as you think, and he practically threw them off the property."

"Good for him," Justin said.

"He practically threw me off, too, and because of you, I think." She pointed at Justin.

"How's that?"

"He said that if you tried anything, he'd throw you off his property, too. What's that about?"

Justin looked at Walter. "I think I know." They turned to the drawings and papers laid out on the table. "It's all here. Your father—Archie, I mean—is a surveyor, and he's found an interesting document. Do you remember that odd stone Toby fell over in the field once, when we were playing hide-and-seek?"

"No. Oh, perhaps I do. It had writing on it, didn't it?"

"Our family names. And they were put there for a purpose."

He related the story of their three families, which he had learned from Browning, and the agreement they had reached to share their land.

"It's all here in these papers. Signed, sealed, and hidden in a chest beneath that stone. Browning found it and dug it up."

"What does it mean?" she asked.

"Basically," Walter said, "it means the Whitfields, Johnsons, and Sterlings are all equal owners of all of their lands."

"Unbelievable. Is it legal?"

"As sound as the Liberty Bell," Walter said. "Metaphorically speaking, of course."

"No wonder Thomas is afraid of you. He might be more

afraid of Henry, if he were still alive."

"Your mother owns the Whitfield property now," Walter said. "And she's part owner of our land and the Johnsons', too, according to this agreement."

Abigail stared down at a drawing of the properties. "It's too odd to contemplate."

Walter picked up his pipe. "It makes no difference to us Sterlings, now that you and Justin are to be married. Our lands will be joined and gladly so. It shouldn't matter to you, either, unless your mother has more children." He winked at her.

"Not much chance of that." Abigail laughed. "Although there is a new man in her life, as you know."

"A good man, too, from what I see." Walter struck a match and puffed on his pipe until it glowed.

Justin looked at Abigail, then at his father. He remembered a conversation he'd had with Abby once as they sat on a bench outside a store in Ridgetop.

"Father, why don't we set aside the pipe for a moment." He placed a hand on Abby's stomach and winked at her. "My child is still too young for tobacco."

"Of course," Walter said, "I accept that." He set the pipe in an ashtray.

"Thanks, but I don't think Thomas is going to accept any of this." Justin slapped the papers with the back of his hand. "It's odd enough. I suppose I wouldn't either, if I were he."

"He's got more immediate trouble with Mr. Bailey," Abigail said. "I don't like that man. I'm afraid he might try something."

The following evening, Abigail called at the Johnson farm again, walking there under the light of a full moon. Thomas was stiffly formal, but he had calmed down and let her in. Thomas's wife, Janice, made them tea, and they sat uncomfortably around a table in the parlor. Abigail told them of her travels. She didn't mention their reasons for going west, or whether Tobias had lied about Justin stealing cattle. As far as she was concerned, that was ancient history, and their families had to get along, or not, going forward from that day. She didn't mention the documents Archie Browning had found or property ownership, either. That problem would work itself out in its own sweet time. She knew Thomas and Janice were more interested in the fate of their son.

"We're so sorry about Henry," Janice said. Thomas nodded.

"Thank you."

Thomas said, "That battle at the mission. What did you call it, the Alamo? It's causing quite a fuss here in the States."

"They say the men who died there are heroes." Janice looked at her husband.

Abigail nodded, remembering her father. She wondered what he'd think of being called a hero of Texas, a land he'd never meant to visit. "I'm sorry I don't know what happened to Toby," she said. "We think Colonel Travis sent him for reinforcements just before the Mexicans' final attack." She knew that was unlikely, since Toby wouldn't have known the territory. But it could have been true, and there was no reason they had to assume Toby deserted at the last minute.

Thomas nodded again, grim-faced but accepting the possibility that Toby had done the right thing.

"Of course it was a dangerous task," she said. "Impossible, really, surrounded as we were." She looked away. "Toby was very brave even to have tried it."

"We appreciate your telling us all this, Abigail," Janice said. "Toby was very fond of you." She wiped away a tear that threatened to dampen her cheek. "He had plans, you know. For the two of you."

Abigail didn't get the chance to respond. A thunderous crash sounded, along with the splintering of wood.

"My goodness!" Janice dropped her tea cup.

Thomas jumped to his feet. "That was the front door!"

He stepped around the table but, before he could go any farther, Mr. Smith rushed into the room. He ran straight toward Thomas with a long knife raised over his head. Abigail tried to rise from her chair and Janice screamed.

"What? No!" Thomas had nowhere to run. He raised his hands to ward off the blow.

Smith's eyes grew wide and he lurched forward, off balance. He fell forward without his legs under him. His hands came down, but they didn't stop him from slamming into the floor facedown. Justin had tackled Smith and still had both arms around the man's ankles.

"My Lord," Janice said. "What on earth!"

Smith lay on the area rug without moving. Justin felt Smith's neck for a pulse. Then he rolled the man over heavily onto his back. Smith had fallen on his own knife, which was now buried to the hilt in his chest.

Justin looked at Abigail. "I thought he'd come back here tonight. Bailey, too. Where is he?"

"I'm right here." Bailey stood in the doorway holding a cocked pistol in each hand.

CHAPTER THIRTY-FIVE

Bailey looked down at Smith's body, lying motionless on the floor. "A minor inconvenience. Mr. Smith always was a bit too headstrong for this business."

"The robbery business, you mean," Thomas hissed.

"If you say so." Bailey motioned with one of the pistols for Justin to back away.

Justin's fists clenched and his body tensed. Abigail saw he was ready to spring at the man in spite of the menacing weapons.

"Justin, please," she said. "Don't do anything foolish." But, at the site of Bailey's guns, she remembered the pocket pistol in her small purse. The square woolen purse hung by a thin cotton strap from her right shoulder, away from Bailey.

Justin's angry gaze flashed back and forth between her and Bailey. He was still looking for a chance to leap at the man.

"Justin, you have your son to think of," she said.

His shoulders relaxed, but only slightly. He moved back, away from Bailey, but his fists were still clenched.

"That's right, Justin." Bailey sneered. He stepped farther into the room. "Think of your child. Sit down on the floor, over next to the wall, and don't do anything foolish."

"What do you want from us?" Thomas demanded.

"Nothing from you, for the moment. You sit down next to Mr. Sterling there, by the wall." He motioned again with one of the pistols. Thomas's jaw was set, but he slowly sat next to Justin.

"Master Johnson?" A servant arrived through a doorway to the kitchen, then a farmhand right behind her. They looked at Bailey wide-eyed, then at the bloody body on the floor.

"Welcome," Bailey said. "Come right in. Sit down next to the others, by the wall. Do it now."

Thomas nodded and they sat next to him, not taking their eyes off Bailey and his pistols.

"Are we expecting anyone else?" Bailey asked his hostages.

"Doubtful," Thomas said. "Not at this time of night."

The two servants silently nodded their agreement.

"That's nice. Now you, madam." Bailey looked at Janice. "I want you to go upstairs and bring me all your jewelry and anything else you have made of silver or gold. No plate. I know the difference. Bring it to me in a pillow case, and it had better be full. If it's not, one of these pistols might go off accidently, and somebody might get hurt. Probably your husband."

Janice stared at Thomas.

"Do as he says," Thomas growled.

"I'll help you," Abigail said.

"No!" Bailey shouted. "You stay at the table. Justin needs to know I have you in my sights."

"You bastard," Justin said. "If I ever find you—"

"Please don't finish that thought," Bailey said. "I don't want to *have* to kill you just to keep you from finding me. Not that you'd know where to look. Now move, madam, and be quick about it." Without letting go of the pistol, he pulled a pocket watch from his vest by its thin chain and looked at it. "I'll give you five minutes. After that you might hear a pistol shot. Take ten minutes, and you'll probably hear two." He let go of the watch and let it dangle on the chain.

Janice looked at her husband and trembled.

"Go!" Bailey shouted.

"Go," Thomas said. "And hurry."

She stood up, started to run one way, then stopped and ran in the opposite direction. Bailey chuckled. "I told you it was bad luck not to pay your debts," he said to Thomas.

"My son owed you nothing."

Abigail looked at Justin, who still had fire in his eyes. She raised her eyebrows, trying to tell him with her own eyes to calm down and to stay where he was. When Bailey wasn't looking, she could see Justin's leg move, ever so slightly, as he tried to get his footing underneath him. He still intended to spring at the man, she knew.

As casually as she could, she let her hand drop from the tabletop to her lap. This caused one of Bailey's pistols to swing in her direction.

"Try to stay still, miss," Bailey said.

Justin's leg moved again.

She could feel the weight of her little pistol as the purse rested against her hip. If she could reach it before Bailey had a chance to shoot . . .

Justin's leg moved another half inch. He was forcing her hand. If he sprang at Bailey she wouldn't be able to shoot the man before he put a musket ball in Justin. But if Justin remembered her pistol, that might have been part of his plan. If he was willing to die at the Alamo, no doubt he'd be willing to sacrifice himself to save his wife and child.

"Believe me, this is nothing personal," Bailey said. "And I apologize for all the trouble." He took off his top hat and set it on a side table. "Without Mr. Smith's help, it would be hard for me to relieve you of your cattle. But I'm sure a man of your obvious means must have bestowed any number of precious gifts on his wife. I'll have to be satisfied with those."

Thomas glared at the man, miserable, full of hatred and helplessness. Abigail let her hand slide ever so slightly toward her hip. Now her hand was partially hidden by the girth of her stomach. Her fingers fumbled at the opening of her purse. She tried to remember the last time she'd checked the charge in the pistol's flash pan. It didn't matter. When Justin made his move, which apparently he was determined to do, she would have to shoot, and shoot as quickly as possible.

"Your wife is taking her time," Bailey said to Thomas. He wiped his forehead with the back of one hand, still holding a pistol, and glanced at the watch. "I wonder if she really loves you. Perhaps she wants to keep her jewelry and thinks losing an old codger like you is a small price to pay. It would be a shame if she has already left by a back door."

Abigail's thumb caught the opening of the purse. The strap quivered, which caught Bailey's eye.

"Ah, a purse!" he said. "Now we have something to do while we wait." He stepped over Smith's body to the table where Abigail sat, but he kept an eye and one pistol trained on Justin. "You're a Whitfield, aren't you?" he said to her.

Abigail nodded as he stood over her.

"Whitfields are even better off than the Johnsons. What have you got in that little purse of yours?"

He bent down and started to reach across her body for the purse. Abigail saw Justin's leg move with lightning speed. The side of his boot brushed across the carpet and made a hissing sound as he came to one knee. Bailey's eyes twitched, but Janice appeared in a doorway at the same time, carrying a heavy pillowcase. Justin reached for the knife in Smith's chest. Before Bailey could react, Abigail clutched the man's shirt in her left hand and kept him from turning around. At the same time, she raised the pistol in her right hand, placed it against his forehead, and pulled the trigger.

The small explosion filled the room. Janice screamed and dropped the pillowcase. Bailey uttered a short, surprised cry. Both of his pistols discharged, one on either side of Abigail's chair, splintering the floor and sending wood chips flying into the air. Through a small cloud of black powder smoke, Abigail watched Bailey as he fell backward with a disbelieving look on his face. He dropped onto the floor next to Smith, still clinging to the empty pistols. One leg twitched, and then he lay still.

CHAPTER THIRTY-SIX

May 25, 1836

Justin and Abigail stood arm-in-arm in the Johnsons' yard, along with Thomas, Henrietta Whitfield, and Walter Sterling. They watched the sheriff's wagon drive away with the bodies of Bailey and Smith bouncing in the back. Janice had recovered from the drama of the evening and was in the kitchen supervising preparation of breakfast for them all.

"Who would think such awful things could happen in Ridgetop," Henrietta said, shaking her head.

"Now perhaps we can finally get some peace around here," Walter said.

"Not quite yet, Walter." Thomas stood apart from the rest with his hands on his hips. "There's still the matter of the property, and that questionable agreement Mr. Browning claims to have found."

Abigail gave Justin a cautious glance. Was Thomas going to press the issue now?

"My goodness, Thomas." Henrietta shook her head. "After what just happened, is now the proper time to discuss that?"

"I think it is." Thomas rubbed the back of his neck. "That scoundrel Bailey's visit last night was an eye opener for me. Gave me some clarity on things. Property issues among them."

"We may want to consult the county lawyers before we reach any decision," Walter said. "There's a lot at stake."

"Fiddlesticks. I don't need a bunch of lawyers to figure out what's what for me." Thomas kicked at the gravel in the driveway with the toe of his boot. "I've made up my mind."

"Nothing has to be decided today," Walter said.

"It's as final now as it needs to be," Thomas said. "So hear me out." The assembled group gave him their attention, but Abigail had suffered enough controversy. She wanted to take Justin by the hand and go back to her house or his, but she braced herself for the arguments she expected to follow.

"I'm not a young man," Thomas said. "And for better or worse, it doesn't look like I have an heir anymore. No one to pass my land to directly when I, when Janice and I, are no longer here."

There was a brief silence, acknowledging the fact that Toby was missing, but Abigail noted Thomas's reference to "my land."

Thomas continued. "I don't know anything about that document Mr. Browning found, and if you ask me, it's not worth the paper it was written on. I don't think it's reliable."

"But Thomas—" Henrietta stopped short when Thomas held up a firm hand.

"I don't care about any agreement our ancestors are supposed to have entered into. They were all sick, anyway, if what I hear is true. But seeing as how there's no one to inherit my farm, I can't think of anyone I'd rather see take it off my hands than this young couple here." He pointed at Abigail and Justin. "Janice feels the same way. You two pretty much pulled our bacon out of the fire last night, and if you hadn't, well, I don't want to think about that."

"You'd have done the same thing," Justin said. Abigail nodded her agreement.

"But that's not the way it turned out, and I don't see any reason why you shouldn't get the benefit of what you saved. Janice and I are willing to enter into a whole new agreement, if necessary. One that says pretty much the same thing as the document Browning found. That is, if you two agree that's the right thing, and it's what you want to do."

Henrietta took Thomas by the hand. "We'll be one big happy family, Thomas."

He rolled his eyes in mock annoyance, but then he smiled.

"What do you think, Justin?" Abigail held her breath, waiting for his reaction. He looked down at her, then he gazed out at the fields, forests, and rolling hills in the distance.

"I think we'd have plenty of room here for our children," he said. "And for a few of your horses, too."

ABOUT THE AUTHOR

S. B. Moores is an iconoclastic, award-winning author who reads and writes across many different genres, and who grew up admiring Louis L'Amour. Widely traveled and always looking for a new experience, the author has been a journalist, a biologist, and an attorney, and now lives and writes in Colorado.

The author's most recent mystery novel, *Dead on Cuban Time*, is available as an e-book on amazon.com. You can visit the author's blog at stevenmoores.net.

The employees of Five Star Publishing hope you have enjoyed this book.

Our Five Star novels explore little-known chapters from America's history, stories told from unique perspectives that will entertain a broad range of readers.

Other Five Star books are available at your local library, bookstore, all major book distributors, and directly from Five Star/Gale.

Connect with Five Star Publishing

Visit us on Facebook:
  https://www.facebook.com/FiveStarCengage

Email:
  FiveStar@cengage.com

For information about titles and placing orders:
  (800) 223-1244
  gale.orders@cengage.com

To share your comments, write to us:
  Five Star Publishing
  Attn: Publisher
  10 Water St., Suite 310
  Waterville, ME 04901

287